HOOVERVILLE

HOOVERVILLE

KAYLA JOY

Indie

This book contains descriptions of domestic violence.

Hooverville is a work of fiction. Any resemblance to any persons
living or dead is purely coincidental. The characters presented in
this story are fictitious inserts into real American history. The historical figures and events are true to the best of the Author's understanding, though the role they play in this narrative is entirely
fictional.
Cover Design by Elena Karoumpali

First Printing, 2021

For Grammy,
my #1 fan since day 1

"YOU MAY NOT ALWAYS HAVE A COM-
FORTABLE LIFE AND YOU WILL NOT
ALWAYS BE ABLE TO SOLVE ALL OF
THE WORLD'S PROBLEMS AT ONCE
BUT DON'T EVER UNDERESTIMATE
THE IMPORTANCE YOU CAN HAVE
BECAUSE HISTORY HAS SHOWN US
THAT COURAGE CAN BE CONTAGIOUS
AND HOPE CAN TAKE ON A LIFE OF
ITS OWN."

-MICHELLE OBAMA

Hooverville

KAYLA JOY

I

My seamstress pokes me with her needle, and a single spot at the hem of my gown goes red with my blood. I wince and pull myself away, but Polly holds me still, going at my dress with an intense concentration in her scrunched-up little face. I push back my shoulders and tilt my head at my reflection while she sews me into my evening gown for tonight. This wasn't my idea, of course. I have no insight into my mother's messed-up psyche, but I can say with near certainty that sewing me into a gown is a ploy to prevent me from overindulging at Betty's party. That, paired with the benefit of keeping Frank's wandering eye on me—it's the perfect solution.

"Do hold still, missus," Polly says, poking me again. At this rate, the whole dress will be stained bright red by the time I make it to the Lyndon's.

Out in the hall, two maids scurry away, followed by a butler, and I know what that means. *Three, two, one...* I count, and right on schedule, Mother makes her grand entrance, waving her arms wildly, shouting about dust or something like that. She's not normally this bad, but today must have her on edge. I try not to get too involved in my mother's emotional affairs. She's going to scold me either way.

"*What have you done?*" She stomps to Polly, her tiny heels clacking against the floor, and all but kicks her to the ground. I straighten my back uncomfortably and plant my feet into the ground, in case she feels like kicking me over too. "You've made her bleed all over the dress! This was an eighty-dollar dress!" Polly looks like she may cry, so I intervene before it goes further.

"Mother, it's alright. I'll be against the wall the whole time, and no one will even notice."

"No!" Mother shouts, startling me and a trembling Polly. "You have to look perfect tonight or—" Mother must realize she's said something wrong, because she stops mid-sentence and blows out a few breaths. "Polly, give me a moment alone with my daughter." *Oh no.* A "moment alone" means a lecture, I'm sure of it. Polly scurries out of the room and wipes at her cheeks as she shuts the door behind her, leaving in her wake the popping and crackling of the fireplace. Mother turns me on the pedestal and looks me up and down. "This is a very important night, Annaleise. Do you understand that?"

"Well, yes, I sort of sensed something like that, but why?"

"Everything will make sense soon." Mother glances at the blood and sighs. "Stay close to Frank tonight."

I open my mouth to speak, but she straightens her back, and I know there's no getting through to her even if I tried. She leaves me alone with the fireplace and the mirror.

Virginia did my makeup as per Mother's specifications to make me "younger and sexier," if such a thing exists. My dark hair is secured to the side of my head with hairpins and curled down my shoulder. I'd like to cut my hair like the girls in the magazines, but I'm not allowed to. Not as long as I'm unmarried and living under Mother's roof.

Polly returns a moment later and finishes the hemming and stitching. She stares at the dress with puffy eyes and a red nose. I hate it when Mother makes our staff cry because there's nothing I can do about it. It happens more often than you'd think, too, and just like when Frank says something mean to me, we have to just accept it.

"I'm sorry," I whisper without looking at her. Perhaps she thinks I didn't say it to her because she looks perplexed and then says nothing. I slump my shoulders as she says in a soft voice, "You're all done, Miss Annaleise."

"Thank you, Polly." I step down from my pedestal and do a turn. In the mirror I catch her looking at the areas where she poked me, but I make a point to show her that if I keep my arms at my sides, it's hardly even noticeable. The dress is a little tight in the knees, so walking comfortably is a struggle.

While on my way out to the foyer, I pass Virginia, my maid, and give her a sideways grin. We both know how ridiculous I look, but it's best to let Mother use me as her little doll to play with and dress up.

I find Mother again and she circles me once more. "This will have to do," she sighs and looks me deep in the eyes. Her buggy eyes always make her look crazed, and she once again wears too much powder that cakes into her wrinkles and makes her smell like baby powder nearly all the time. Her hair sits piled atop her head the way *her* mother wore it, and it makes her look at least fifteen years older than she is, though I'd never tell her that.

"Be on your best behavior tonight, Annaleise. You understand me?" I furrow my brow and start to speak, but she cuts me off. "No laughing too loudly, no slouching, nothing that will embarrass Frank and this family."

So that's what it's all about. "Mother," I sigh. "I'm not going to—"

"I know how difficult it is for you to not embarrass your family name."

Mother has said mean things to me before, but tonight this feels different. I bite the inside of my cheek to prevent myself from sassing back. "Yes, Mother," I mutter, and at her disapproving look, I enunciate my words clearer. "I won't embarrass you or Frank."

I know I'm not nearly as good as some of the other Society girls, and I know she'd rather have one of them for a daughter, but hearing it so bluntly stated while I'm *trying* hurts. My best will never be good enough for her. But I can't worry about this right now. I won't let it interfere with my performance tonight. We attend parties and galas like this one every single night. It's the same people talking about the same subjects, congratulating themselves for being magnificent for the bare minimum. It shouldn't be too difficult to act perfect.

"Don't you think it's rude to discuss people when they aren't present?" says a crisp voice with a smile in it from behind me. My shoulders tense as Frank kisses Mother on the cheek. I quickly separate myself from my emotions before I make an embarrassment of myself or Mother again. I harden my expression and turn around to face Frank. A look of absolute bliss washes over his face and he snakes his arms around my waist.

"My dear, you've never looked more lovely."

Even in the six months I've been acquainted with Mr. Alexander, his presence never ceases to unnerve me. Try as I might, I can never seem to place what it is about him that sickens me. Perhaps I wouldn't find him so awful if I wasn't the sorry soul with the misfortune of courting him. He's handsome enough for a man his age. I've seen handsomer, but he's not *bad* looking. His hair is jet black and combed back and smoothed with some thick gel that smells of lard and leaves his hair stiff. His face is square and chiseled like a sculpture in a museum that's worn down by years. From far away, he's the perfect man, but when up close, even he has imperfections.

He's wealthier by far than any of the other men in New York Society. Certainly, he should have been married ages ago, but when we were introduced, Mother said he was a bachelor-type looking to settle down with a trophy. A prize. A pretty little ornament to hang on the wall, to show off to friends and guests and then ignore soon as he gets home. I'm not yet twenty years old, but every other woman my age in the Society is already married or engaged, and it's all anyone asks me about anymore.

"When are you going to settle down, Annaleise?" "You won't have this body forever!" "Don't you want to have children before you're too old to enjoy them?" Yak yak yak.

Frank takes my hand and helps me outside and into the car, ducking and jogging a bit to avoid the rain. I smile at Arthur, our driver, as Mother and Frank slide in next to me. "Evening, Annaleise," Arthur says. "You look lovely tonight."

"Thank you, Arthur!" I grin genuinely and flatten out my dress. "How are your daughters?"

"Oh, they're just fine, Miss Annaleise." Arthur smiles at me in the mirror, but quickly focuses on his job again. I don't have to look to know that Mother and Frank must have scowled at him. I wish they didn't dictate who I could or couldn't speak to, but I don't want to get Arthur in more trouble than he's already in. I apologize to him with my eyes in the mirror, and he just gives me a gentle smile.

Frank and Mother discuss something quietly, but I don't bother listening to them. I lay my head against the car window and watch the lights pass through my vision. I count the number of cars we pass and find myself wondering where they're going. If they're going home to a family or if they're leaving after a long day at work.

Maybe they have a wife and kids, or maybe they have nobody. Frank tugs on my hand at some point and intertwines our fingers together. My focus shifts to the raindrops on the glass, two of them racing to the bottom of the window. The left one wins.

My eyes travel upward to the newest landmark of New York. They only finished construction on it last year, and Governor Roosevelt was beyond proud to have funded the tallest building in the world—even if he had nothing to do with it. When they first started construction on it, I used to think that as long as I could see The Empire State Building, I'd be able to find my way home, but now I think as long as it's in my view, I'm still trapped here.

"Annaleise?" Mother asks, and something about her tone says she's been trying to get my attention for some time now.

"Hm?" I ask, focusing again. Frank chuckles at Mother's expression, and Mother motions for me to sit up straight. I sigh and obey, meeting Arthur's eyes in the rear-view mirror. His eyes say something he dare not say out loud, and it makes me turn away.

After several minutes of painful quiet, Frank turns his attention from the street to Arthur, stammering and waving his hands. "Why are we going this way? This is directly past the park; I don't want to be swarmed by scum!" I squint through the dark at twenty or thirty shacks made of wooden slabs and blankets. There is a bonfire with shadows breaking up the light of the flames, and laughter so loud I can hear it even in the car, and music and dancing. They don't look like scum to me.

"The main road is closed for construction, sir," Arthur says apologetically. "This is the only way to travel after dark for the next couple of weeks."

Frank curses under his breath and leans back in his seat. "Leave it to Roosevelt to authorize construction projects in the middle of a recession," he mutters. I don't counter with an argument about all the jobs he's funded. I focus on the shadows. They seem to be happy, all things considered.

They're called Hoovervilles, I think. It's a direct jab at President Hoover, who single-handedly got us in this mess. It's not the most creative name, I'll admit, but I guess they didn't have much time to come up with a better one. They're little villages of makeshift homes, tents, whatever else. I find myself pitying the people in there whenever I pass, but as Mother would say, "They got themselves into this mess, they should get themselves out." I've tried to adopt a mentality more like hers, however wrong it may be. It's easier to avoid a fight if I pretend to be like her.

The people who ended up in there mostly lost their jobs or money when the market fell— many people in New York Society included, actually. The quickest way to lose the respect of rich people is to lose the money. Those of us who still have money flaunt it even more than we did before. Not *me*, per se; I don't have a penny of my own to flaunt, even if I wanted to. But people like the Lyndons, who bought a second home, or my mother, who went for a shopping spree in Paris. I'm not sure why rich people can never have enough, while giving nothing to others. Is the goal to establish dominance in the wild, or something? Sometimes the frivolity of it all shocks me, but who am I to fight a broken system?

"Filth. Ruining our city. And Roosevelt is just accepting this trash."

"Yes, Frank. The misfortune of others must be such an inconvenience to you," I say, earning a scold from Mother. Frank squints his eyes at me and continues his rambling.

My head starts to hurt listening to his nightly rant about the Governor. Franklin Delano Roosevelt could give free puppies to orphans, and Frank would still find a way to spin it into something negative. It's one of a great many skills he possesses, complaining about things that have absolutely no pertinence to him. Arthur drives past the Hooverville and I say a silent apology on behalf of Frank.

We pull into The Lyndon's drive around, where lights illuminate the raindrops. We wait behind three or four other cars. "Can't we get out here?" I ask Mother. "It's only a short walk."

"In the rain? Are you mad?" Mother scoffs. "No, we'll wait until we get to the door."

In the cars ahead of me, men dressed in suits get out and hold the hands of their wives dressed in shimmering gowns and furs—certainly not for warmth in these summer months, but because they can. I glance at Arthur again to read his interpretation of this on his face. It seems inconsiderate of Society women to wear such expensive clothes when they know we're in the midst of an economic crisis, but I shouldn't talk while wearing an eighty-dollar gown to a dinner party.

A woman gets out of the car in front of me, carrying a wrapped package under her arm.

"Mother, were we supposed to bring gifts?" I ask confusedly. I peruse the calendar in my brain to see if tonight is perhaps Betty's birthday, but nothing comes to mind. Mother's face twists into a mischievous grin that scares me. She knows something, and I don't want to find out. If I had a choice, I'd stay in the car and play checkers with Arthur until Frank and Mother come back, but I have no choice.

Finally, Arthur pulls up to the door and Mother exits the car, followed by Frank, and then me.

"Thank you, Arthur," I say as the valet closes the door on him. Mother's intensity is back in her face, and she looks between the two of us as if my thanks to Arthur is a personal affront to her. Frank takes my hand and grins excitedly.

"Everybody ready?" Frank asks. Mother reminds me without words of my duty: smile, don't embarrass her, and hope with all my being that I don't let her down.

A butler welcomes us into the home and takes Mother's coat, and a second butler brings us champagne and a tray of various fruits and cheeses. Frank takes some, but I imagine one seam in my dress popping and decide against the cheese. I look at Mother for verification that I'm doing well and shrink myself down to match the personas of every other lady here tonight.

The room is filled to the brim with other couples from New York Society, all equally wealthy and equally unbearable. Nobody discusses anything outside of their simple, insignificant lives. Not the stock market, not the unemployment. There are some notable names missing from the party, though, and although nobody says it, I know it's because they've lost their money and are now dead to the Society.

With Frank on my arm, nobody asks me judgmental questions. It's as if, with him by my side, I'm suddenly worthy. I'm suddenly more respectable than I was six months ago. Mother never strays too far, shifting her eyes to watch me over the shoulders of the guests. A quartet performs classical pieces in the corner, and some newer jazzy pieces, but none of the couples dance or even acknowledge hearing such music. Instead, they're all too enthralled by their own gossip and self-indulgence.

I find Betty on the other side of the room, but she's so busy fielding her guests she has no time to come say hello. If only I could be more like her. More sociable, more likable. Perhaps then, I wouldn't be such an embarrassment to Mother. Her words echo in my head again, and I'm suddenly very aware of my every movement. Am I breathing too loud? Am I standing in an awkward position? Is my diction too unladylike? I straighten my back and smile unnaturally at everyone we pass.

Frank and I find the McKenzie couple. They married only a few months ago and took a three-month honeymoon at a tropical island resort. They gush about how cheap the whole ordeal was and encourage Frank and I to go there for our honeymoon. Frank clams up a bit at that idea and nudges me to move toward another couple.

At least for a moment, my face reflects how I feel, because Frank leans forward and whispers, "Smile, you look miserable." I craft a smile out of the knowledge that we can go home soon. I have to wonder if every other wife here is as miserable on the inside as I am, but as I analyze their perfect faces, there's nothing but joy in their eyes as they clutch their husbands to them and show off their wealth.

About an hour into the party, a butler announces that dinner is served. We're seated around the Lyndon's long table, with Johnny Lyndon at one end and Betty at the other end, giggling amongst themselves. My posture is perfect and my elbows never touch the table and my napkin sits folded in my lap and I eat as impeccably as ever. Not too much to appear to be overindulging, but enough that it's not rude to the kitchen staff.

Midway through the first course, the door opens and a man I assumed to be dead stumbles into the dining room. The table falls silent and all eyes turn to him. As he passes by me, he grips the top of my chair to steady himself. I squint at him and he grins at me.

His name is Henry Banner. He's a publisher around the area, though from what I've heard, he hasn't sold a decent book in the last ten years. He spends his time drunk as a skunk these days, and even though he is technically still a member of Society, he is generally regarded as unwelcome. He used to spend lots of time around my father. In fact, they were the closest friends. When I was young, I called him Uncle Harry. But that was a long time ago.

"Been a while since I've seen you, Annaleise," he slurs, blinking one eye. I swallow a lump in my throat as he moves to the other end of the table and drops himself into his chair with a thud. The other guests avert their eyes and continue cutting their meat.

"Can we get you a drink, Banner?" I ask sarcastically. A light chuckle emerges collectively from the table. Frank smiles under his breath, and Mother fumes. She clenches her teeth so tightly the veins in her forehead pop out. I look down at my lap again.

I know how difficult it is for you to not be an embarrassment to this family.

Dinner comes to an end the same as always, and we return to the hall for mingling. I'm not sure why anybody even holds parties like this anymore. They all consist of the same people telling the same stories to the same audience, pretending as though they're someone of consequence in the grand scheme of things. Frank, for one, believes he alone is the great savior of humanity, and that his business dealings will save the entire world. If Frank had any selfless bones in his body, I might fool myself into believing that.

"Annaleise," Frank says once we're in the center of the room, with couples all around us and Mother positioned directly over his shoulder, watching me. We stop moving, but I keep my back turned to him. I really should get to the wall so nobody notices the blood on my dress. "As you know already, I've very much enjoyed our time together."

"As have I," I say, but it doesn't sound like my voice. I try to back toward the wall, but as he takes my hand, there's a lag in the music and the women around me gasp or squeal excitedly, as if they've seen a picture star or a ghost. Confused, I turn to see what they're looking at, only to see Frank has gone to the floor, down on one knee, and he pulls out a ring that glitters even when there's no light.

Time stops and I must freeze, because although I see his lips move, it comes out as a warbled sound like when you're underwater. But I don't have to hear him to know what a proposal looks like.

II

I couldn't be more uncomfortable if I was nude. I'm woozy in the head and want nothing more than to get out of here. Hundreds of beady eyes stare me down, waiting for a yes, and Mother's burn a hole into my skin from where she stands a few feet behind Frank. Suddenly, I understand why she was acting so bizarre this morning. I understand why she spent so much on a gown and had me sewn into it. Her lips purse together, and her nose scrunches up the longer I'm silent, and I remember to speak.

My lips form a "yes" that tastes like vinegar to say. The crowd erupts into cheers and I feel like I could vomit. Frank stands with a sickeningly sweet smile on his face, and he slides the ring onto my finger. He gives me a kiss, but I recoil away as his mustache hairs tickle my nose.

The other guests clap, but I hear none of it over my heart pounding in my ears. I lose my footing and catch myself on Frank's suit. He squints his eyes at me, the act so minuscule that nobody other than myself could even notice, and in that moment, I see the rest of my life completely planned out for me. If they had planned an engagement party for me before I'd even said yes, who knows what else they have planned? No doubt the wedding, already. And if, god forbid, I ever have children, Mother and Frank have probably already named them something absurd and signed them up for the most prestigious schools in the country. Every single day of the rest of my life. Day in, day out. Smiling like a ninny. Starving myself to fit into dresses. Mindless conversations. Presenting myself as *ready* to my husband. And for what?

I try my best not to cry. Frank would probably kill me if I cried. But my eyes fill with tears anyway, and Betty exclaims, "Aww, she's crying!" The women in the room let out a bunch of "awww"s. At least I have them fooled that it's tears of joy.

A crowd of the other Society wives forms around me. Some of them grab at me to see the rock while some of them shout bizarre things I'd never even thought of, like "Please, can I be a bridesmaid?" or "Rupert's cousin does the most beautiful floral arrangements, I simply *must* put you in touch with him!"

Mr. Banner appears in front of us. He shakes Frank's hand and nudges me with his elbow. "May I just say congratulations? It's always nice to see two people who are perfect for each other end up together," Banner says. He gives me a slight, condescending look from the corner of his eye. "You're a lucky man to marry this firecracker." I know what that really means. That means, "Good luck controlling this one, Frank."

The room spins around me, and I can't find a single familiar face who can pull me back. If I don't get out of here quickly, I'll vomit across the Lyndon's brand-new marble floor. "Will you excuse me a moment?" I breathe and separate from Frank. He makes some excuse while I hasten up the stairs, careful not to trip on my dress and to not show anything in my face until I'm alone.

I throw open the nearest door, and the moment it's closed behind me, I fall against it and let my emotions free, and the tears that accompany them. I pull the chair from the vanity and tuck it under the doorknob so that nobody could come in if they tried. I let out a string of aggressive expletives, and I find some type of ceramic and throw it at the wall, then I claw at hideous velvet curtains from the window. I steady myself on the vanity, digging my fingers into the marble top. My body shakes with anger as tears slip down my cheeks and land on my chest.

I stare at my reflection in the mirror until I go numb, until I don't even recognize her. My breathing calms to a slightly heavier than average pace.

My eyes catch sight of the glittering diamond ring that weighs my finger down. I can't say I didn't see this coming; I just thought I had more time. But no, he selected me as his wife before I even realized I was up for auction. He's handsome enough that any woman should be happy to marry him, but he has no warmth, neither in his soul nor in his body. My friends fought me for him when we first got together, and they always pout about how lucky I am. Am I broken for not loving him as deeply as everyone thinks I should?

It's easy for everyone else to settle into this life, so why isn't it easy for me who was born into it? Why can't I just be like everyone else and accept the hand I'm given? I have a man who wants to love me, and a beautiful home, and a life without worry, which is more than others can hope for these days. So why is it not enough for me?

The curtains billow from the open balcony doors and I find myself drawn to the ledge, but urgent knocks on the door pull me away from the dark thoughts creeping in. Mother says my name, and something about her tone indicates that she's waiting until she comes inside to really scold me. I turn back to my reflection to will her into obedience. She's just as exhausted as I am. My lips shake as I see what I've become. An empty, vapid, shell of a person for whom pearls and diamonds do not equal an existence. I press my palm to my mouth so no sounds come out and shut my eyes so tightly that tears drip down my neck to my chest, leaving streaks where they've ruined my cosmetics.

I blow out a breath and find it within me to answer her.

"Just a moment, Mother!" It takes all my energy to steady my voice enough so that I'm not suspicious. My chest feels hollow and my heart burns, and with a final deep breath, I force the tears to stop, as simple as turning off a bathtub faucet. In my short life I've mastered the art of cutting off emotions, and this is no different than any other time. I wipe away the smeared make-up and quickly reapply more from the collection on the vanity, then I tuck my hair back into some remnant of my original hair style, so I look as good as when I first arrived.

I powder the redness from my face and tuck the puff back beside the rest of the cosmetics, so Betty won't suspect I used any. Behind me, Mother speaks to somebody, and there's another steady and firm knock on Betty's door, different from Mother's. I check my face once more and smooth out my gown, then move the chair from the doorknob. I pause, composing myself, and open the door to face—not Mother, but Frank. The word comes to mind, but it makes me sick to admit it.

"Your mother was about to break down the door," Frank says, with his nose turned up slightly and his eyes shifting as if he's scanning the room for enemies. He takes one step into the room and places a hand on my hip. At his touch, all the little hairs on my arms and my neck stand at attention. My stomach turns like when you hear an unexpected gunshot and you're stuck with anticipatory anxiety for the next several minutes. Frank leans down and kisses my cheek, then beams at me in the mirror. He looks at me the way a prideful man looks at a trophy. I look like my mother. Obedient, put together, like a perfect woman of society.

"I know you hate surprises, but we couldn't help ourselves," Frank says. "You know, for a minute there, I didn't think you were going to say yes." He releases me from his arms and sits on Betty's bed, sipping the wine in his glass.

"I would have liked a warning." My voice sounds dull, no hint of that fire everyone told me I had when I was younger. To think of it now, they always said it like it was a problem. *You're a fiery one, Annaleise. Your parents have their hands full with you.* But somehow, this new me doesn't feel much better.

"Why would you need a warning? Everyone knows you're mine. Don't be stupid; you knew this was going to happen. It's merely a formality." I sense rising anger in his voice. "You shouldn't be hiding up here. People might get the wrong idea."

I press my eyebrows together. "What d'you mean?"

"Well, for one, you've hardly spoken a word to me all night. And that little crying stunt didn't help us much." He towers above me and takes my hand, admiring the ring up close. He sighs and softens his voice. "I know this isn't how you wanted it, but you can't always have your way. And you can't throw a tantrum when you don't get it. You're my fiancé now, Annaleise. You can't continue to act like a child."

"I'm not acting like a child." I pull my hand back from him and stretch my neck to try to reach his height. "I would have liked to be warned, so I wasn't so blindsided in front of all my friends," I say firmly.

"Well, I didn't like how you ran out of the party the moment you said yes. I couldn't care less about your emotions, Annaleise, but I expect you to keep them in check. Mr. Banner noticed something was aloof."

I look down at the floor and grind my teeth together. "I'm sorry." I'm not sorry, but I want to keep the peace.

Frank sucks on his teeth, quiet. "Look at me when I speak to you, Annaleise," he spits suddenly, his voice hard like nails. Despite my efforts to be good tonight, I've upset him. "I gave you everything you have. Your clothes, your home, your chefs, that stupid maid you're so clingy to. You'd think that after everything I've done for you, I would deserve some respect! I gave you everything and you're still ungrateful!"

"I'm not ungrateful!" I insist.

"Then act like it!" He seethes. "Who do you think has been keeping you and your mother afloat all this time? If it wasn't for me, you and your mother would have drowned in debt. The least you could do is act like you're happy to marry me." He pours a glass of ice water from the pitcher and drinks it to cool himself down.

"You don't get to buy me, Frank," I say, matching his anger. Frank is quiet for a moment, but I feel his frustration with every breath he takes, filling up the room like a balloon ready to pop. I've failed at my one job, and now I get to pay for it.

My ears heat up and my heart beats faster as Frank's anger boils over and he paces around the bedroom, running his hands through his hair. He grunts and throws the glass of ice water, which lands with a splash and a crash against the wall. Certainly, the people downstairs at the party can hear. I hope they hear. I pray they hear.

Before I have time to stop him or reason with him, Frank spins on his heel. His palm flies out and slaps me across my face, so hard that my ear rings and the skin feels like fire. I double over, clutching my cheek as some type of strangled cry escapes my lips.

"That is exactly what I get to do!" he shouts, waving his grubby finger in my face and leaning in close to me. "I own you, Annaleise. That was the deal, you spoiled brat!"

I can't cry. I won't let myself this time. I bite the inside of my cheek to keep the tears at bay, and I have to pray that no bruise shows until I get home. I straighten myself and keep my hand on my cheek where he's slapped me until my hearing returns to normal.

"I don't want to hurt you, Anne. But I don't see how you give me an alternative. Be a good wife," he whispers, a hopeful smile growing on his face, "and I won't have to."

We leave the bedroom and suddenly Mother appears at my side, her cheeks spotted with red blotches and a light sweat forming at her forehead. She lets out a huge breath and immediately her eyebrows point in two different directions to scold me, but Frank puts a hand up to silence her.

"Not to worry, Mrs. Winston. Everything is fine," Frank says charmingly, and Mother relaxes—or at least she pretends to. Nobody heard anything. Nobody's planning a rescue. I'm on my own.

"You don't want to keep your royal subjects waiting for you, do you?" Mother says with a flourish of her wrist. She says it like a joke, and while she shares a pointed laugh with Frank, it doesn't feel like a joke. Frank and I, we really are the king and future queen of these people, so to speak. We may not have the power to start wars, and we don't have servants at our every beck and call, but the people in New York Society look at us like royalty, and even I don't want to let anybody down.

"Mustn't keep them waiting, you know." Frank holds a smooth hand out toward me, and I take it gingerly. His body is as cold as ice, and his skin feels like paper beneath my fingers. We descend the staircase with smiles and excitement for our engagement.

Betty raises her glass "to the happy couple!" and all the guests raise their glasses above their heads and say in unison, "To the future Mr. and Mrs. Frank Alexander." It's the first time I've heard the name, and it makes me dizzy enough to stumble and almost slip off the stairs. Frank catches me and gives me a sideways look. Just as quickly, he laughs and looks back at the crowd.

"Looks as though my fiancé has already had too much to drink!" He explains my dizziness away and the crowd laughs. I blush with embarrassment and hide my face. We continue to the bottom of the stairs and serpentine through what must be hundreds of couples, all of whom congratulate us.

At most of our interactions, the woman of the couple gawks at the ring with me and giggles about how cute Frank is and how lucky I am, while Frank discusses business with the men, looking very stern and important, with their brows folded in tightly and their cheeks sucked in. They puff on cigars and drink drinks they don't actually enjoy but pretend to like, complimenting each other on their magnificence.

Betty Lyndon pushes through her party guests with a drink in one hand and dragging her husband Johnny along in the other, giddy with excitement. Betty is exactly my age, but she's already been married for two years. She was the first of us girls in Society to get married, and as soon as she got engaged, the other girls rushed out to find themselves a beau too. Johnny and Betty look at each other in a way that gives me a pang of jealousy every time I see them because I know Frank and I will never like each other as much as they do. Betty notices me, and with a loud, joyous noise, she throws one arm around me and hugs me, careful not to spill her drink.

"ANN-LEESE!" she squeals, rocking us back and forth. Mother says Betty is "nouveau riche," which basically means they didn't earn their money, they don't deserve their money, and they make a fool out of anybody who has money. Betty's Daddy struck oil some years ago, so she doesn't have the same refinery that Society-born girls have, but because Johnny allows all of her chaos, nobody can scold her for it. At least not to her face, as proven by Mother. Unfortunately for me, Frank shares my mother's ideas about what a wife should be. I think they're conspiring against me.

"Oh, my gosh," Betty gushes as she yanks my hand and admires the ring up close to her face. "That's even bigger than mine!" She holds up her own hand and compares ring sizes, then scrunches up her face. Frank scowls at her, but luckily Betty remains blissfully unaware. "Good job, Frank." She smiles charmingly at him. "Oh, my goodness, Ann-leese. It was so hard keeping tonight a secret from you! I was so scared I was going to spoil the surprise!" Betty says.

"I wish you had," I say through my teeth. I sound and feel more like myself when I talk with Betty. Mother and Frank can't stand Betty, but I like to spend time with her because it is the only time I don't have to be so poised and so proper. Compared to Betty, my mother must think I'm an angel. I can't do much wrong in her presence.

"You should have seen your face!" Betty exclaims, bouncing slightly and almost tipping over her drink. "Oops," she giggles.

Frank squints his eyes at Betty and finds someone new to distract himself with. "Ann, I'm going to go speak with Maximillian over there." He gives Betty a polite nod as a goodbye and squeezes my hand before departing. The moment Frank is out of my personal space, I feel a shift—the air becomes lighter, my shoulders relax, and a weight on my lungs lifts. I didn't know Frank's presence had such a physical toll on me. Marriage to him will be awful.

"Ann-leese, have you tried the cream puffs yet?" Betty gushes. "I think I could eat about a million and not get tired of them."

"Not too much, don't want you getting fat now," Johnny teases with a poke to her rib cage. She looks at him with a flirty, scandalized look, and laughs. "I'll let you two ladies catch up. Good seeing you, Annaleise," Johnny says charmingly and disappears into the crowd. I wonder if Johnny ever hits Betty in private.

"How is Johnny's brother Jackson? He's married now, yes?" I ask. Typically, the Lyndon boys travel together like a pack, but I haven't seen or heard from Jackson in a while, other than that he married some nobody a few years ago.

Betty's eyes grow as big as saucers and she pulls me to the side of the party, lowering her voice. "You haven't heard?" I shake my head, looking like a ninny. I do love a good scandal. "Oh, it was so embarrassing, Ann. Jackson and that horrible woman Louisa got involved in the wrong stock. I don't really know the complete story, but I know that when the market went down, Jackson went down with it. They had to sell all their stuff, and you *know* Louisa has lots of stuff. The damn woman probably married him for his money. But anyway, they lost their house, and they had to borrow money from us. Johnny made the deal; I wasn't involved. But if he didn't loan them money, they would have ended up in one of those homeless towns."

I think back to the shadows in the park on our way here. They didn't seem like monsters like everyone would have me believe.

"It's a good thing you gave him a loan, right?" I ask, confused. "Now he won't be homeless."

"Yes, but you're missing the point! He could ruin our good name if someone were to find out. If that witch decides not to pay back the loan, Johnny is out ten thousand dollars! And with a *baby* on the way—" She realizes her mistake after it comes out, and she covers her mouth. "Oh, dear. Ann-leese, promise me you won't tell. We meant to keep it a surprise, and I don't want to overshadow your big day!" She looks as though she could cry.

"Don't worry, I won't tell. That's amazing! Congratulations, Betty." I laugh softly, grasping her hand. She spends the next ten minutes gushing about how wonderful her pregnancy is, though I admit I tune her out about halfway through.

The idea of being pregnant makes me ill. I'm not sure if it's the idea of having children or having children *with Frank* that makes me so opposed to it, but I would be better off jumping from the Brooklyn Bridge than having a child with him. I have a vision of my children cowering in the corner while their father releases his anger at them, the way he does with me.

Would he be so cruel as to hit a child? To "correct their behavior," as he so lovingly does to me? I don't believe anyone could be so evil, but I wouldn't put it past Frank either. He's sneaky in his cruelty. He never fails at chipping away a piece of my ego.

I vow that if I should ever bear a son, I will raise him to be the opposite of Frank. He will be what Frank pretends to be in public.

I realize my face reflects my bitter thoughts, so I force myself back into the persona of Annaleise Winston, the future Mrs. Frank Alexander, and craft a painfully fake smile. I take his arm and we walk to the dance floor. He leads me in a waltz, and we don't speak a word to each other for the rest of the night.

III

To my relief, Mother feigns a headache to get us out of the party, but even so, it takes us another half an hour to get away from the Society wives congratulating us and begging to see the ring again. The car ride home is so silent that the air hisses, except for the moment when Frank opens up a bottle of liquor and downs it in the backseat. I close my eyes and envision the car driving into a pond and water pouring in.

When we arrive home, I storm past Mother and Frank—admittedly, a bit dramatically. If I could claw this dress off my skin, I would. I climb the stairs, but only a few steps up, a hand wraps around my wrist and tugs me down so forcefully that I spin to Frank, whose face is so tense he could be a marble statue only inches from me.

"Remember," he mumbles, "be grateful." I tug my hand away forcefully and squint my eyes at him. I'm allowed to feel what I want to feel. He may own me, but he cannot buy my heart.

"Get your hands off me," I spit, and I have no more than a few seconds of warning before his hand flies up and slaps me across the cheek. I double over in pain, clutching the side of my face.

"Don't ever speak to me like that again, you selfish bitch." Mother comes in the door, apparently having missed all the action and saving me from another slap. Frank rubs his hands together and shouts at Polly to go fix him a sandwich, and I sneak away up the stairs.

Virginia stands to greet me in my bedroom, but her joy to see me is quickly replaced with concern as I start hyperventilating, reaching to tear the dress off of me. I know she sees the ring, because her entire body language changes, and she helps undo the stitches on the gown. The moment I'm free from the dress, I hunch over and clutch my stomach. Virginia slides a nightgown over my body and takes my hand.

"Everything will be alright," she whispers as she braids my hair for bed. Everything I am is because of Virginia. We almost lost her during the crash. We almost lost everything because Father wasn't careful, but Frank saved us *and* Virginia. I hate that I owe so much to him now. Our debt is no longer with the banks. Our debt is with Frank, and I owe him my life.

I stare at the base of the floor while Virginia combs out the tangles in my hair with her fingers. Early in our relationship, I teased Frank for not knowing who some author was. At the time, I thought it would lead to a playful, flirty interaction about books, but it led to Frank beating me within an inch of my life and Mother canceling my birthday party because my injuries were so severe. She told people I fell down the steps. I don't know if that's what she believed happened, or if she knew the truth and chose to ignore it, anyway. Still, I never called him another name again, but he always finds some reason to be upset with me. If I don't prepare his tea correctly. If

I speak out of turn. If I cry openly. Whatever I do, it'll never be enough, no matter what he says or tries to convince me of.

Upon the thought, a sob comes up from within me, though I have no tears left to cry. Virginia should understand the fear of this situation better than anyone. She's seen the bruises he's left on me, and she's seen how cruel he can be. He may put up a perfect persona in public, but he's a monster, and if nothing changes, I won't live to be twenty-five.

I must stop this. Somehow, I must find a way out of marriage to Frank.

"I don't—I don't want to marry him." I cover my face and let the waves of anguish roll through me. Virginia half-hugs me and half-rocks me, as if I were a child and her warmth brings me comfort.

"So, don't," she whispers. "You'll figure out what to do in your own time." But no matter how hard I think, there is no scenario in which I win.

Virginia stays with me for a while, but when she yawns and wipes the sleep from her eyes, I kiss her on the cheek and urge her to go to bed, insisting that I'll be okay. She tiptoes out my door and carefully shuts it behind her, giving me one final, sad smile. The door shuts behind her, and I stare at the ceiling until sleep finds me.

***

The sun pokes me in the eye, demanding I wake. My face is puffy from crying, but I'm well-rested comparatively. Last night seems to have only been a bad dream until I stretch out my fingers and see the ring.

The walk down to breakfast is quieter than usual. I note the lack of maids or butlers hustling around the halls like they usually are. Mother must be in a good mood this morning. I reach the dining room and step inside, the only sound my bare footfalls against the ceramic tiles. Mother and Frank lean close to each other across the table, looking over a notebook.

Mother taps it with her pen and mutters quietly, leaning back in her seat when I approach the table.

"*Dear lord*, you slept in late this morning," Mother gawks, sipping her tea. I look at my fiancé, but he doesn't even glance up from their work. Virginia brings me a cinnamon roll to eat. I thank her and take a seat at the other side of the table.

"What are you doing?" I ask while chewing. Mother purses her lips together and gives me a pointed look. I roll my eyes, swallow the bite, then repeat myself. "I'm sorry. *What are you doing?*"

"Manners, Anne," Frank says warningly from across the table. I bite the inside of my cheek and try to avoid more conflict. Mother turns the notebook to me, where there's a list of random words like flowers, seating, dress, cake. I take a moment, but it eventually catches up to me.

"Are these wedding details?" I take the book from her and flip to a second page. "Mother, I haven't been engaged for twelve hours yet!" Mother snatches the notebook from me and flattens out the pages, careful not to smear the ink.

"Well, we have to work quickly if we want to have an August wedding."

I choke on my tea. "*August?!*" I catch my breath and pull myself together. "That's—that's too soon! There is no way we can plan a wedding in that time. That's not even two months!"

"That's why we've been planning this wedding for months." Mother sips her tea and winks at me like she's a genius, but I can't bring myself to feel any relief. If they have planned the wedding all this time, then why even bother with the proposal? Why force me to say yes in front of all my friends? Why not just drag me down the aisle in literal chains?

Shouldn't I be making some of these decisions too? Or is Mother going to walk two steps behind me for *the rest of my life* and make my choices for me? Perhaps I should just let her name my children now and sign them up for those private schools. Maybe I should help her find a venue for my funeral, choose a caterer, too!

I don't mean to show my anger. I know I'm not supposed to. But I can't help it. If everyone else's life is as planned as mine, how does everyone else act so okay with it? And if their lives aren't like this, then why is mine? *It isn't fair.*

The cork is pulled and I can't stop the words from spewing from my mouth.

"Don't I have a say in any of this?" I ask. My tone is as sharp as razors, but I don't raise my voice. When Mother looks up from the page with wide, scandalized eyes, I'm careful not to falter. Frank looks up from his breakfast steak but, thankfully, chooses not to engage. "I'm the bride. Shouldn't I have a say in something like the venue, or the dress, or, I don't know, *the husband?*"

Frank clenches his teeth, his jaw twitches, and his fork shakes in his grip from how hard he holds it. But he doesn't explode. He remains calm. Anyone other than me wouldn't recognize his little ticks of anger. But I know them like the back of my hand. I know what level of anger he's at by his shoulders. Mother is a different story.

"Annaleise!" Mother rises from her seat, drawing me from

my fuming wrath. Catching my breath, I shrink down before her, back to my normal size. "You are acting like a spoiled brat and I won't put up with it any longer! I don't know where you got this sense of... *entitlement!*"

I let out a breath and stand. "I'm going out," I say flatly. That's one choice I can still make. Frank goes to his feet quickly.

"Annaleise, I don't think that'd be a good idea. You have so much planning to do," he says. "The wedding is so soon; you really shouldn't waste any time." He smiles, and his eyes flash with a smirk that his mouth does not show. I want nothing more than to jump at him and... I don't know what I would do if I had the chance. I want to hurt him, but trying to fight with him is like when you punch someone in a dream: you just can't hit hard enough to cause pain. I want to see him hurt and I want it to be at my hand.

"It seems like you two will do just fine without my help." I turn on my heels and leave the room. I don't even bother going to get changed out of my nightgown. Instead, I grab a long overcoat from the front closet and pull the first pair of shoes I can find onto my feet, slamming the front door behind me as loudly as I can. The house shakes and I immediately regret that choice. I'll pay for that later. I stuff my hands in the coat pockets and walk down the driveway, scuffing my feet on the ground, quite unladylike.

My hands wrap around a small package in the pocket, and I pull it out. It's a silver cigarette box. This is my father's old coat. It's sat idle for almost ten years and smells of mothballs, but this feels like a sign from him. Solidarity. I can almost hear him saying, "I can't be with you, but I support your fight." I know he'd be on my side if he was here. I haven't really thought of him in a long time, but right now, I desperately wish he was here. I wrap my arms around myself and keep walking. My feet find the main street and I lean my head back, letting the wind blow through my hair and the sunshine on my skin.

I pull Frank's engagement ring off my finger and consider throwing it into the bushes or the pond, but instead, I tuck it in Pa's pocket and shuffle my feet on the concrete beneath me. An old man looks me up and down, either admiring me or sizing me up as I schlump along. I walk for miles and only stop when my feet ache and blister.

I sit in the grass in Central Park and pull my shoes off to rub my feet, but then I lay back against the grass and close my eyes in the sunlight. As I silence my thoughts, I hear music playing in the distance. Instruments I can't identify, lyrics I don't know, and clapping. Lots of clapping. I look around for the source and find that it's coming from the Hooverville, the shantytown in the center of the park.

It's made up of cardboard boxes and sheets, tents, and scrap metal pieces, all thrown together to look like tiny houses with no doors or windows or structure of any kind. Garbage is strewn about, and a clothesline is tied between two trees with dozens of shirts and dresses hanging from it. I scrunch up my nose and push myself back to my feet.

Smoke billows out of various firepits in the homeless camp, forming black shapes in the sky. I glance down at a handwritten sign made from a cardboard box that reads, "Welcome to Hooverville, est. 1928" in messy lettering. The people sing a song, and someone plays the harmonica. Children run around barefoot and giggle loudly, trying to catch each other. Despite their glee, they look pale with sunken cheeks and eyes, and the adults are even worse. I've only ever seen sickness like that once in my life, and in their faces, I see my Pa. They look like dead men walking, and it shakes me so badly that I have to look away. My eyes find a girl my age sitting beside a sign on the path that says "ANYTHING HELPS. NEED MONEY FOR TRAIN TICKET TO CALI." I make eye contact with the girl for a moment.

The singing group claps and stomps to the beat of whatever song they're singing, but they slowly stop as they realize there's an outsider in their midst. Ten people stop to look at me, and I can't tell if they're defensive or if they're happy to see me. They whisper amongst themselves and one boy, a tall one with overgrown blond curls, steps closer to me with his mouth open like he's going to say something. I fear he'll ask me for money, so I quickly turn my head away and continue walking, past the singers and past the girl, embarrassed to have nothing to offer them. I hear mumbles and slowly the music starts up again, but they still seem wary of the intrusion. I sigh as soon as I'm out of their sight.

The rest of the country would probably give their children for a chance to have wealth like I do, so I should be grateful for everything I've been given. But I'm not. I would give anything for a second chance. An honest upbringing away from the secrets and lies I've had to hold just to keep us afloat.

I stop for lunch at Pa's old favorite diner, and I pay with a nickel I find at the bottom of my coat pocket before I make the long walk back home. It's midafternoon when I turn back onto my driveway.

I hover before the front door and pause before opening it. I shake my uncertainty away and push my way in, but it's dead silent except for Virginia washing the dishes in the kitchen. I slide my shoes off and place them by the front door per her instructions.

I make my way into the library—well, actually, it's *Frank's* library. When Frank moved into the west side of the house, he claimed the library. I'm not allowed to use it, but I do when he's out-of-town anyway. I browse through his books and find one I haven't already read. My body senses his presence before he even makes a sound. My shoulder muscles stiffen, and my stomach turns as if all the air in the room has turned sour.

"Hello, Frank," I say without looking away from the shelf.

"I thought I might find you in here when you came back. *If* you came back. Where did you run off to?" he asks, leaning nonchalantly against the doorway, crossing his arms.

"I went for a walk."

"Yes, I *know* you went for a walk," His voice has an edge to it that signifies he's upset with me. "But where? I didn't know where to find you."

"You had no reason to try to find me because I will *always* come back," I say, finally looking up at him. He is uncharacteristically dressed down, wearing only the white button-up he usually wears under his suit. In a moment of sincerity, he kneels beside me and reaches his hand up to my cheek. I flinch away for fear he'll slap me for what I did this morning, but he only places it there, sickeningly gentle as he looks into my eyes, which frightens me more than if he'd hit me.

"Annaleise," he says sweetly. I curl my upper lip and lean back slightly. "We've both behaved very badly these last hours.

I hope you understand now that if you're going to be my wife, you must behave a certain way. You shouldn't deny me, Anne. Don't make me a bad guy. You and I can make a happy couple if you'll just let it happen."

Just let it happen. Just let everything happen to me, including his abuse and likely my eventual death. Frank leans in and kisses me. He releases me from his grasp and smiles at me in a way that almost makes me think he's undergone a personality change, but I see it. The flicker in his eyes that acts as a warning of what could be unleashed if I don't behave myself.

"You're capable of being a good wife, if you tried." He stands and leaves, and somewhere in the kitchen he yells at some poor sou chef. I close my eyes futilely.

I would love nothing more than to see my mother's face if I chose not to marry Frank.

She'd no longer have any of his money. She'd be on the streets she hates so badly and become one of the people she despises. I think of the people in the Hooverville today and whether they have troubles like mine. I've never been hungry in my life. I've never been cold, and I've never not had a bed. It's selfish of me to believe I could even remotely understand what they go through daily, and stupid too. My problems must seem silly to them, and so I try to shake my complaints away.

With Frank, I'll be secure and financially stable. In this economy, that's the best thing a woman can be. But my dreams won't matter in the slightest. I'll never travel. I'll have nothing that's truly my own. I'll have children and Virginia will probably raise them too, and in that scenario, I will become the thing I hate most in the world.

I look around the room at all the books and think of the wedding plans. I have played the good girl role my whole life. I've smiled and said whatever my mother wants me to. I've been a perfect example of a Society Girl. But I can't live any longer in a life where I'm silenced. I can't walk two steps behind a man for the rest of my life like the others. I can't listen to that voice in my head. To *Mother's* voice inside my head. I can't marry Frank.

I must get out.

IV

Dinner is painfully awkward, unfortunately. Mother doesn't take her glaring eyes off me for even a second. Frankly, I don't care how furious she is with me; I'll not put up with it. As I'm about to excuse myself to my room, Frank clears his throat and stands, trying to hold back a smile but failing. Even the skin on his face unnerves me. It's like aged leather that has been stretched out over time, with a sort of green tint to it.

"Ladies," he smirks. "I have an announcement. I'm going away on business in the morning. I won't be back for at least a week," he says, practically bouncing as he speaks. This isn't news, though. Frank's away on business at least half of the time. He's never made a big show of it before, so what's he hiding? Frank answers my question before I ask it. "Don't be mistaken, this isn't like any ordinary business trip." He holds his head higher in the air and looks at Mother. "Governor Roosevelt and President Hoover have invited me to a gala where I will get to meet all the state senators and the opportunity to have an *input* in some political manners."

Mother clasps her hands together excitedly and congratulates Frank, but I feel frozen to my chair.

"The President invited *you*?" I ask incredulously, raising

my eyebrows disbelievingly. Mother's eyes burn a hole in my skull.

"Yes, he and I met once at an alumni event. He went to school with my father." Frank smiles proudly at this and looks me up and down.

"Why would he invite you to do politics?" I ask, scrunching up my nose. "You're a businessman."

"Anne, all politics is business, and especially right now, he needs someone like *me* to show him how to keep his money." Frank shares a laugh with Mother and snaps his fingers at Virginia to load more food onto his plate. Virginia gives me a look while scooping extra potatoes.

"Is money all anybody here cares about?" I ask.

"Don't be silly, Anne. Without money, man has nothing." Frank says. "You can pretend not to care about it all you want, but even you can't live without it." I take his words like a challenge. I'll show him, when I leave him and make it on my own without his money. I don't need him or anyone to survive.

"Well," Mother chimes in. "I think that's quite an honor they've given you, Frank. Be sure to bring us back a souvenir from Washington."

"Actually, I was going to ask if Annaleise wants to come with me." Frank and Mother both look at me hopefully, my mother nodding for me. In their faces, I see an opportunity, an opening in the brick walls they've built up around me. Very carefully, I speak.

"I'll think about it," I tell them, a soft smile coming to my lips. "I'll let you know before we go to bed."

"Very good." Frank smiles at my sudden personality change, and I grin to myself while cutting up my steak. I catch

Virginia eyeballing me, but I give her a minuscule shake of my head.

I'm excused from the table and head to my bedroom to wash up for the night. As soon as I shut my bedroom door behind me, I scramble through my drawers and closet. I stuff whatever I can find into a bag—clothes, shoes, money, some photographs. I freeze and my heart beats faster as I hear footsteps outside my door and my doorknob jiggling. The door opens and my mother reveals herself to me.

"What are you up to, Annaleise?" she asks as she shuts the door behind her. "Don't be stupid."

"What do you mean?" I ask, playing coy.

"Your behavior is erratic. No question about it, Annaleise. You're going with Frank to D.C. It's an opportunity we can't afford to pass up. It's an opportunity every girl in the country would kill to have. Are you purposely trying to make life difficult for us?" She raises her voice slightly.

Watching my mother squirm is just a benefit to my behavior. "Am I making things difficult for you? I didn't notice." I wish I could be one of those girls who's good friends with her mother, but let's be honest here: those don't exist in families with arranged marriages.

"I know what you're doing, Annaleise." Mother takes a step closer to me, but I don't shrink down. For once, we seem to be on the same level. "You may think you can make a fool of us and magically get your way, but you can't. Stop being difficult and just accept that this is your life now. Here, I brought these." She holds out a stack of cards with intricate calligraphy on them reading "*You're invited to the wedding of Frank*

Alexander and Annaleise Winston," along with a save-the-date card dated the 18th of August.

"I need you to sign each of them and write the names on the top, then put them into the envelopes. I'll have Virginia mail them." The weight of the invitations is more than I expected.

"Be on your best behavior in D.C., Anne. Don't embarrass us," she warns under her breath, then she pulls me into a tight hug, surprising me. We haven't hugged in so long; I didn't even know she knew how to hug.

"I'll do my best," I tell her as I pull back. Mother straightens her back and flattens out her wrinkled dress.

"Have a pleasant trip, Anne. I'll see you when you get back." Mother turns and heads for the door. I'm about to let her walk out of my life forever without saying another word, but I couldn't live with that on my conscious.

So, "Goodbye, Mother," I tell her. The way she looks at me makes me wonder if she knows I have a plan to run away tonight, but she leaves anyway, shutting the door behind her and leaving a frozen silence in her wake. I return to stuffing items in my bag; including a diary, clothes, some jewelry, and some cash. At least once a week, Frank gives me money and tells me to "buy myself something nice." But I have everything I could ever want, and I'm not like Betty Lyndon, who has to have something just to prove something to another person. So instead, I started pocketing it, saving for something huge. A house of my own maybe, or a way out of New York...

Oh, my God! The girl from the park comes to mind. The one with the sign who wanted to go to California. I rush to my window and look out onto the horizon. I could make it there, surely. I have enough money. There are plenty of jobs opening out West, and I could do anything I want, be anyone I want to be. I've never seen the Pacific Ocean. The best part of it is that *Frank wouldn't find me*. He wouldn't think to look for me there!

It's foolproof. I hide the bag underneath my bed and straighten my hair. "Frank!" I call for him down the hall. A minute later he enters, a hopeful look in his eyes. I immediately squash his hopes of something happening tonight. "I've decided it's best if I stay here." He seems confused.

"I won't be going to D.C. with you tomorrow," I explain further. He presses his eyebrows together and leans against the wall. I hold on to the bedframe behind me to steady myself for fear he might insist on more. Not tonight. Not ever again.

"Why not?"

I think up an excuse on the fly. "I'm on the rag." It's a lie, but it's one that I've learned to use to my benefit, as it makes men around me uncomfortable and they don't ask too many questions. I enjoy watching Frank's face when I tell him about it, because he turns a pale shade of gray and looks as though he'll throw up in a wastebasket. How can someone so *tough* be so squeamish about women's troubles? It makes me laugh.

Frank swallows back his bile and nods. "Right, then I guess I'll see you when I get back. What should I bring you from D.C.? Any souvenirs?"

"Oh, no. Please don't. I have more gifts than I know what to do with."

"Don't be silly! I love you, Annaleise, and I want to shower you with gifts." He takes my hand and smiles. "I'll surprise you. How about that?" I nod quietly and force a weak smile.

"Bye, Annaleise. Sleep well, and go easy on your mother this week." He grins at me and leaves, closing the door behind him. I am amazed at how easy that was. My last communication with Frank. I'm free. I collapse on my bed, covering my smile with my hands and kicking my feet excitedly. The feeling I've been carrying for the last six months is lifted and the world feels new again.

On my nightstand, I find the stack of wedding invitations Mother gave me to sign. I flip through them and search for a single name I like, or even *know*. There are my mother's friends, Frank's business friends—people neither of them like but whom it would be a scandal to not invite.

The Governor is invited, and my mother's extended family who I don't know beyond an occasional Christmas card. But no one invited to the wedding is of any importance to me. I'm not sure anyone of these names would care if I was missing or dead. Not even Betty. Not even Frank.

I kneel in front of my fireplace with the invitations in my hand and stare into the flames. I daintily hold one invitation addressed to Frank's parents between my fingers and outstretch my arm until the tips of the flame grasp at the corner of the envelope. I hold it up close to my face and watch the fire burn more and more of the letters. It's like a drug that I can't get enough of. I drop it in the fireplace and watch it writhe and curl until it disintegrates. My shoulders drop, and I take another invitation and burn it, followed by another one and another one until the entire stack of envelopes is nothing more than a pile of ash.

I smile into the fire and write a note on some spare stationary at my desk. I put it in an envelope and slide it under Virginia's door before sneaking back to my room. I try to sleep until the sun comes up, but anticipation keeps me awake.

I hear Frank downstairs, and I hear the front door close, and I know it's time. I put a cloak on and grab my bag, and for good measure, peek my head into my mother's bedroom. She's sure to still be asleep, as she rarely says goodbye to Frank and me, but it's better to cover my tracks, anyway.

"Mother," I whisper. "Frank and I are leaving now."

She rolls over in bed and puts her pillow over her head. "Be safe," she mumbles sleepily. "Don't embarrass me." And then she snores, and that's the last of it. I shut the door behind me and tiptoe down the stairs. The glowing eyes of Frank's car disappear around the corner, and I know I'm in the clear, so I leave.

V

Ladies never chortle. Ladies don't hold their glasses in their palms. Ladies dance only with a partner. Ladies don't cry in public or in front of their husbands. Ladies always present themselves as *ready* for their husbands. Ladies raise the children unless their husbands are around, then the children go to the nanny. Ladies fall silent when the men are talking. Ladies *never* run away from home in the middle of the night.

I dawdle so not to disturb the gravel too much until I reach the end of the driveway, and then I take one last look at my house. I've never really considered the house to be my home. Mother bought it right after Pa died, so it always felt like I was staying in someone else's home without him there. Pa, despite his wealth, didn't like to show it off. He always said that after a certain point, a person *can* have too much money. He put a decent amount into charities, quite a bit in the stock market, and left nearly everything to me in his will. I haven't seen a penny of that money. I'm sure Mother pocketed most of it. Bought our new mansion with it or something. She expected his stock would keep us afloat forever. She was wrong.

The sun wakes over the horizon, illuminating the sky a

light purple color, and a few migrant workers are already beginning their day doing the things nobody else wants to. Newsboys make their way to the Herald. Lamplighters turn out the lights from the evening, skipping and whistling as they walk. I'm rarely awake this early, let alone out and about. The world is still. Peaceful. Blissful. I don't look over my shoulder as I walk. I don't feel the need to. I find myself smiling at everybody I pass and waving at cars at intersections. The crisp morning air means freedom. It means a new beginning.

I cut through the park to reduce my walking time by half. The grass is damp from the rain and soaks through my shoes and halfway up my stockings, but I can't find it within me to care. I won't worry about mundane things like that on a beach in California.

In the distance, I see the tents and shacks that make up Hooverville, and the few souls up before the dawn are hustling around in silence like spies. I cut the corner to avoid their guilt-trip. I have the means to help, but I don't have the heart to. And yes, I know that makes me a bad person.

I'm almost away from the Hooverville when a bulldozer of a human slams into my side, and I land in the grass with a thud and a scream. At first I think it's Frank, that he's somehow found me, but the man is covered in dirt from head to toe, and he's so skinny that I can see his bones. The man lowers himself on top of me, holding a cracked, callused hand over my mouth to stifle my screams. I kick wildly and use all my strength to force him off me, but a swift hit in the temple is all it takes to disorient me. I'm sure of what will happen next, and I'm trembling as the man removes his hand from my mouth.

"*I'm sorry*," he whispers. He grabs my bag and rummages through it. My eyes grow huge as I realize I have all my belongings in there and a decent amount of cash. The man reaches into my bag and throws my items to the side, finding my stack of cash. "Oh, holy shit," the burglar whispers to himself. I start to reach for him, but he pushes my chest down with his foot, and I'm still too scared to move.

"Stop!" shouts someone I can't see. The burglar quickly shoves my money and some of my jewelry into his pockets and runs away. I try to push myself up to chase after him, but I'm not fast enough. Two boys rush past me to chase after the burglar. I check my bag for whatever may be left. The diary, the clothes, and one locket are all that remain. Shit. I rest my head in my hands and take deep breaths until the headache passes. I've been punched in the head twice before, and it never gets any easier. I just have to hope I don't have a concussion, or Mother would get suspicious.

Oh, no. Mother!

I can't return home. She thinks I'm with Frank, and even if I go home at the same time as Frank, there would be too many questions and they'd find out my whole story doesn't add up. My foolproof plan was not so foolproof, and all because of some freak from a Hooverville. I feel nauseous.

"Are you alright?" the taller of the two boys asks as they return. "We couldn't catch him. I'm sorry," he says. He kneels beside me and holds out a hand, which I initially flinch from, but then I take it and pull myself to my feet, dizzy and seeing stars. The short boy comes close to me and tilts my head to look at my temple, where there's sure to be a bruise. I pull myself away from him quickly.

"I'm fine," I say proudly, toughening up. I couldn't fight back if they attacked me, but I can at least try to be intimidating so they won't hurt me.

"Do you need any more help?" the taller one asks.

"No," I blurt. I take a step away from them, nauseated, dizzy, like the world spins around me and I could collapse.

"Hey, are you alright? You don't look so good." He puts a hand on my shoulder and I roughly shake him off me. He holds his hands up in surrender and takes a couple steps back. "Sorry." I immediately feel bad about that. He's just trying to help. It isn't his fault any more than it is my fault. "I haven't seen you before. Are you from Hooverville?" I shake my head and he frowns. "Peter can get you set up with a tent, and then we can figure out something for you later, okay?" Peter, the shorter boy, waves at me with a smile. "I'm Thomas, by the way!" he says. I hesitate for a minute, but if either of them wanted to hurt me, they probably would have done it by now.

"I'm Annaleise," I whisper, and Thomas smiles crookedly.

"Nice to meet you, Annaleise," Thomas says and shakes my hand.

"We have a fire every night," Peter tells me. I stifle a bit of a laugh. He reminds me of a bagboy bringing me to my suite in a hotel, giving me the best service for a good tip, but Peter has to know he won't get a tip from me. "Pretty much the only way everyone can stay warm." His voice goes solemn at the end, and he looks at the ground sadly. But just as quickly, he smiles enthusiastically again and brings me to a back corner where there are a couple of empty huts and tents. "We had a few people leave recently. So, I guess you can have your pick of 'em."

I look at Peter and Thomas uncertainly but then choose a small hut. It's made of wood planks with the paint peeling off them and has what looks like mold growing on it, and it's leaning slightly like a gust of wind could blow it over.

Still, it's in the best condition of all of them, and I don't really see how I have a choice. Even if I don't stay long, it's some place to get dressed and have quiet time to myself.

"Congrats, Ann...Anna...Annie? What was it again?" Peter stammers.

"Annaleise," I repeat.

"That's right. I'll remember it." He salutes me with two fingers and leaves me alone in my new home.

"No, he won't," Thomas says jokingly, and I actually crack a smile. "Let me know if you need anything. I know it can be scary moving in here, but something tells me you'll manage just fine," Thomas says. He talks much gentler than Frank did. He's not so harsh on his consonants, and it's like he's trying not to spook me with any sudden movements. I appreciate that, however demeaning it might be.

"Thank you," I tell him. He pauses a moment, opening his mouth to speak, but shakes his head and leaves. Maybe he really wanted a tip. But no matter. I'm here in a Hooverville, and I've got to handle the situation at hand. The interior of my new house is about the size of Virginia's closet back home and smells of beetles and mold. The shack isn't even big enough to hold my arms out and spin around, and there are slants in the walls that let me see outside.

The sun rises fully, and Hooverville wakes with it. Some

children run around chasing each other, exclaiming, "Tag, you're it!" and turning and running away again. Some mothers carry linens to washboards and sopping buckets, where two more women sit gossiping. Many of the men are already away, while the few men who've stayed back circle the job sections in the newspaper. I watch through the hole in my wall, cautiously distant until I'm sure it's safe to come out.

"John!" one man yells to another man, waving a newspaper around madly. "I found a job that's perfect for you!"

"Aye, bring it over, mate!" the other man, John, shouts back.

A makeshift band made of mostly elderly men has started playing lively music to lighten the mood. There's what looks like a cooking station, complete with whatever spices or ingredients people could save when they were kicked out of their houses. A pot over a fire boils and somebody makes oatmeal in it. Two old men sit at a table playing an intense game of chess on cardboard with chess pieces that must be worth a fortune. Some mangy looking dogs roam around hunting for food, while one bounces excitedly with the children.

Everything is so lively; it's so unlike anything I ever saw back home. I slowly emerge and enter the world around me, however cautiously. Nobody seems to notice me as an outsider, so I sit on a log around the fire near some gossiping women doing their laundry and pretend not to listen.

Apparently, one of their husbands got sloppy about his work and got fired, instead of someone else who shouldn't have been working there, to begin with. One of the other women has been sleeping with somebody's beau and nobody is happy about it. It's not so different from Mother's book club meetings, really. Then, they turn their attention to me.

"You're new here, aren't you?" one woman without teeth says. I instinctively scrunch up my nose—I wasn't expecting her to have no teeth!—and that makes them angry. They didn't like that.

"Oh, and you think you're better than us, too!"

"Pretty girl like you won't last a day," another says, turning up her nose. The toothless woman smacks her on the shoulder.

"Don't *tell* her that! Let her figure it out on her own."

I frown and think of earlier when I thought that robber was going to do something far worse. I could be dead by the end of the day, depending on how savage these people are. "Why wouldn't I last a day?"

They laugh uproariously with each other, holding their bellies. "Is that a real question? Darling, you're what we call *expensive folk.*" One of them grabs my hands and flips them over to look at my palms. "Look at these hands. There's not a callous on these fingers. You've never done a day of work in your life."

I swallow a lump in my throat and tug my hand back to my lap. It's okay for *me* to say I won't make it, but when a stranger so-triumphantly claims to know me, it fills me with rage, and honestly, I take it as a challenge. I'll do the damn thing just to show that *one* asshole who told me I couldn't, and then they can eat their words.

"Would you two leave her be?" a third girl from behind me says. I turn around to see a dark-skinned girl with thick, curly black hair that frames her face and a pretty smile approaching with two tin cans. "Ya'll haven't worked a day in the last ten years so keep your mouths shut." She steps over the log and sits beside me. The toothless woman mumbles a slur under her breath, and the women all take their laundry and leave. The girl hands me a can, filled almost to the top with chili.

"Oh, no thanks," I say quietly. She grins and takes it back.

"You *are* new." She sets the chili beside her. "I'm Eva."

"Annaleise," I say. We shake hands. She's about my age, maybe a little younger than me, but she holds herself with confidence that I can't even pretend to have.

She shovels a spoonful of chili into her mouth. "So, how long are you here for?" she says as she chews, but to her credit, she at least covers her mouth with her hand so I don't see the food in her mouth. Mother would still kill her for that, but I'm willing to let it slide.

I hadn't considered the actual plan, or what I'll do when Frank looks for me as he certainly will, or how I'm going to find a job and make money, or how I'm supposed to suddenly compete with thousands of people trying to get a job at the same time. I feel sick to my stomach as I realize what a mistake I've made, but there was no alternative if I didn't want to be killed by Frank. Here, I might still die and die broke with nobody knowing. My shoulders become heavy and my mouth goes dry.

"You okay?" Eva asks upon seeing my reaction.

"I haven't quite figured that part out."

"Eh, don't worry about it. Very few of us have anything figured out." She eats the chili and crosses one leg over another. She's unlike any of the Society girls. She's carefree. "Thomas told me you got robbed."

"Who?"

"Thomas? Thomas Kelley. He was the one that helped you this morning." She frowns.

Oh, right.

"Yeah, some guy tackled me and took my money." I shrug. "I wasn't planning on staying here, but I guess I'm kind of stuck now."

Eva laughs. "That's how it happens. I wasn't planning on staying here either, now two years later..."

"You've been here for *two years!?*" I choke on my spit and look at the Hooverville again. I can't be here for two years. I shouldn't even be here for two weeks!

"Oh yeah," she nods, then sees that the color has gone out from my face. "It's not so bad, though." She leans down to see my face. "Thomas and Peter are wonderful; they're like my best friends. Everybody's really supportive."

"I don't need a support system. I need a way to California." I don't bother maintaining the sugary sweet voice I used at home. I don't bother being nice because, honestly, I don't feel like it. She perks up, and I suddenly realize where I've seen her before. Of course. She's the girl with the sign who made me want to leave in the first place. I feel guilty. She wouldn't make enough money to get to California in a million years. Jobs are scarce. Donations are even scarcer. And that brings another worry. We're now on an even playing field. Without Frank, I have just as much of a chance as she has, and that is none. But maybe we can help each other.

"You're going to California?" she asks excitedly. "Me too!"

"That's the goal." Goals change, though. "But I'd accept anywhere, really."

She throws her head back and laughs, then leans back

comfortably, stretching out her legs and crossing one leg over the other. "Wouldn't we all?" Her stockings are ratty, and her dress looks like it's been passed down through several women before her. Her shoes are so muddy that I can't tell what color they originally were. Still, she's more relaxed than I've been publicly in years. I'm suddenly aware of my perfect posture, so I slump my back and uncross my legs in an effort to fit in. She eyes me without turning her head.

"So. Jobs," I mumble. I don't have to ask. Eva understands immediately, and she laughs softly again. How someone can smile so much in such bleakness is beyond me, but Eva seems to do okay with it.

"Zero." She sighs and looks ahead. "At least not for us."

I shake my head. "Us?"

"Women." She rests her chin in her hand and leans her elbow on her knee. "There is an order to the hiring process. The white men take priority. They have first choice. Then the black men. Then the white women, and then the black women." She looks at me with a bemused expression that shows she doesn't expect me to understand. "*They* have to take care of their own first."

I understand that much. When she says "they," she means people like me. People like Frank.

"Women who look like you could probably still get a receptionist job if you tried. Maybe a schoolteacher. But not me. Not unless they've looked everywhere else and can't find anyone. I'm their last resort." Her voice trails off at the end, some bitterness in it but mostly resigned to her fate. Frank's voice comes into my head from just days ago, when he declared that people in the Hooverville shouldn't ask for handouts but should earn their own living like he did. I hadn't thought of it that way. Eva doesn't stand a chance.

Eva leaves a few minutes later. She runs off claiming somebody needs her, which I don't doubt, so I stand and explore more. There are lots of interesting characters. A woman wears a fur coat even though it's summer, with pearls wrapped around her neck. It's not prideful like when women wore furs at Betty's party, but more like she's clutching to a lifeboat while drowning. It's strange to think that only five years ago everyone partied and celebrated decadence which no idea of what was coming. If only there was a way to warn the people back in 1927 about what was coming for them. If somebody told me I'd be engaged and stranded in a homeless camp, I wouldn't have believed it.

I pass through the people, and some of them look at me, but not all of them. I've nearly gone in a circle around the Hooverville when I hear some laughter and a familiar man's voice. But I can't place it. It's gentle and sultry and doesn't fill me with terror like most familiar voices would.

"Mr. Alexander left this morning, and the Missus gave me the day off, but we both know that just means she don't have to pay me," he says, the crowd laughing. I stiffen and stand off to the side as I catch a glimpse of his face.

It's Arthur Abbott, my dear friend and driver, dressed down with one of his four daughters sat on his knee. I haven't seen her since she was a baby, but she must be around six now. How could he be here? Certainly anybody who works for my family is paid well enough to afford a house. This doesn't seem right. I try to stay hidden, but I don't exactly blend in here, and he catches sight of me through the crowd. His face tenses and his eyebrows go together, and I see his back straighten like he's at work. He smiles nervously at his friends, lowers Mia off his lap, and stands, mumbling something to the others, and all heads turn to me.

He strolls over to me with his hands stuffed in his pockets. His shoulders are tense, and I can't tell if he's angry with me for being here or fearing for his job. I never know how to act around my staff—except Virginia They're my parental figures, but I have the power to fire them if I want. It makes for awkward encounters more often than I'd like.

"Annaleise," Arthur says, touching me on the shoulder and pulling me to the side. "What are you doing here?" *I don't know,* I want to say, but no words come out when I open my mouth. I stammer and tears come to my eyes as if I'm on trial. "I thought you were in D.C. with Fra—Mr. Alexander? Does your mother know you're here?"

I shake my head quickly. "She *can't* know."

He scrunches up his face. "Did you *run away*?" He tightens his grip on my shoulder. "I'm taking you home. This isn't safe for you." He balls the shoulder of my dress in his hand and starts marching me towards the outskirts of the Hooverville, but I dig my heels into the dirt and tug myself out of his grip.

"No, Arthur, please don't." I'm almost crying, and it must play to the more empathetic part of him, because I see his face soften and his hands go into his pockets. "I can't go back there. Please don't make me." He looks around and sighs. "Why are *you* in here? Arthur, do you live here?" I ask.

He sucks the inside of his cheek and nods awkwardly, embarrassed. "Your mother doesn't pay as well as you'd think she would." I feel my chest burn with fury at Mother. How *dare she*?

"But..." I hesitate over my words. "Your daughters!"

He shrugs. "It's okay, Annaleise." But it's not. He may be able to lie to himself, but he can't lie to me.

"I'm so sorry, Arthur," I whisper, and I feel my eyes sting with a future sob.

Mia runs over to him with her arms raised. Arthur picks her up, tension in his shoulders. He plasters a smile on his face and glances back at me. I can see through the facade. He still thinks I'm going to fire him. He's still afraid of my power, even when I have none.

VI

It's particularly strange having no responsibilities. Nothing to feel guilty for *not* doing. I've never been on my own. Shoot, I've never even been more than twenty yards from my mother's grasp. This could be a relaxing afternoon full of freedom I've never had before, catching up on reading, or figuring out a plan, but instead, I bounce with a nervous energy that has nowhere to run to.

Evening falls and streams of sunlight reflect off the tin roofs of the houses, casting the Hooverville in a golden yellow glow like something out of one of my dreams. I emerge from my hut with caution, though the evening light puts others at ease, and so my soul relaxes. I look around for a familiar face but see none, and none of the others even bother looking at me. I pick at the seam of my coat, my familiar loneliness returning. Maybe I should just hide out in my hut and wait for everything to be better.

No! That's how you stayed with Frank for so long! We don't do that anymore! a tiny voice yells at me. Right, no more waiting. I propel forward into the camp. I've never found making friends to be the easiest thing. My friends are only my friends because our families vacationed together, or we went to the same boarding school. Even Betty was only my friend because

I was the only one who tolerated her. How am I supposed to make anyone here like me when none of us have anything in common? How did I get punished with being an outsider in *both* worlds?

A bright flicker of light catches the corner of my eye. I squint at the light until it turns and disappears to reveal a suncatcher made of painted broken glass, bells dangling from it in the doorway of a dilapidated shack. Its faint tinkling catches my ears and draws me toward it.

As I approach, I hear more and more bells chiming, like a symphony of fairies making their way toward me. I slowly peek my head into the doorway of the shack. My lips part as I see dozens of the chimes dangling from the ceiling of the shack, blowing in the slight breeze coming in through the doorway. This shack is larger than the others I've seen around here. It has a dining table and chairs made out of unfinished lumber, and a portrait of a young black boy hanging on the wall. The room smells of pine needles and glue.

"Hello?" I ask as I step inside and admire the art on the suncatchers. One of them is a koi fish leaping out of the water, while another one is a mountain landscape. The setting sun is just bright enough to fill the room, and as it hits the suncatchers, the room is filled with dancing colorful lights. They spin on their strings, covering my body in orange and yellow and pink spots. I grin and turn in a heavenly circle, arms outstretched, only to be startled by a voice.

"Oy!" a scraggly voice shouts. I jump out of my skin and stop spinning immediately. An elderly woman with dark gray-ish skin and a face like a snapping turtle emerges from a second room and limps towards me with a carved cane in her hand. She comes close enough to my face that I notice she has no teeth either, but she carries it better than the other woman did. She wears a floor-length blue sheet as a dress, and underneath it, she's barefoot with long, ugly yellow toenails. "What do you think you're doing? You're going to mess with the juju."

"Juju?" I ask as the woman reaches above her head and stops one of the suncatchers from moving.

"The sun comes in, the suncatchers take the good light and sends it off into the universe, while the bad light is trapped in the picture and becomes something beautiful. AND I WILL NOT HAVE YOU MESSING IT UP!" The woman hits me in the shoulders with a rolled-up newspaper. I jump away, back towards the doorway.

"I'm sorry!" I shout, trying not to laugh at this odd predicament. She's at least a foot shorter than me, but with the strength of a lion in such a frail little body. The skin on her arms sags and swings as she hits me, until she takes a step back and looks at me. Her eyes are black and beady like a crow's eyes. "I'm sorry," I repeat as she stops.

"What's you doing in here?"

"I-I-" I stammer, but then a growling monster joins us in the room. My stomach. The lady's eyes grow big and her entire demeanor shifts. She grabs my hand and pulls me out a doorway in the back of the shack to a fire pit with a pot on top of it. She stirs it with her face nearly in the pot, and then fills up a bowl with some dark red soup.

"Eat, girl!" She hands it to me, then fixes herself a bowl and waddles back into her shack. I have to jog to keep up with her. She's fast for someone so tiny.

"I was waiting till my boys showed up to eat, but I'm not

about to let you go hungry," she says as she pushes a chair back for me to sit in. I take a seat, trying to conceal a smile at this bizarre yet welcoming woman.

She blows a kiss at a portrait of a boy my age—a grandson, maybe—nailed to the wall, then sighs and sips her soup. It's silent for a while, so I eat the soup, but revert to my old habit of eating extremely slowly no matter how hungry I am. It's more polite that way. By the time she finishes her bowl, I've had about four spoonfuls. She pours the last drops of soup into her mouth and watches me scoop my own with a baby-sized spoon.

"No wonder you're so skinny; you eat like a rabbit." She frowns. "You don't like my soup?"

My eyes get huge. "No! No, that's not it at all. I'm sorry. I was raised in a pretty strict household. Eating fast isn't *lady-like* where I'm from."

The woman laughs and spits into a nearby bucket. I almost choke on my soup but manage to swallow. "No one here cares if you're ladylike, kid. They care if you're alive."

I look down at my soup. "I guess that's a fair point."

"You got a name?"

"Annaleise," I say gently. "And you?"

"Clara."

"Nice to meet you." I smile and reach out my hand to shake hers, but she just points at the soup bowl and urges me to keep eating. I hold the bowl up to my mouth and gulp it down quickly, filling with warmth all through my body. I sigh as my muscles relax away unwanted tension. It's even better than our cook's.

"Thank you," I breathe to Clara, wiping up some soup from my top lip.

Suddenly, all the rainbow lights in the room dim, and the room goes dark as if something has blocked the sun. Clara jumps up excitedly and throws her arms up in the air, her mouth forming into a joyous gasp.

"Boys, you're back!" she exclaims, walking past me toward the door with her arms wide open. My eyes follow her until I'm turned around and facing two shadows in the doorway with their arms full of what looks like junk. They offload the junk onto the floor, and the sun fills the room again so I can see their faces among the colored lights.

"We tried to find you only the best, Miss Clara," the short boy from this morning—*oh, what was his name?... Peter!*—Peter says with his back turned to me. "We've practically cleared out the Hooverville of glass and metal by now."

The other one, Thomas, drops the junk in his hands and turns around to see me, but his face turns to confusion. "Annie?"

"Thomas? What are you doing here?" I ask, pushing myself to my feet. "Clara, these are your boys?" I look at them, and between their three vastly different skin tones, and not to mention Clara's age, there's no way they're her sons.

"Yes, these are my sweet boys." Clara pinches Peter's cheeks, making him blush and hide a smile. I laugh softly.

"When we showed up, Clara kind of adopted us," Thomas explains quietly, a confused look still on his face. "What are you doing here?" he asks again.

I start to explain, but then Clara starts loudly rummaging through the pile the boys brought. She picks up items and holds them up to the light and either nods enthusiastically and tosses it over her shoulder into a second pile or she shakes her head and throws it back.

"I'm sorry, can you explain what's going on?" I ask Thomas while Peter kneels and rummages through the items.

Thomas grins at me with a strange look in his eyes and says joyously, "Tonight is the start of the Summer Festival." He looks at me expectantly, like I should know what that is, then his excitement falls to the floor. "It's just this thing we've done the last couple of years. On the first night of summer, we all have a bonfire, and we sing songs and we dance around the fire..."

"What's that got to do with the junk?" I ask quietly so Clara doesn't hear and get offended.

"Well, this, of course." Thomas looks up at all the suncatchers dangling from the ceiling and the lights land on his face like paint on a canvas. He notices the confused look on my face because he elaborates quietly, stepping closer to me like this is a major secret. "Miss Clara decided this year she wanted to make a gift for every person in the Hooverville, and she believes that these keep away evil and bad feelings. So, she's making dozens to give out tonight."

My heart flutters at such a kind gesture for no reason, and I look at the lights differently. The bells jingle faintly, but nobody outside the room notices.

"Don't tell anyone, okay? It's meant to be a surprise."

"I won't tell," I promise, admiring the paintings on each of the glass bits. "Clara, did you paint these?"

"All by my hand," Clara says proudly.

"You must teach me how to paint sometime," I say with a smile.

"You want to see the one we made for you today?" Thomas suddenly asks, taking off his coat and setting it on the back of the chair.

"I get one?" I stammer out in surprise. I don't think I deserve one. I'm hardly a resident here.

"Of course!" Peter stands and begins searching through the catchers on the far side of the room while Thomas searches the ones closest to me. Eventually, Peter shouts "aha!" and pulls down one of the catchers by the string. He hands it off to Thomas before returning to his task of sorting through them.

Thomas looks at it, then hands it over to me. "I picked the animal, but I'm useless at painting, so..." As he turns it over to me, I see the clear image of a monarch butterfly bathed in orange and yellow paint. I nearly start crying at how touched I am, so I just hold the gift in one hand and put my other arm around Thomas's neck. I have to stand on my toes to hug him properly, so he leans down a bit.

I'm surprised at how comfortable I am to be hugging a perfect stranger, and quickly separate. My cheeks are surely flushed pink. As are his., Thomas looks as though he's nervous to be happy, but eventually he gives in to it. "Thank you," I breathe as I pass him to Clara. "It's really..." I'm speechless and I can't take my gaze off it. "Thank you."

"Do you want to help us make the rest?" Clara asks. I'm honored to be included, but I know I don't belong here. I don't fit in here any more than I fit it at home. I almost say no, but something in Thomas's eye makes me change my mind.

"Okay," I say. I smile despite my nervousness.

We form an assembly line. Thomas molds the glass pieces together over the fire and hands it off to Clara, who paints pieces on it to form an animal, who then hands it to me. I paint the background pieces and tie string to the bottom and the top, and then Peter strings the windchimes to the bottom. To make one takes us around fifteen minutes, and after a couple of hours, we've completely run out of space to make anymore, but we've made enough for every single home in Hooverville to get a one-of-a-kind sunchime.

Thomas and Peter load their arms up with them, jingling with every movement.

"Are you coming, Annie?" Thomas asks. I pause at the nickname he's given me. I used to really love the Little Orphan Annie strip, and the name seems to suit me more than Annaleise ever would. I nod eagerly, happy to be included in something like this, and fill my arms with sunchimes. Thomas grins at me and tilts his head to signal me to follow him.

"Bye, Clara. I'll see you later!" I say as I leave through her doorway behind Thomas.

Following his lead, we stop by every house and drop off their custom sunchime. I get to see the look of pure joy on everyone's face as Thomas explains that Miss Clara made them custom for every single home, and about her belief that they keep away evil. Thomas also takes the time to introduce me to everyone, and everyone welcomes me with a kind heart and open arms—much more so than this morning, but Thomas's endorsement must help. It seems Thomas is liked and known by everyone. When we arrive at Eva's, she and Peter show off a special handshake they've made to greet each other, and Eva kisses Thomas on the cheek. They must be an item. Good for them. I'm happy for them.

I say little on our outing, but seeing everyone in their natural state eases my nerves. I used to think these people had done something wrong in life, but in most cases, they're good people, but life did them wrong. I find my mind trailing back to Frank while we deliver the gifts. Frank would never do something so kind for anyone, much less the homeless. He would never spend his days with an elderly woman, musing her and her hobbies and then delivering gifts for an entire village. Frank would complain that he didn't receive his gift fast enough. As the supply in my arms dwindles, and all of the Hooverville twinkles with lights and wind chimes, the fear creeps in with the idea of Frank's face, like a bear coming out of a cave.

We find Arthur's shanty-home and Thomas begins to introduce us, but Arthur stops him. "We're already acquainted, Thomas." Arthur's four daughters, Mia, Hattie, Molly, and Gertie, look so frail that they could be skeletons, but they still bound to Thomas, climbing on his arms and his shoulders and treating him as a jungle gym. Thomas just accepts it with a laugh and spins around, making them giggle. Hattie hangs onto Peter's ankle and Peter pretends to be a monster, dragging her along with every step.

"So, you've met Miss Clara," Arthur says, hanging up the suncatcher in the doorway of their shack. "And the boys."

"Yes," I say. I can't take my eyes off of them. "The girls have gotten big since I saw them last."

When I was fourteen, Mother invited the families of our entire staff to a party—or, she told everyone it was a party, but it was really a public sacking of one of her maids who stole. A public warning to everyone who worked for her of what would happen if they messed up. The girls were babies or toddlers then. Mrs. Abbott had one baby after another until she died at around the same time my Pa did.

"They're growing every day. I tell you, I don't know how to raise girls, let alone raise them in here." He motions to the Hooverville. He keeps his voice low so that the girls don't hear.

"Arthur, if I had known..."

He shakes his head and puts a hand on my shoulder. "You couldn't have done anything about it." He's right; Mother would never let me interfere with the payment of a staff member, but still... I'm as much a guilty party as she is. "Now are you gonna tell me why you're here?" He drops his voice like a father would.

I watch Thomas and the girls. Thomas takes Hattie's little hands and spins her around. He occasionally glances back at me.

"I was running away to California. But somebody took my money, and now I'm here." I don't know whose voice comes out of my mouth, but it isn't mine. "And I can't go home, and I can't go to California."

"Is it Frank?" Arthur asks, then corrects himself. "Mr. Alexander."

"Don't do that with me," I sigh. "It was him, and my mother, and every girl in Society. I was tired of pretending to be somebody that I will never be."

Arthur nods and crosses his arms. I've never seen him dressed down like this, wearing a simple shirt and slacks instead of his usual suit and chauffeur cap covering his bald head. He's probably never seen me dressed down like this either, considering that anytime we need Arthur's services, I'm usually dressed up for a party or other event.

"I would help, but... I can't," Arthur says quietly.

"I know." I watch Peter and Thomas, then say, "What do you think of those two?"

"The boys?" Arthur crosses his arms. "They're good kids. Work hard. Helpful. I trust them to take care of the girls if I can't or if Eva can't."

"So, I can trust them?"

Arthur smiles some. "Yeah, I think you can trust them."

Thomas and Peter come back over to us and pry the girls off, much to their discontent. Thomas tells them we must get the rest of the suncatchers out and then get to dinner, which I suddenly don't feel like eating anymore. Thomas introduces me to the last couple of people whose names I don't bother remembering, and we get rid of the last of the gifts. Thomas stands with his hands on his hips, admiring the work we've done. He smiles at Hooverville and the soft *ting ting ting* of the bells, then turns to look at me to see if I'm loving this as much as him, but I can't even fake being happy.

"You okay?" Thomas asks.

I shrug. "I suppose," I say sadly, and quickly make up a lie on the spot. "It's just sad to see those girls growing up in a place like this." It's even sadder to know I'm partially responsible for their living here. How they don't resent me, I don't know.

"A place like this?" Thomas asks with one raised eyebrow. "Annie, everywhere is like this. Some Hoovervilles are just better looking." I'm stunned speechless by how true that is, and he doesn't even know. He watches me for a minute with the remnants of a smile on his lips, and then he looks at the ground. "Come on, they're about to start the bonfire."

We make our way through the Hooverville, with the moon high in the sky, glowing on every single chime so that the rows between the homes are covered in rainbow lights. The children dance excitedly between the rows while the older folks listen happily to the chimes. As we pass through, they thank us once again. Thomas smiles and nods at them, while I duck my head down awkwardly so as not to take credit for any of it.

Thomas and I take a seat on a log in front of an unlit firepit. Thomas leans back and relaxes.

"You want a drink?" he asks me suddenly, sitting up straight again like he's just remembered I'm here and he's trying to make a good impression on me.

"What?"

"Do you drink?" he asks, keeping his eyes on me as he stands and approaches a jug. He pours two glasses of a strange light amber liquid that looks like watered-down maple syrup. I watch him closely and then shrug. Back home I used to have wine all the time, but it was always the fancy kind that had been saved for decades for the most special of occasions. Mother had a wine cellar back home that I was never allowed in because I once broke a bottle and it shattered all over the floor. I cut my foot open on it, but she seemed to care more about the wine.

I take the glass from him and say, "Why not?" But when

it touches my tongue, I spit it out and scrunch up my face. Thomas chuckles at me. "Ugh, that's disgusting!"

"I guess you don't have moonshine often."

"Never." I pucker my lips and try to laugh through it, but it lingers in my mouth for far too long. Thomas grins and takes a swig of his.

I shake my head and set my glass down on the ground. Some men mess with the fire, trying to start it. "How can you live like this? How could *anybody* live like this?"

Thomas watches me and frowns. "Are you having that bad of a time?"

"No, it's just..." I shrug. "I don't understand how everybody can be so happy for having nothing; how you can all just accept that you won't have any help from anybody. There are parents here with children starving, and nobody's doing anything about it. How can you live like this?" I repeat, clearer.

Thomas thinks for a second, taking in what must sound incredibly rude to him. I hear my mother scolding me in my head. "You know, Annie," he starts, and I brace myself for whatever angry rant he's about to throw at me. "Not everyone here is happy having nothing. People are angry and it's a scary thing to be living here. I don't want you to get the wrong idea. It's shit."

He stops for a beat and watches me to make sure I'm understanding. "It's horrible living here. There isn't a day I wake up and don't wish I lived somewhere else. Technically I make enough money that I could afford my way out of here, but it's these people who don't have that luxury. That's why I stay."

"Why?" I ask. "You don't owe them anything."

"You don't do good things because of an obligation. You do

good things because that's what's right," Thomas says, slightly shocked that I could even suggest something otherwise.

"I just think that you're allowed to be selfish once in a while, that's all. I doubt anybody would hold it against you."

"I would." Thomas frowns at me.

"Well, you're nobler than I am." I look at my hands as the men finally get the fire lit, and I'm met with a huge blast of heat. I take a deep breath and watch the flames dance up to the sky, and then some men pull out their instruments: a banjo and a couple of guitars. They'd likely be worth a decent amount of money if they were to sell them, but the music fills the Hooverville with such joy that you can't put a price on. Immediately people begin hopping and dancing to the music, arm in arm, including Peter and Eva, who've been just loitering around. I fear for a second that Thomas will ask me to dance. I feel his eyes on my face, so I quickly ask him a question to avoid dancing.

"Where are you from? Before Hooverville, I mean," I ask him. He leans back some and relaxes.

"Technically I was born in New Mexico, but I call Indiana home," he says. "Worked my way over to this side of the country to try and make something of myself, but I still don't know what I want to do. It's pretty hard to make a career for yourself when you don't know what you like."

Ain't that the truth?

"Got a bunch of odd jobs and such, but eventually settled in as a shoeshiner. It's decent money, and I get to have conversations with people I wouldn't normally." He shrugs. "It's fun, I guess. What about you?"

"Do *I* find shoe-shining fun?" I grin.

"No, what's your story? Your pre-Hooverville story?"

Oh, if only you knew, Thomas. "There's no story. This is my story."

"Alright, then what's the prologue?" He leans in close like he's waiting for me to reveal my secrets to him, but I just laugh in his face.

"You'd hardly find it compelling." I tell him tauntingly. He mocks offense and shakes his head.

"Then will you tell me something I can know?" he asks sincerely. I look up at the sky and think long and hard before I finally decide on something that I'm willing to tell him.

"I'm an only child," I say, but it doesn't seem to be enough to satisfy him.

"So am I technically. Come on, a real thing, a real secret."

"*A secret?*" I can hear the flirtation in my voice. I haven't even been away for twenty-four hours and I'm already flirting with the first person I met! What kind of a floozy am I? "You never said anything about a secret. You just said *something*," I say, and he smiles at his lap. "You take what you get."

"Come on, Annie. There's got to be something," he says and tilts his head. I look at the fire, and then at Peter and Eva. Everything I could say would come across as arbitrary or completely give me away.

"I have never left New York. And I've always wanted to," I tell him, swinging my knees and sitting on my hands. "My mother doesn't—*didn't* like traveling much."

"Was she a tough lady?" Thomas chuckles.

"You have no idea."

"Were you close with her?"

"No, not really." I shrug. "She's one of those women who

should not have had children. She doesn't have a maternal bone in her body." Thomas frowns. "And your parents?"

"Oh, well, there's not much to tell. They both died when I was pretty young. My dad floated around and never really found his place in the world, ended up dying about ten years ago. I went into an orphanage. That's how I know Peter, actually. We shared a home from the age of ten to thirteen, and then we kept in touch until we made our way up here."

"That's amazing." I pause awkwardly. "How do you know Eva?" I try to ask nonchalantly, but I want to know if they're together or not.

"She moved into Hooverville a few months before I did. She tried to fight me on my first night. Good times." He smiles, reminiscing, but it's really not helpful.

"And I take it you like her?" I ask. Thomas looks scandalized and laughs.

"Eva? No. She's like my sister."

Somehow, that makes the awkward tension even worse. "My dad died too," I blurt out. "He got sick. I was nine."

Thomas looks at me. "I'm sorry. Were you close with him?"

I nod softly. "He was my favorite person in the world."

"I'm sorry; that must have been hard."

"It was," I say awkwardly. Those were dark weeks immediately after my father died, when they were still clearing his things out of the home. I didn't want them to get rid of anything at all, and I shouted at one of the auctioneers who came to steal my father's belongings. I wept and wept on the carpet of his office until the auctioneers were so uncomfortable that they left without buying a thing.

My mother then pulled me up by the collar of my dress

and demanded that I stop mourning his death because it wasn't going to land me anywhere but in trouble. And I tried to avoid crying, but at nighttime, when nobody came to kiss me goodnight or to tuck me in, I realized he wasn't coming back, and my mother didn't care about my well-being anymore.

I haven't thought about that in ages.

Thinking back on it now, I shouldn't have been surprised when she forced me into an engagement with a man twice my age with the fortune of a king and the fist of a dictator. Thomas leans back and takes a deep breath.

"I'm sorry, I didn't mean to tell you anything that would make you uncomfortable." People don't like talking about death or sadness. I've learned that from Society.

Thomas quickly shakes his head. "I'm not uncomfortable."

I turn back to watching the people dance, specifically Eva and Peter. "They know how to have a good time. Why aren't you up there with them?" I ask. Thomas shrugs.

"Once you've danced with Peter a thousand times, you start to want to look for new friends," he says seriously, then we both laugh. His laugh fades and I feel his eyes watching me—not in a threatening way, but I still don't like it. It makes me aware of how I'm sitting or how I hold my chin, which I normally only pay attention to when Mother forces me to. Thomas then pushes himself up onto his feet and holds out his hand to pull me up with him. "Come with me," he says.

I'm unsure, but he looks so excited about it that I don't want to tell him no. I take his hand and stand, and we run towards the edge of Hooverville and continue walking past it into a dark part of the park. I stiffen cautiously, as if Thomas is plotting to murder me in the woods, but curiosity keeps me with him.

Finally, when we can no longer see Hooverville and we're well hidden in the dark, Thomas stops and lays on the wet grass, looking up at the sky.

"Take a seat," he urges, patting the spot beside him. I press my brows together and look at the surrounding area to see if there are any more people, but we're completely alone. The stars aren't out yet, but he's looking up at the sky as if he expects something to happen. I look at the sky, then lay beside him.

"Why exactly are we sitting in the dark?" I ask him.

"Just wait." He smiles at me. "You'll see."

Around us, there are the tall buildings of the city, all of them dark and unlit, black shadows against the deep purple sky. After a minute of silence, I start to think about Frank again and what he'd say if he was here, but just as quickly as the thought comes, Thomas says, "Look!"

As I look up, the skyscrapers are starting one-by-one to turn on their lights, until all the lights in the city are glowing, surrounding us in the faint light. It looks as though a million little stars have come down to Earth to shine on us. It takes my breath away but in a good way, and I sit back up to look at it. All around, the blackened sky is brightened with white, yellow, and even blue lights. Yet, it's silent all around us as if the lights exist only for us.

I've seen these lights a million times before, but from down here, it's like it's a whole new world created just for the lucky souls in this field.

I cover my mouth and take in the beauty. "Oh my," I whisper. "Thomas, I've never seen anything so beautiful in my life."

"Neither have I," Thomas says from behind me, a smile in his voice.

"Thank you for bringing me here today," I whisper to him. "I needed something good." He looks down at his lap. He looks happy, but a different kind of happy than when he's with the others. I hope he doesn't dislike me. I do enjoy his company... probably too much, all things considered. If it wasn't for the Hooverville, or New York High Society, or Frank, or my mother, I could see myself liking Thomas as more than a friend. Why wouldn't I? He's very sweet and good-looking and attentive. I would have to be crazy not to admit his good qualities. But this is my life, and I can't afford the luxury of choosing love. It's better to not exercise even the idea of it.

"You're welcome, Annie."

I usually hate the name Annie, but coming from him, it's endearing, and makes me feel more at home than when I lived at home. For the first time, I feel like I made the right choice, and I don't want to leave. We stay out for a few minutes longer before we head back wordlessly toward the festivities. I open my mouth to start a conversation when we're in sight of the Hooverville lights, but suddenly Thomas says, "Ah, shit. Come on!" He begins to run.

VII

I chase confusedly after him, shouting "What is it?" Thomas stops at a table where a crowd is gathered around cheering, and there's a rhythmic banging sound. Thomas parts the crowd with his long arms, and Peter is sitting there, his palm flat on the table and his fingers parted. He looks around with a big smile, riling up the crowd.

"Are you all ready?" he asks, and the gathered crowd cheers. "Thomas! You're just in time. Where have you two been?" He raises his eyebrows, insinuating something I would never do with a perfect stranger.

I blush deeply and shout, "Absolutely not!"

The crowd oohs and laughs, and Thomas doesn't say anything. Instead, he says to Peter, "You're drunk, and I won't let you chop off your fingers."

"Pfft!" Peter laughs and holds up the silver pocketknife in his other hand. "I'm an expert at this."

On the other side of him, Eva says, "Relax, Tommy. Peter's an expert at this."

Thomas sighs exasperatedly and crosses his arms. He takes his place next to me. "He's not an expert at this," Thomas whispers to me with a sigh. I look between him and Peter, confused. Then Peter stabs the knife into the table between each of his fingers in a pattern. He starts slow, finding his rhythm, then he moves faster and faster. He looks like he's holding his breath and focusing hard to not stab himself in the fingers. Then he stabs the knife unbelievably quickly, with a huge proud smile on his face, and suddenly—

Peter lets out a bloodcurdling scream and clutches his hand. The knife falls with a *clink* and the whole crowd gasps. Eva screams and drops beside him. Peter curses through his teeth and groans in pain. I grab the first thing I can find to steady myself—Thomas's wrist. We glance at each other, then separate quickly as Thomas takes his place at Peter's side.

"Let me see your hand, Pete," Thomas insists, and even though he sounds angry, anybody with eyes can see how concerned he is for his friend. Peter sucks the back of his teeth and shakes his head, keeping his fist tightly closed. "Dammit, Peter, show me your hand so we can stitch it up!"

"Did you lose the finger?" Eva cries. I hold my breath and take a step back. I've never liked seeing blood, and I fear if Peter's lost a finger, I might vomit.

"Peter!" Thomas shouts again, and it looks like Peter is crying, but then suddenly he starts laughing and holds up his hand—all five fingers attached and not so much as a scrape. Thomas drops his hands to his sides and immediately walks away, shaking his head and laughing. "You ass."

"I got *you*, and I got *you* and *you*." He points at Eva and Thomas and a few other people in the crowd. "I told you! I am an expert at it! Have a little faith in me!" His eyes find mine, and I suddenly feel like a spotlight's been put on me. "Annaleise thought it was funny, didn't you Annaleise?"

I shake my head wildly.

Eva, with fury in her eyes, starts punching at Peter. My shoulders tense, but Peter only laughs while trying to block her fists. "Damn you! If you *ever* do anything like that again, I will *murder you!*" she screams at him.

"Okay, okay, I'm sorry!" Peter says, though he can't stop laughing. Pranks were never tolerated in my house. I'm not sure how I'm supposed to react, so rather than trying to fit in where I don't belong, I separate myself from the crowd and head to bed.

"Hey, wait!" Thomas shouts and jogs to me. "Where are you going?" he says, still smiling from Peter's prank.

"Bed."

"Don't you want to stay out with us?" His smile starts to slip, and I falter. I do want to stay with them. I want more than anything to stay forever and be a part of something *good*. But I'm not. No matter how hard I try to turn myself into one of them, I'll never be able to kill that voice in my head that urges me to be polite and be *perfect*. Running away from Frank was only half of the problem. I can't run away from who I'm supposed to be.

"Not tonight, Mr. Kelley," I say formally. I leave Thomas and the rest of the crowd for my little shack with only a pile of blankets in the corner and my bag of things, and my monarch butterfly suncatcher dangling from one of the ceiling boards.

I fall asleep almost immediately after staying up all last night.

Tonight, Frank finds his way into my shack and the safety of my blankets. And he either beats me or smothers me with unwelcome kisses or both, because I wake up gasping for breath and trembling. It's still dark out, but when I squint in the darkness, I see a dozen black silhouettes, leaving their shacks without so much as a sound, making their way toward the city. They wear hats and overalls, and some carry brief-cases and some carry nothing. These must be the dawn-break-ers. The newsboys, the shoeshiners, the lamplighters—the people who do the jobs everyone else doesn't want to do. Thomas and Peter are somewhere in that crowd.

I fall back asleep with the knowledge that no one can hurt me as badly as Frank did. I've already survived the worst of it. Things can *only* go uphill.

The morning comes, and Hooverville is nearly empty. Most of the people who filled it yesterday are at work or nurs-ing their hangovers from last night. Without the people here, without the liveliness, I can see how people from my world would think it's just a heap of garbage. I've seen the beauty of it, and even I think it's a heap of garbage.

I take a seat beside the smoking fire pit and watch Mia and another little boy chase each other around, giggling. I write in my journal about everything I saw yesterday and all the peo-ple I've met, like Clara and Eva and Peter, and about Peter's knife prank, and Thomas's kindness to show me the lights. I write about Arthur and the girls and how stupid and blind I must have been to not notice.

I head back to my shack, set my notebook down on the cot, and pull on my father's old coat. I leave the park and take a walk around the city, the way I used to. It once was my favorite thing to do, the thing I'd look forward to every single day. But with nothing to run from anymore, it's not as enjoyable. I buy some five-cent apples with a quarter I find on the street and carry them home—not home, back to *Hooverville*—in a bag. I'll give them to the Abbott girls. It won't repay the debt I have with them, but it's a start.

I cross the street back into the park, and I swear I see Mother's face peering at me from the backseat of one of the cars. My breath stops, and the car turns away from me. I hold my breath for a few seconds longer before my brain reminds my feet to move so I'm not standing in the center of the street.

Arthur went back to work this morning. Perhaps he's told her where I am and they're coming to take me back home. But the car doesn't come back for me.

Somehow I find my way back to the Hooverville, despite my mind racing a million miles a minute. Mother wouldn't have reason to think I'm lying. She thinks I am in DC with Frank. And Frank thinks I am home with Mother. They wouldn't look for me. Would they? I don't doubt that if given the chance, would my mother really drag me back to Frank in chains. I have to have faith in Arthur and my ability to trust him. I have to hope he didn't tell Mother.

I'm pulled from my thoughts when Eva runs up to me.

"Annaleise! There you are!" she exclaims, grabbing my arms. I tense up but hope she doesn't notice it. "Listen, I need a favor."

"What is it?" I ask.

"I usually keep an eye on Arthur's girls during the day, but I heard a rumor that Sally's Diner is giving away food today. I was going to see if I could go get some and bring it back."

"So, what's the favor?" I ask, starting to walk past her.

"Can you sit with them until I get back?"

The mere thought of sitting with four girls who are only

homeless because of *me* is enough to send beads of sweat to my forehead and gives me the urge to vomit into a nearby bush. "Why me? Can't somebody else do it?"

"Well, Miss Clara sits with them, but," she leans closer and whispers, "she's not exactly the most fit to handle children."

"Neither am I!" My voice goes up at the end and cracks in a way that makes Eva laugh.

"Just sit with them. I won't be gone more than an hour." She points me in the direction of their shack, and while my head is turned, she rushes off. I sigh and drop my shoulders and drag my feet all the way to their home, where it's anything but quiet. Giggles fill every inch of the air, as if to position themselves at the root of people's sadness and immediately lift them up and fill them with life again. Even I can't stop the twinges of joy in my heart at the sound of their laughter.

I push the blanket out of the doorway and peek my head in. The four girls are giggling as they chase and catch the lights from Clara's suncatcher in their hands, pretending they're fairies. They talk to the lights and have assigned themselves roles to play for the day. Hattie, the eldest, has made herself queen, while Molly and Mia are sister-princesses, and Gertie is the witch. Clara sits a few feet away in a rocking chair, relaxing and keeping an eye on them.

The girls fall into silence as they notice me, and I give an awkward half-wave. They look amongst each other and then resume playing. Since they seem occupied, I pull out a book from my bag and read in my lap. I'm going to have a problem coming once I finish this book and I don't have anything else to read, but I'll deal with that when it happens. I've read a couple of pages when a shadow blocks my view of the book. I look up at Mia, the littlest, staring at me with her thumb in her mouth. It's a little bit creepy, I won't lie.

"Hi," I say. She waves with her other hand. "Is everything okay?"

She pulls her thumb from her hand and asks, "What are you reading?" So, this is it. *This is how I can connect with these girls.* I smile softly and watch the other three, huddled in the corner.

"It's about four sisters," I say with a sly grin. "About four sisters who play pretend together. Just like you all."

I always turned to Louisa May Alcott's book to live a fantasy of having sisters growing up, but I suspect girls like Hattie, Mia, Gertie, and Molly are closer to her intended audience. They whisper amongst each other, and Mia takes a seat in front of me. The others come over one at a time and sit in front of me like in a classroom. I glance at Clara, who winks at me, and I open it to the front page.

"Chapter one," I read aloud. I do my best to overcome self-consciousness and do funny voices for each of the characters to make the girls laugh, and when they do, I realize they hold no bitterness in their hearts for me or my family, and I let myself relax. One by one, the girls start to fall asleep on the floor, so I stop reading and put a blanket over them.

I sit back beside Clara. "How did I do?" I whisper.

"Not bad," she says. "You were an only child, weren't you?"

"What gave it away?"

"Well, mostly how painfully awkward you are around children," she says bluntly, but then she softens her voice. "But then it was how much your face lit up with them. Girls who grow up without sisters always are more excited to be let into that relationship, even for just a minute."

I think I'd have killed for a sibling growing up, but who knows how many things would be different if I wasn't Mother's only child? Maybe I'd have had a sister to outnumber her, tire her out so she couldn't be so mean. Maybe a brother to defend me from Frank. Maybe Frank wouldn't even be in the picture, because Pa would have planned better for the future if he had two children to look after.

"Did you have siblings?" I ask her quietly. Hattie and Molly hold hands while sleeping and my heart *melts*. I've never wanted children, but if I ever have them, I want daughters.

"I did. I had one big brother and one little sister," Clara says. Her tone tells me what I don't dare ask. They're dead. Whether they lived to an old age or not, they're dead as dead can be. I guess that's one pain I'll never have to deal with. Losing my father was one thing, but I imagine losing a sibling is the worst pain imaginable.

"Miss Clara," I ask. She braces herself for the question, but I change direction. "Tell me about when you were young?"

Her eyes light up, and she tells me about how slavery was abolished when she was right around my age, and how after that, she became a dancer in a show that toured the country. She says that boys would line up around the block to see her dance, and that was where she met her husband, Kenneth. The longer she talks about her childhood, the more Southern her accent becomes, which makes me laugh.

"Kenneth was not the best lookin' boy on the block, let me tell you." She laughs from deep in her stomach and ends up coughing and hacking into a napkin. She blows out a breath and folds up the napkin in her hand. "But he was the sweetest. He came to see me backstage and he brought me a single rose. Now, I was already seein' another boy named...oh, what was his name... I don't even remember! Kenneth and I were married two weeks later, and we stayed together for fifty-two years!"

I do the math in my head and determine that it's more likely Kenneth died too. Spanish Flu, I'd guess.

"How did you get here?" I ask quietly.

"Here?"

"Hooverville."

Her eyes avert to the ground and she taps her fingers. Whatever happened must still be too raw for her. I wouldn't expect her to ask me how I got here either. I guess it's like Thomas said, and Hooverville isn't our whole story. There's always a before, and there will be an after.

At dinner, Eva got hot dogs from Sally's, so they put skewers through them and roast them over the fire. I've never had a hot dog before in my life. I would see hot dog carts at Coney Island when I went as a kid, but not even my Pa would let me eat one. I lean over to the nearest person to me, a woman not much older than me with three children under the age of five, and whisper, "What is a hot dog?"

I've never seen such a look from another human being, let alone from three tiny children and their mother. If I wasn't seen as an outsider before, I am now. I find my way to Thomas and Peter and sit beside them.

"Did you eat?" Thomas asks while Peter stuffs a hot dog in his mouth and hardly acknowledges me. Thomas sticks his hot dog onto a stick and holds it over the fire along with the others, rotating it.

"Not yet," I say quietly. My stomach growls, and I take a deep breath. "Thomas, can I ask you something?"

"Sure."

"You have to promise you won't laugh."

Thomas makes a face and says, "I'll do my best."

"What is a hot dog?"

Peter makes the same face the mother and children made, only with fat cheeks of food. Thomas squints at me, then smiles amusedly and pulls his hot dog from the fire.

"It's pork. Or that's what they say it is; I'm not sure. Have you really never had a hot dog before?" Thomas asks. He doesn't sound judgmental, just confused, and I wouldn't even blame him if he was. I know it's not normal. I would be confused too if I met someone who's never tried such a... delicacy.

"Try it, I think you'd like it," Thomas says. He hands me the one he's already cooked and starts preparing another one for himself. I'm self-conscious about eating in front of people, but I'm starving, so I take a bite. It's not what I expected it to taste like, but it's not bad either. But that could be my hunger speaking.

Thomas chuckles. "You like?"

"It's not bad." I smile. "Uh, hey, have you seen Arthur? I need to talk to him."

Thomas shrugs, swallowing his bite of food. "Why Arthur? Everything okay?"

"I'll know after I talk to Arthur, I guess," I say quietly. "I could potentially be in trouble."

Thomas smiles and looks at me. "You seem to make trouble

wherever you go." He laughs while he says it, but it feels like he knows too much about me, so I scoot away from him. The Abbott girls bolt across the field where Arthur kneels down to meet them. He hugs Mia and meets my eye across the camp, giving the tiniest nod possible, that instantly relieves a weight from my shoulder. It means he didn't tell Mother. It means I'm safe, at least for now.

The next morning, I ask Eva if I might spend another day with the Abbott girls. Somehow, it feels like repaying my debt with them, even if it's just a bit of reading. Eva agrees, if somewhat reluctantly, and takes to the streets to ask for money. I used to see people like her on the streets asking for money and I'd tell them I had none, even if I did. How selfish I was. I'm the problem.

I peek my head into their shack again, and Gertie and Molly jump up to hug me, and I'm immediately bombarded with questions about the March sisters and their adventures. Miss Clara is sat in the corner again, pale and frail, with sweat rising on her forehead.

I kneel beside her and kiss her on the cheek, and she's so warm it burns my skin. "Miss Clara, you're burning up. Are you feeling alright?"

"I'm fine, girl," Miss Clara says with a dismissive wave of her hand. "The Lord will save me."

I purse my lips and turn back to the girls. I shouldn't show concern in their presence. It would only worry them more, and they're too young to know when something's wrong. I feign a smile for their comfort, not for mine, and open the book to where I left off yesterday. It seems overnight that the girls have assigned themselves to a March sister to identify with, because when I speak for each character, one of the girls leans forward with feverish excitement and bounces a little.

I take a break from reading for lunch and overhear the girls discussing the book.

"*I* think Laurie is wonderful," Hattie says dreamily. "He's so sweet and kind."

I laugh. "Do you want to marry him, Hattie?" I tease, cutting the moldy bits off of some bread for them.

"*No!*" she says defensively.

Mia, Gertie, and Molly circle her, laughing and cheering, "Hattie likes Lau-rie, Hattie likes Lau-rie!" while Hattie blushes a deep red color.

"Don't worry, Hattie," I say. "I like him too." I smile.

"Like who?" Thomas appears in the doorway with a basket. I stand straighter upon seeing him. His hair is extra messy today, and he looks a little out of breath. He glances at the girls, who jump up and cry, "Thomas is here!" He quickly glances at me then back away like I didn't notice.

"Laurie!" Mia says, hugging him. Thomas looks confused until he sees the book in my hand.

"We weren't expecting you here today," I say. He gives Clara a hug and a kiss and has the same moment of concern as I did when he feels her temperature. But just as I did, he puts on a smile and sets the basket on the table.

"I bring the girls food sometimes if I can."

"So, listen," he says, turning to them very seriously. "I didn't get cheese like you all wanted." An uprising starts among the girls, but I sense Thomas has something else up his sleeves entirely. "Hey! I've got something better!" The girls quiet down, anger stewing among them like water about to boil over. Whatever he has, it'd better be good, or we'll have a mutiny on our hands. He holds his hand out to urge them to be patient and opens up the basket, and immediately a delicious smell wafts out and reminds my stomach of how hungry I am today.

He pulls out a potato pie and sets it on the table with a grin, but then reaches back into the basket, mischief on his face. He pulls his fists out, and opens his hand palm up to reveal—

"CANDY!" the girls screech and take the treats from him, unwrapping them and sticking the butterscotches in their mouths before I can even tell them to have lunch first. Thomas smiles proudly and turns, holding one out to me.

I take it and pull on the ends of the wrapper so it twists itself out, and I stick it on my tongue. "How did you do all this?" I whisper when the girls aren't listening.

"I got a big tip today," he says quietly. He has a sparkle in his eyes when he's proud of himself. "I bribed the baker to give me whatever he couldn't sell." Suddenly I feel sick, and it's not from the candy. He gives his own money to feed the children that my family didn't. It's a profound irony that makes me realize that no amount of reading will ever keep them alive. Running away to California and leaving Thomas with this duty isn't fair. It's my responsibility. I can't go anywhere until I make sure they're taken care of so that Thomas Kelley doesn't have to.

"Anyway, I have to get back to work," Thomas says, tossing his own wrapper back in the basket. "And it sounds like you all have to get back to your book."

After Thomas leaves, the girls have one more candy and

a slice of potato pie before we continue the book. For once, Clara has nothing to say.

VIII

We spend the rest of the day reading while Clara naps, and by the time Arthur comes home from work, we've finished the book and the girls are asking me endless questions about it. They ask me if I can come back and read to them again. I agree, even though I'll have nothing new for them tomorrow. I'm sure someone else here has a book they can lend me.

"Peter," I say, letting myself into his shack. He's napping with his blanket over his head. "Peter." I shake him awake.

"What?" he grumbles, but he's startled when he sees it's me. "What're you doing here?"

"Do you have any books?"

"*Books*?"

"For the Abbott girls."

He rubs the sleep from his eye and points to a small stack of books in the corner. "That's all I have."

I crouch down before them and squint to read the titles: *Macbeth, Othello, Romeo and Juliet.* "I can't read Shakespeare to children, Peter."

"I must have left the children's books in my other mansion," he says, half-bitter but half-joking. It sounds like an attack, even though he wouldn't know anything about that. I blink several times and shake it away. "Check with Tommy. He might have some."

"I already asked." I run my hands through my hair and my eyes catch a newspaper open to a jobs column. "Can I see that?" I'm already taking it before he answers.

"Good luck finding anything. Eva interviewed for that secretary job, said the guy was a total dick." He crosses his arms.

It pays decent money, enough that I could provide for Arthur's daughters if I got the job, so I tear out the advertisement and fold it in my pocket.

"I figure I might as well try," I say off his look.

In the morning, I recruit Eva to help me get dressed and do my hair to talk to them. It's more fun getting ready with Eva than it was when Mother or Virginia prepared me for a gathering. There's giggling and there's laughing and dance breaks. I was initially concerned she'd be angry with me for trying to take a job that could belong to her, but if she had any negative feelings about it, she doesn't say so. Maybe if I earn enough, I can pay for her to go to California too, since I didn't give her money while I still had it.

Eva braids my hair and I suddenly feel Frank's hands, pulling me to the ground and keeping me there. The ringing in my ears when he'd slap me. I become dizzy and I suddenly feel very ill.

"Are you alright?" Eva asks, leaning down to look at me. "You're turning green." I nod and swallow down my puke.

"I'm fine," I lie.

I look like a regular woman when I'm finally dressed. A couple people let me borrow their nicest things to wear to the interview, including Eva, who gives me her "lucky broach" of a butterfly to wear on my lapel.

I take the subway, among men in suits and women in outfits much like mine, to the office building. I'm not entirely sure what the business does, but that much doesn't matter to me. Only the money.

A woman around my age invites me to take a seat and goes to a desk in the back to alert the boss I'm here. A grubby, balding man with a cigar between his thin lips comes out and narrows his eyes at me. He doesn't shake my hand; he just nods his head and motions for me to follow him.

The other workers—all men, all looking just a tiny bit lecherous—turn their chairs to watch me pass them. And as I reach the boss's office, I walk into a waft of smoke that makes me choke and my eyes water.

"Your name?" he asks, writing on a piece of paper. I decide not to go with Annaleise. A new job means a completely new beginning, which means a new name.

"Annie," I say.

"Annie what?" he says, frustrated with me for taking up so much of his time. *Shit.* I need a last name.

"Kelley." *Bigger shit.* I don't know why I said that; it was just the first name that came to mind. Hopefully Thomas won't mind.

"You're here about the secretary position, yes?" He couldn't be more bored with me. Judging by the look of his office, I'd guess he'd rather be playing darts or gambling than talking to me.

"Yes," I say, then quickly add, "sir."

"Do you have any previous work experience?" he asks. My heart drops into my stomach and fills me with panic.

"N-not professionally, but—" I start to twist the few things I have done to sound better, but he tosses a file to the side and folds his hands across the table.

"Then why are you here?" he asks. "This position is for experienced secretaries *only*." He snaps his fingers, and the other woman opens the door for us.

"Please," I beg, standing. They both usher me out the door despite my pleas. "You don't understand. I have to care for a family. They're starving! They're homeless!" They don't hear any of it. Upon hearing of a family and living in a shantytown, the men who had previously stared at my backside avert their attention to anywhere else.

"Maybe you should have thought of them before," the man says as I get outside, and they slam the door in my face.

So that's how it feels to be on the receiving end of that.

I walk back to Hooverville instead of taking the subway. By the time I get reach it, my feet ache, so I sit in the grass and tug at strands in solitude. I don't know what I'm going to do. I stay on the outskirts of Hooverville until sunset, when Arthur comes back home from work. I can't face him right now. I know Arthur doesn't blame me, but I do.

I remember my promise to read another story to the girls, and that's just one more promise I can't keep, because I still have nothing to read them. I watch them from across the park and remember their game on the first day I read to them.

I push myself to my feet, brushing the grass off my bottom and my lap, and rush back to my shack. I pull out my diary and my fountain pen.

Once I decide to unlock my imagination and invite myself into their game, the story is easy and flows out of me. It's like it's always been there. It's about an enchanted forest and a war with a kingdom and four sisters assigned to protect it from evil. Miss Clara is in it, as a wise talking willow tree. Thomas is a knight. Peter is a woodsman. Eva is a queen's lady. I don't put myself in it, though. It's their story, not mine.

I tear out the finished pages and smile proudly at them, and I push Eva's butterfly pin through them to keep them together. It's no *Little Women*, but I think they're going to like it.

I pause before putting my pen to the diary, thinking about my whole experience here. Then I write about Thomas using his money to feed the girls, and how I can't get a job. I write about how afraid I am. I write about how memories of Frank are almost debilitating, and they come at the most random of times. He's gone, and I'm *still* living in fear of him. It isn't fair. It's not supposed to be like this.

I eventually fall asleep, still in my clothes from the interview.

I dream I'm a bride walking down an aisle towards a faceless groom. But I'm not afraid of it. I'm excited for it, and the longer I walk, the longer the aisle becomes and the further away he is. I start running towards him, and I almost grab his shoulder to turn him around, but I wake too soon. Whoever he was, my heart yearns for him even after I wake, and it takes several minutes of lying in bed to recover and remind myself of real life.

Eva lets me take a bath in her shack, in a large tub that looks like a horse trough. I scrub the dirt off myself and clean my hair. It does a little bit to raise my spirits, but I'm constantly nervous that somebody will pull back the sheet and find me naked. I get out and dry off and get dressed for the day faster than I normally would. I dump the water out and start towards Clara's shack, where the girls are sure to be.

It's Saturday, so Mother will be at a Society meeting today, eating mini sandwiches and champagne by eleven o'clock in the morning. Arthur will be pretty busy today, which gives me plenty of time to read the girls their story.

God, I hope they like it.

I can hear Clara coughing from halfway down the path, as if she's trying to hack up a lung. Is it even healthy to have children near her while she's so ill? I enter the shack and flinch as the girls let out an ear-splitting shriek upon seeing me.

"Ow," I say. They hug me as if they haven't seen me in years, and I sit down. "Okay, okay. Girls," I say seriously, putting on a theatrical voice. "Are you ready for a new story today?"

"Yes! Yeeesss!" they cheer, bouncing up and down.

"You have to sit though, if you want to hear it. And be very, very quiet. Or you might wake up the dragons." Their eyes light up, their bottoms hit the floor, and their mouths shut. "This story is called, *The Reign of the Abbott Sisters*."

This starts to rile them up again, but when I hold a finger to my lips, they silence. Maybe I should be a schoolteacher; I'm good at this.

I open my mouth to read, but Clara's coughing interrupts me, like a rude, unwelcome guest at a party. I read the first sentence and I'm interrupted once again. The girls' eyes are big, and I can sense their fear and concern as Miss Clara's coughing becomes violent, and she can't even take a breath in.

I set the story down and drop to Clara's side. She hacks

into a cloth which becomes wet with blood, even though she tries to hide it from me. I'm filled with terror beyond recognition. No. I can't show it in front of the girls. I have to be strategic.

"Girls, why don't you take the book and go over to Eva's. She'll read to you." I expect an argument, but Hattie stands and guides them out of the shack. None of them can take their frightened eyes off Miss Clara. I don't know how to reassure them that everything will be okay, because I don't know if everything will be okay. "It's okay, Clara, just breathe," I tell her. What am I supposed to do here? I don't know what I'm doing!

Clara's body heat makes me hot just being near her, yet her entire body is trembling. I grab her wrist and suddenly realize how much weight she must have lost recently. She should have gone to a hospital weeks ago. There's nothing a hospital can do for her now. She's dying.

I force myself to my feet, despite my entire body trembling, and I rush out of the tent.

"Thomas!" I scream at the top of my lungs. Everyone knows. They know I've been spending the days with Clara, and they know what *running* as quickly as I do means. I shove people out of the way to get to Thomas's shack. "Thomas!" I shriek and push through his blanket to get in, but his bed is empty and he's not here. "Shit!" I punch his door frame and run off to Peter's shack. They can't be at work. I can't be alone during this.

"Peter!" I'm crying, and my breathing is shallow like I'm drowning. I turn the corner toward Peter's shack and slam my body hard into someone, and it sends me to the ground. I look up at him, fully crying now, and I've never been so relieved to see another person before in my life.

"What's going on?" Thomas asks, pulling me back up to my feet. He doesn't wait for me to answer. He must read my mind, because he's off running. He shouts, "Get Peter!" and is gone. I steady my emotions and sprint to Peter's shack. He's changing his clothes when I enter, but his embarrassment fades away as soon as he sees my face.

"What is it?"

"It's Clara," I breathe.

IX

⚜

Hours later, there's still no answer. Nothing we can do about it. Clara's coughing fit ended, and she slept for a while. Thomas didn't leave her side even for a minute. When she woke up, she said she feels fine, and she joked that she's just not good at this breathing thing, but nobody laughed, not for real. There was no bonfire tonight. Everybody went to bed without so much of a word, because it felt strange to celebrate life while being so certain of an impending death.

"Why didn't you tell us you were so sick?" Thomas asks her at some point.

"I'm old," she says. "I'm going to die regardless, so it's best that I don't keep you all worried all the time. I swear to you, I'm *okay*." I watch her suncatchers spin in circles, the only sound the *tingtingting* of them.

There's a knock on the exterior of the house, and Eva steps in. She was here earlier, but I suspect it got to be too much for her, so she left. "I brought a few guests." She steps out of the doorway where Arthur, Hattie, Gertie, Molly, and Mia enter in a pack. There's far too many people in this tiny room. The girls look scared of Clara, and guilt fills me for how I left them.

"Come here, my girls." Miss Clara opens her saggy arms to welcome them in, and all four of them climb in close to her. Gertie hugs her tight and cries into her side. I blink back tears, and so does everyone else. "It's okay. Today was scary, but I'm okay." She doesn't fool anybody, least of all me. I watch Thomas's face. His seemingly permanent grin is not so permanent. He looks like how I feel. Hopeless.

Eva taps me on the shoulder and hands me the story I wrote the girls' last night. I had completely forgotten about it in all the confusion today.

"Oh, how did they like it?" I whisper.

"I didn't read it to them," she says. "It's your story. You should read it."

I look around and all eyes are on me, expectantly, including Thomas's curious eyes. I take a deep breath and hold it up to read. "This story is called *The Reign of the Abbott Sisters*, and like all good stories, it starts with 'Once upon a time.'" I'm not sure if they listen because it's good or if they listen because it's an escape. An escape from Hooverville, from Clara's deathbed, from New York, but everyone listens to me as a captivated audience. Nobody ever listened to me like this at home, even at the best of times.

"The sisters ruled their land beautifully, and the seasons visited each of them like an old friend. When one sister had autumn visiting, another had spring, and so on. And when winter, the most unwelcome of guests, visited one of them, the sisters came together to bring warmth into those cold, cold months," I read aloud. "The sisters would seek the elder willow tree called Clarise for wisdom, but Clarise was guarded by two"—I omit the word *handsome* from the original text—"woodsmen, called Pete and Tom." Peter and Thomas elbow each other in the ribcage, excited to be included and giggles dance around the room.

I reach the end of the story just in time, because I can see the girls' eyes drooping and I don't think they'd last much longer. "And they lived happily, forever thereafter." I shut the pages and look at Thomas, who has his usual sparkle back in his eyes. Peter claps, then Eva and Thomas, then Clara and Arthur, then the girls, and I feel a blush coming to my cheeks.

"That was wonderful, Annaleise," Arthur says and kisses me on the top of my head. I feel a warmth in my chest. I feel welcomed. I feel home. "I had better get these girls to bed. Say goodbye, girls."

We all know he meant to say "goodnight," but what he said was "goodbye," and it shocks all of us, including Clara, who looks sad that this may be her last time with all of us together in a group. The girls sit up one by one and kiss her on the cheek and hug her, whispering "Bye, Missus Clara," before hopping off the bed. Arthur kisses her on the forehead and says, "Goodnight, Clara." He stands straighter again and gives each of us a sad smile before he guides the girls out of the room. Eva, Peter, Thomas, and I look at the floor, unsure of what to say. Peter stands with a sigh and stretches.

"I have to be up in five hours for work, so I'll see you all..." He stops his words and looks at Clara. "Tomorrow, right?" Clara takes his hand and squeezes it as confirmation, but I can tell she's getting tired.

"We should let her sleep," Eva breathes, blowing out the light from each of the candles. Peter whispers something to Clara and slips out the door. Eva hugs her, tells her she loves her and makes a joke, but Clara's already falling asleep. "Thomas, you coming?" Eva asks him. He shakes his head and sucks the back of his teeth. He takes Clara's hand.

"No, I'll stay here, but you go get some rest," he nods. After Eva and Peter clear out, he looks confused as I stay. "Aren't you going?" he asks.

"Do you want me to go?" I ask gently. He's quiet for a long time, then shakes his head. "Then I'm staying." Clara falls asleep, and neither of us take our eyes off her chest for at least twenty minutes. If she takes a little too long to start up breathing again, we panic.

"How did the interview go?" Thomas asks quietly after a while. Oh, *shoot*.

"They kicked me out because I didn't have any experience." I use finger quotes, which makes him chuckle a bit. "I used your last name, by the way," I say awkwardly. I didn't need to tell him, I guess, but it would make for an awkward situation if he were to somehow find out from somebody other than me.

"What?" He looks like a laugh is bursting at his seams, but he keeps it under control.

"I didn't want to use my last name, and yours was the first one that came to mind." I shrug. It's not so big of a deal, but I enjoy being Annie Kelley way more than I like being Annaleise Winston.

"You can take my last name anytime you want," he says with his smile back on his face. I know he's flirting, and I like him flirting with me, but a blush still comes to my face to be flirting in Clara's presence.

"Well, they wouldn't hire me, so..." I shrug.

"Yeah, Eva said he was a jerk."

Fear creeps in again like a sneak attack and strangles me, just as violently and brutally as if Frank did it himself. It starts as a voice in my head telling me I'll never be good enough. I'll never help the people I need to help. I'll never escape him. It becomes full-blown memories of Frank. His words, his abuse. The further away from him I get, the more vivid the memories of his abuse. It's as if he's here beating me up, anyway.

"Is everything alright?" Thomas asks, snapping me out of my memories.

I finally decide on, "I don't know," and it's true. "I thought it was, but now I'm not so sure." He waits for me to continue. "It feels like I can't ever escape the thing I'm running from."

"What *are* you running from?" he asks.

I don't know how to explain it without scaring him off, so I just say, "Everything."

He touches my arm with his other hand and looks at me softly. Frank was never gentle.

Frank never made me feel so comfortable in the years I knew him, and here's Thomas Kelley, a shoeshiner who I met three days ago who has completely earned my trust. No. I will *not* be that foolish girl. I'll not do it. I find myself staring at him again and I look away.

"That story tonight was wonderful. How long did it take you to come up with that?" he asks.

"That? Oh, that was maybe a couple hours last night." I shrug. "It was easy."

"You should write a book," he says. I guffaw and cover my mouth so I don't wake Clara.

"Yeah, sure."

"I'm serious." I look at his face and sure enough, he's not kidding. "I'd buy it. I'd read it. And I'm not a huge reader, so that's saying something."

He's just being nice, I'm sure. Just trying to flatter me so I feel better about myself. But it's not a bad idea. If I can't get a job, I could use what little marketable skills I have. What would I even write about? Coming up with the idea last night was so easy, I didn't even think about it. But now my brain is blank. Thomas must hear my thoughts, because he says, "Write about us. About Hooverville. And put me in it and make me handsome."

I blush and look at my lap. "Just for you," I tease. I smile at him, and then we both go quiet. "Thomas," I say after a minute of silence. "Can I ask you a question?" He turns his body to me to give me his full attention, and I take his silence as a yes. "Are you afraid?" I ask quietly.

"Of what?" He looks at Clara.

"Everything. Just, in general. Are you afraid?"

"Every day of my life," he says. It's clear he's let his guard down and feels like a real person instead of an untouchable being who's always available for a laugh. It's as though he's also shocked to admit that. "I'm not here because I want to be," he admits. "And every day I wake up scared that I could lose someone, or somebody could get hurt because I wasn't there, so I'm too scared to leave."

"Thomas, you could go and live your life, if you wanted. Give some responsibility to somebody else for once." I lean on my elbows for emphasis.

"I couldn't live with myself if I did that." He takes Clara's hand again. There was a slim chance he'd listen to me, but I hoped he might. Once again, Thomas is a better person than I can ever hope to be. "You should sleep, you've had a long day." I try to find any ingenuity in his face, but there's none. Only a pure heart. So, for the first time in my life, instead of arguing, I listen, and I lay my head down at the foot of Clara's bed and fall asleep.

I slowly come to after what must be a couple of hours and find silence where there was once solitude. The air is still, the sunchimes have stopped their faint *tink tink*, and Thomas sleeps with his head beside Clara, who is still, like a painting. I sit up straighter. Her lips are a dark gray color and her skin is leathery. I know already, but I want to be wrong. I shake her foot some, but she doesn't move.

"Clara..." I whisper. My voice cracks. "Clara?" I blow out a breath and blink back tears before I look at Thomas in his last few moments of peace. "Thomas," I whisper. "Thomas," I repeat, louder. He stirs and his eyes open slowly, and as soon as he sees my face, my tears, my pain, his focus shifts to Clara. He shouts her name and pushes himself to his feet, shaking her shoulders violently and practically screaming in her face to wake up. His pain is my pain, and I can't reject it this time. I feel every bit of it. The anguish, the burning in my chest, the lump in my throat. Hot, electric pain all the way into my shoulders and down my arms into my fingertips.

And in his reaction, I see Frank again. Screaming and shaking in the same way, for different reasons.

"Thomas," I finally force myself to say. I step forward, arms shaking, and pull him off of her by the back of his shirt, but what he does next startles me. He wraps both of his arms around my neck and cries into my hair. I press my face into his shoulder and cry and just say, "I'm so sorry" over and over and over again until it no longer has any meaning. He eventually pulls back and looks back at Clara, but it's too soon. I don't want him to leave my arms yet.

He wipes at his cheeks and takes a few deep breaths and pulls her blanket up over her head. He can't meet my eyes, either embarrassed for reacting like that or angry with himself—or worse, *me*—for not saving her earlier. "Some—" he breathes heavily and hiccups. "Someone has to tell Peter."

Oh God. I can't endure this reaction two, three, four more times, but since I've known her the shortest amount of time, it's only fair that it should be me.

As I leave her shack, a few of the stragglers who were either out late or up early, already know just by my face. Their hands go to their mouth, they might whisper, "Oh no!" and hug the person nearest to them, but for the most part, it's quiet. I go to Eva's hut first and strengthen myself outside before I push open the blanket. She's awake, and the minute she sees me enter, she knows. It's not quite like Thomas's reaction. She sits up and cries into her hands, but then she pulls herself together and asks if Peter knows yet, and I shake my head. She takes a deep breath and pulls on a pair of shoes and follows me to Peter's shack. His reaction *is* like Thomas's. He hugs Eva and cries into her hair, asking "why?" into the void. I have to leave a couple of minutes in. It's too much for me, and since I didn't know her well, it's my job to be the strength for everyone here. It's no different than at home, really. I just have to maintain some objectivity. And not look anyone in the eye.

By eight, everyone knows. I told most of them with a

heavy heart, but several of them caught word from somebody else. They filed into her shack to say their goodbyes, including the little Abbott girls, all of whom were crying and clutching their dad—thank God she died on a Sunday so that Arthur could be here for his daughters—and then they retreat to their own homes to mourn in privacy. At around ten, Thomas leaves Hooverville without saying a word to anyone. I try to follow him, but Eva grabs me and tells me not to.

"He just needs some time," she promises.

I don't know what funeral protocol is here, but I also don't know what to do with myself, so I write a eulogy for Clara, even though nobody will ever read it. I write about her kindness and enthusiasm. I write about her fearlessness and selflessness. But after a page or so, writing about her becomes too difficult, so I end up staring at the walls of my hut, listening for a sound from outside.

X

As I emerge from my hut, I immediately stop by Thomas's and peek my head through the blanket of his doorway. I tread carefully in case he's sleeping, but when I look in, Thomas is still missing. I feel myself grow tense and wander to the center of the town.

Everyone keeps their heads down if they must be out and about, while a crew carries Clara's body out of her shack on a large wood palette.

"Where are they taking her?" I ask whoever is nearest me.

"Hart Island," Eva says quietly. I look at her to see how she's holding up. Her eyes are puffy and her dark skin is flushed, but if it wasn't for that, I'd never even know something happened. "That's where they take the bodies that can't afford a proper funeral." She sniffles and looks at me. "She'll just be dumped in a shallow grave without any kind of marker, next to hundreds, if not thousands, of other people."

I feel sick as they carry her away. Peter's there, but not Thomas.

"It's a shitty world we live in, Winston." Eva sighs. "Come on."

She moves over to one of the logs in front of the burnt-out

bonfire and begins carving intricate designs into a long and thick stick with a knife.

"What's that?" I ask her, pointing to the strange designs.

"I sell these. I don't make much from them, but they keep me busy and give me a little bit of extra money." She shrugs and carves the design of an owl into the top of it. "It's a walking stick. Or a cane, I guess."

"It's beautiful," I tell her. She smiles and continues working. "Do you know where Thomas is?"

She purses her lips together and shakes her head. "No. I figured he'd be back by now. I'm a little worried about him."

"Me too," I whisper, and we say nothing else.

After Clara's body is removed, Peter and another boy whose name I never learned begin clearing out her belongings. The rest of Hooverville has begun to return to their normal behavior, but Peter is solemn. I watch from a distance as the boys sort her items into piles—one pile to sell, and one to give to others—and write about today's events in my diary. I spin around when I feel a tap on my shoulder, and part of me is hopeful for who it is, but my hopes are dropped when I see Peter standing there instead.

"Annaleise, you may want to take a look at this," he says slowly, slightly in shock. He holds out the parchment I wrote the Abbott story on, complete with Eva's butterfly broach. I push my brows together.

"This is just the story I wrote for the girls. I don't—"

He interrupts me. "Flip it over." I flip it over and see more writing, only it's not mine.

In chicken-scratch handwriting, it says "happy" repeatedly in simple lines, like I was forced to do in school for proper handwriting lessons. She must have woken up at some point while Thomas and I were sleeping and wanted to tell us she was happy. A last message from Clara. A promise that she's okay and at peace.

After sundown, the fire pit is like a large circle of friends sharing stories about their time with Clara. Some people cry, but it's mostly laughing, the way I believe funerals should be. Peter shares the most about his time with Clara, about how on his first night in Hooverville, she swatted him for being too loud, then gave him a blanket and some food she'd hidden in her hut because he was too skinny. Another woman shares about how Clara once rocked her baby to sleep so she could get a few hours for a job interview in the morning. She doesn't have a baby, or even a toddler around, but I don't think too hard about that.

Soon, people break out in song, clapping and cheering to raise their spirits. Eva tells me it was Clara's favorite song, so I hang onto every lyric like it's a gift from her. I mentally count the hours since Thomas left, and worry consumes me. I can tell Eva and Peter are concerned too, but they don't send out a search party for him. Would he have gone somewhere dangerous? What if he's hurt?

To try and avoid the dark thoughts creeping in, I try to sing the song with the folks around the fire, but seeing as I don't know the lyrics, I end up humming awkwardly and clapping my hands to a beat I don't know. Then, from the opposite side of the park, a shadow approaches, and I jump to my feet. I know the posture and walk of the shadow, and I let out a massive breath of relief. Thomas comes into the firelight and gives everyone a weak smile, then tosses a bag of apples into the circle.

"Eat up," he says, his voice raspy and almost gone. The others around the circle pry open the bag and grab at the apples to make sure everyone gets some. Peter passes his knife around the circle to either cut them into pieces or cut moldy parts off, and when I look back at Thomas, he's gone again, as if he never came back in the first place. Eva and I look at each other concernedly, but she doesn't move, and so I don't either.

I don't remember the mourning process after my father died. I remember at his funeral, how my mother spent more time fussing about my dress or my hair than caring about my emotions. At least, that's how I saw it, but thinking about it again now, she must have been trying to keep herself busy. I never once saw my mother cry about my father. I have no proof that she ever did, even in secret, but I *have to* believe that she missed him as badly as I do.

I stand and start to leave. To be a part of something so intimate only makes me feel like I don't belong here even more. Peter stands and rushes over to me.

"Where are you going?" he asks.

"To bed." I sigh. "This has been kind of a draining day." I lie through my teeth, but Peter doesn't notice.

"Okay, wait though. Follow me," he says. Without waiting for a response, he walks towards the center of the Hooverville, back to Clara's camp, now empty except for the two piles. He reaches down and lifts the give-away pile, and asks me, "Is there anything you want from this?"

I have to take a step back. She has some lovely items. Jewelry that could have been worth a bit if she sold it, but I assume the fact that she didn't means it was even more precious to her than money would have been. There is a beautiful knit shawl, and a pair of shoes that would be too big on my feet, and two thick blankets.

"I can't take anything of hers," I stutter. "It wouldn't be right."

"She loved you, you know. You're allowed to."

I shake my head, mouth open. This feels a little too closely to grave-robbing for my liking. "N-no." Peter pulls the shawl out of the pile and wraps it around my shoulders.

"Take this; she'd want you to have it. She said you were far too cold at night."

I press my lips together and agree just so that I can go back to bed. I start to leave, but then I turn around and face Peter. I don't need to open my mouth for him to know.

"He'll be okay, Annaleise," he says, putting a hand on my shoulder. I'm unsure, but something about his tone reassures me. Peter knows Thomas better than I do. He must be right. That gives me enough confidence to go to bed for the night. I tell Peter goodnight and make the long journey around the corner to my hut.

It's entirely too much. I should never have come here in the first place. Why did I think I could handle living in a homeless camp with illness and death and starvation? This was only supposed to be temporary. Now, here I am, forming feelings that I shouldn't have, for people that I will never see after I leave.

I curl into a ball and hide my face in my knees, crying until my chest feels hollow and my eyes are dry. I grab my diary from my bag and read through what I wrote just three days ago. It speaks of hope and longing and complete bullshit. I ball the first ten pages into a fist, ready to tear it up, but stop myself.

I take a breather and drop my shoulders. If I tear this up, every word I've written will mean nothing. Nobody will read it, and nothing will change for these people. Clara will have died for nothing, with nobody to remember her name, and more just like her will die too. I have to keep writing it—if not for me, then for Thomas. Maybe if I take some of the burden of protecting Hooverville onto myself, then he won't have to. If I can't be free, at least I can try to set him free.

Thomas is out at the bonfire long after everyone else has gone to bed. I slip out of my shack and wrap Clara's knit shawl around my waist as protection from feeling his emotions too strongly. I sneak up behind him and peek at him. His eyes are red and puffy, but the heat of the fire has dried him of his tears.

"Hey," I say, unsure of how I should speak to him. "Can I sit?"

"Be my guest." He pulls up the log beside him, and I sit down, cautiously looking at his face. He's slightly sunburnt, but he's looking a little bit better fed than when I first met him. His hair is even messier than usual, and his jaw tightens every so often as he tries to suppress his emotions. I saw that behavior in my Pa when I was young. He didn't like me to see him upset, so even when his older brother died, I didn't see him cry. Just that damned jaw tick.

Real emotion would be a welcome guest in any conversation with a man. Not anger, like Frank. But sadness, grief, joy. Anything.

"You don't have to do that with me," I say gently. He furrows his brow. "Pretend," I clarify. He nods slowly and looks back at the fire. "Do you want to talk about it?" I ask. In my head, it plays out like I'm poking a bear, and that Thomas will lash out at me and turn into a raging monster. But he doesn't. He just looks at the fire and the city lights and focuses on his breathing.

"No," he finally answers, pulling me back from my thoughts. "But thank you."

We sit in silence for a long time, and I lay my head on his shoulder and nearly fall asleep by the warmth of the fire. It's such a long silence that when he finally talks, it startles me.

"Is there a good way to die?" he asks, his voice surprisingly steady. I think for a minute.

The only deaths I've ever witnessed in my life have been at the hands of long, painful illnesses, and by the end, they were shells of their former selves. When my Pa died, for a few days beforehand, he was talking to invisible people in the ceiling and making no sense. I remember once he asked me to go and fetch him a meal, but by the time I brought it to him, he was screaming about the people trying to kill him. He thought that I was trying to strangle him in his bed, so he grabbed my wrist so tightly that it was bruised afterward, and it scared me. He looked like a monster, with his eyes bulging and turning black and spit flying from his mouth. The doctors said it was just the fever, and that it was normal, but it didn't feel normal. He died a couple of days later in his sleep. His last words were, "That's funny."

"I don't know," I finally answer Thomas's question. "I don't think so."

"If I had to choose my way out, I'd choose something in- teresting. Like falling off a cliff into shark-infested waters. Something people would talk about afterward and go '*damn, that's a way to go out,*'" he says. He sounds like he's joking, but his face isn't convincing. I decide that if he wants to avoid talking about it and talk about something else, I'll indulge him.

"I'd have to choose something very boring. Dying at an age where I'm ridiculously old and nobody even cares about me anymore. Hopefully, there will be bets placed on when I die by my great-grandchildren."

"That's too damn long of a life," he laughs sadly. "Who wants to live that long?"

"Well, I used to, but not so much anymore. Maybe the shark-infested waters is the way to go." I sigh softly. His eyes flicker with something that makes me blush, and I pull myself together and sit back up with a sideways grin between pursed lips.

"Why do these things have to happen?" Thomas asks, voice cracking. He's not just talking about Clara, in the same way I'm not just talking about Frank. Thomas opens his arms for me and asks for a hug, but I'm not sure which of us needs it more. So, I do it. He presses his thumb into my shoulder and rests his chin on my head, sighing quietly. At the end of the day, we're still kids trying to find our way through this world with no parents, no guidance, and no money. We need each other. I need Thomas.

People from my world have no idea any of this is going on. They don't know the hurt, or the joy, or the diseases, or the hunger. They have no idea of any of it. And I'm sure that even if I tried to tell them, people like Frank would still demand they help themselves out of the dirt. But I have to try. And who else would they listen to if not me? Our conversation last night about the book felt like a joke, but it wasn't a bad idea. I could write a book and sell it, like what Nellie Bly did about the madhouses. An expose on America's housing crisis. People would eat it up. I'd use the money to help Arthur, maybe change legislation on the way. It may not work, but it's the only plan I have that solves all my problems at once. And with that solved, I fall asleep on Thomas's chest, the most unlikely of safe places.

We jump awake early in the morning to a loud crash, followed by whoops and hollers. On the other side of Hooverville, Peter and some of the other guys have knocked down an empty shack for the wood. After we relax and get out of our fight positions, we laugh at each other's reaction to the sound.

"You fell asleep," he mumbles in a rough voice, rubbing the sleep from his eyes.

"You let me," I murmur and grin at him, eyes drooping closed again. He lets me lay there for a moment, then grumbles.

"Come on. Up."

"I. Don't. Wanna," I whine dramatically, then flutter my eyelids open to find him staring at me. He quirks one eyebrow and smiles at me, and it's enough to wake me from my drowsiness and energize me. I frown and sit up, stretching my shoulders and spine.

"Thank you for staying with me last night," he whispers to me. "Means a lot." I smile softly.

"Anytime," I say gently, and then on an impulse, I lean forward and kiss him on the cheek. Before he can say or do anything, I'm up and walking away from him, lips tingling with both regret and excitement coursing through me. I sneak a look back at his face to see, but he's simply rubbing at his cheek where I kissed.

Shit. I shouldn't have done that. He doesn't feel that way, and I won't do anything to make a fool of myself again. I'm technically still engaged. I have bigger things to worry about than a shoeshiner from the Hooverville.

As I turn the corner, I come face to face with—

"*Virginia?*" I breathe. She stumbles backward and mumbles out a weak apology. It takes her a moment to recognize me, but when she does, she throws her stack of papers down and tugs me into her arms.

XI

"Oh my God!" she shouts, nearly falling backward. "There you are!" She hugs me and shakes me back and forth, and I push her away confusedly.

She's dressed down for the day in a lemon-yellow dress-suit combo that makes her look more alive than her usual uniform does. She looks off-kilter in my new environment. She never stops twisting her head around, like she expects one of the buildings to collapse on her.

"Virginia," I breathe. She stands and opens her arms for me, and I'm not sure who embraces the other one first, or who holds on tighter. She feels different now than she did the last time I hugged her. Less steady. Less certain of herself. I pull back and look at her face. I recognize a deep-rooted sadness in her eyes, and my smile falls.

"What are you doing here?" I ask her. My voice doesn't sound like mine anymore. It's some strange combination of my proper voice from back home and the voice I've found since coming here.

"*Me*? What are *you* doing here? I thought you were on a train to California!"

"It's kind of a long story," I laugh, recounting it to myself. It's an odd predicament I've found myself in.

"So, you're staying here? Why didn't you come home? You could have at least told me you were leaving."

I pause, deciding what I should tell her about my stay here. "I'm only staying until I get some money." I speak slowly so she doesn't panic.

"What happened to your money?" she asks, horrified.

"I was robbed. They took all of it." Virginia's whole posture changes, and she practically grabs me to scoop me up and out of here. "I'm having fun! I've made some friends. I've learned a lot." *And I think I met somebody* my head-voice finishes for me, but I know Virginia wouldn't approve, given everything. "Come, come sit!" I pull her to my shack and sit her down on a log. I sit with my back straight and my knees angled perfectly like I did back home, and when I catch myself, I attempt to break the habit. I drop my shoulders and straighten one leg out.

"Tell me everything," she says, crossing one leg over the other. I ramble on and on about the robbery, though I give minimal details about Thomas. If I were to bring him up to her, it would make everything too real, and I'm enjoying living in a fantasy. I tell her about Peter and Eva and Miss Clara and the suncatchers and how much writing I'm doing, but her expression stops me. I've seen that look before. When she had to leave for a month to take care of her sick mother. When my mother made me quit ballet. When she told me my father would not get better.

"What is it?" I ask lowly. I've known her long enough to know what that face means. She sits straighter and bites her lip, contemplating telling me the bad news. At first, I'm afraid something's happened to my mother, but what she actually tells me is far worse.

"Frank returned two nights ago, as I'm sure you already know."

She's wrong. I didn't know. While I was with Thomas and Clara, Frank was at home realizing I'm not there. I imagine the misunderstanding between Frank and my mother when he'd ask where I was and she'd horrifyingly say she thought I was with him. Oh, how furious. How awful that must have been for the staff to see. I try not to let on how my breathing changes or how loudly I hear my heartbeat in my ears.

"And?" I ask, but my voice gets caught up in my throat.

"He's looking for you," she hisses. "He's gone to the cops. The cops didn't want to help him because it was a runaway case, but he forced them to treat it as a hostage situation. Or worse. He's practically rented the police force, Annaleise. *Everyone's* looking for you."

I swallow and lower my eyes to the ground. "They—" I clear my throat so I don't sound as scared as I actually feel. "They wouldn't think to look for me in a Hooverville, would they?"

"I don't know," she breathes and reaches into the satchel. "But he's having these put up as we speak." She pulls out a stack of fliers with *Missing Persons, Annaleise Winston, $2500 Reward* written across the top, with a photograph of me from the engagement party. "That's where I'm supposed to be, at least."

I feel Frank's boot down on my neck once again. The surrounding air feels thick, and I can feel his eyes on me, slithering up and down like a snake. I take a deep breath to avoid panicking. I can figure this out. I can get through this. "What do you suggest I do?" I ask her. She tells me the words I'm afraid of hearing.

"I think you should go back home," she says. "It will be much worse for you if he finds you, and he *will* find you." I think for a moment about the possibility of being caught. There's no way I can go back to that life. Go back to Frank, leave Thomas with this burden. It's only in the split-second Virginia asks me to go back that I realize I have no choice but to stay. To leave the Hooverville would be cowardice far beyond what I've already done.

"No," I tell her strongly. My voice feels like mine for once. That's one thing Frank can't have of mine.

"I'm sorry, no?" Virginia gawks at me.

"I can't leave. I have a responsibility to these people. I'm working on a... a thing, a project, and I won't leave until I can make people realize what it's really like."

"Make *who* realize?"

"Frank! The Lyndons! Franklin Delano *Goddamn* Roosevelt! I don't know! Anybody who will listen!" I've never raised my voice at Virginia, and neither of us quite expected it. "I'm writing something. A book, maybe. I don't know." She watches me and lowers her chin.

"I don't know what you're expecting from this book of yours, but no book can change the world like you want it to. No matter how beautifully written or how good your intentions are," Virginia says gently. Hearing this from her is a much harsher blow than I anticipated.

"You don't think I can do this?" I breathe.

"I never said that. I said it won't turn out like you expected, and I think that right now, in your condition, you need to think about focusing your energy somewhere else. You can't save the world, so you might as well save yourself, you know?" I've been telling Thomas the same thing since I got here, but it doesn't apply to me. I've spent my whole life only caring about myself. I can't keep doing that and expecting good things to happen.

"Why can't you just let me try?" I ask, pained.

"I don't want to see you hurt; you know that." Virginia reaches out to touch me. I stand up and step back.

"I'm not going back. Not now, not ever. Frank hasn't found me yet. And if he does, I'll leave, but until that happens, I'm staying and writing this book, and I'm going to do everything that I can to help the people in every Hooverville," I say.

Virginia gives up the fight, presses her lips together, and nods. "If that's what you want."

"That's what I want," I demand. She sighs, stands slowly, and gives me a long hug. I can feel her anxiety through her skin, so I whisper, "Everything will be okay."

Before Virginia leaves, I take the stack of flyers from her and keep them near my other things in the shack, under my pillow for a little extra protection. I don't know how many of them Virginia hung up around town, but hopefully nobody from Hooverville will see any and recognize me.

After she's gone, it feels like everybody knows my secret, as if everybody is looking at me like a cash prize. I scan the crowd, waiting for one of them to spring on me and turn me in, but as the nightly music starts up and one of the men brings a bag of marshmallows to share with the crowd, I realize nobody is going to steal me away. At least not tonight. Not now.

One bag of marshmallows as a treat between forty people. How is that fair? If I wasn't such a selfish mess, if I had any compassion at all, I'd turn myself in and give the reward money to these people. They deserve it more than me. But I can't get past my own selfishness. When they die and I live, I'll have no one to blame but myself. When I'm living comfortably on the California coast, and these people are dead in the street, I'll never live at peace. I'll always wonder if I could have saved them all. I can't have peace.

Arthur's four girls sit beside me, savoring their marshmallows and giggling amongst themselves. I find Eva, who sits by herself on the far side of the fire, and Peter, who's flirting with a woman a couple years older than him—or maybe that's just his personality; I can never tell anymore. I don't think Peter would turn me in for all the money in the world. Eva... Eva *might*, and she would have every reason to. I went to the job interview that should have been hers. I've taken over her role here. She should have every reason to want me gone. But still, I don't think Eva would do that. I think she's better than I give her credit for.

That only leaves Thomas. He wouldn't. Would he? He's desperate to take care of everyone else here. Wouldn't he want reward money too?

I'm pulled from my thought by some shouting on the other side of the park. *What now?* The girls stretch their necks to see the commotion. Two men drag something behind them on the ground, but in the dark I can't really see. They shout,

"Clear the way! Move!" and come towards the light. Mia sits up straight and drops her marshmallow into the dirt.

"Daddy?" she cries, and Thomas and another man drag Arthur's limp body into the light.

The girls recognize him much quicker than I do, and once they do, there's no chance of calming them down. They scream and clamor over one another to get to him while about a dozen of us bombard Thomas with questions.

Arthur's face has been beaten in. His eye is swollen and varying shades of black and purple and red. His nose is crooked and broken, and his lip cut. He's lulling in and out of consciousness. I know those bruises anywhere. I know them like the back of my hand. This was Frank.

They get Arthur into Clara's old cabin and onto her big bed, where several of them treat him for other injuries like a broken rib and a concussion. If he wasn't fired already, there's no way he could do his job until he heals. Either way, Arthur can't provide for his daughters like this.

Eva and I put Mia, Hattie, Gertie, and Molly to bed and try to reassure him that their dad will be okay. His injuries aren't life threatening, but it must be scary seeing someone you love hurt like that. It takes ages to get them to sleep, and by the time Hattie falls asleep, I burst into tears.

"Are you okay?" Eva asks quietly. I bury my face in my hands and try my hardest to stop crying, but I can't. It was another thing entirely when I was the only one Frank could hurt, but now, because of my irresponsibility, Frank can hurt so many more people and get away with it. Virginia was right. I need to go back before this gets worse.

"I can't do this," I breathe, and leave Eva and the girls behind.

I rush back to my shack and start shoving my few things in my bag, wiping my tears the whole way. It was foolish of me to try to pull off that stupid book. To pull any of this off. Let Frank kill me.

I don't care anymore.

"Annaleise?" Thomas appears in my doorway. I'm startled for a moment and start crying even harder at the sudden disturbance. I haven't cried so hard since the night Frank proposed. That was also the last time I felt this hopeless. I wipe at my cheeks and steady my voice the same way I did that night. "What are you doing?" Thomas asks.

"Can't anybody have any privacy around here?" I snap, sniffling and keeping my face turned from him.

"I thought you'd want to know that Arthur is going to be okay."

"No, no, he's not." I stuff a sweater into the bag. It's Thomas's that I borrowed, but I don't want to give it back. "Not when he and the girls starve to death and it's all my fault."

I finally turn to him. He looks exhausted, like he hasn't slept much. He probably hasn't, and he shouldn't be here checking up on me. He should be asleep in his bed, while I creep away without being noticed or ever thought of again. His face scrunches up at my suggestion, and he almost laughs.

"Your fault? Annie." He opens his arms for me, but when he sees me melt into tears again, his face and his arms fall. "Annie, what's going on?" He kneels on the ground beside me.

God, he is too sweet and too gentle. It isn't fair. Thomas lives in a Hooverville and Frank lives in a mansion and it's unfair.

I take a moment to recoup and get my breathing and crying under control. I try to speak, but my words only come out as bubbled sobs, so instead I pull out one of Virginia's missing posters and slide it across his lap. He reads it and his eyebrows press together.

"What's this?" he asks. "Reward two thousand five hundred dollars?" He sounds mighty impressed. I may be in danger even showing him that. "Annie, tell me what's going on."

So I do.

I start with how I grew up, my rich family and upbringing, and then go into my engagement to Frank and the bruises. How they aren't from a wild doorknob and I didn't fall off my bicycle. How they're from each time I misbehaved in Frank's eyes. He shifts uncomfortably as I speak, but he doesn't interrupt me or even ask questions. Telling Thomas about all this feels like a weight off my shoulders, and is easier than writing in my diary, because I don't feel like I need to lie, ironic as that is. When I'm talking too fast, Thomas reminds me we have all night and that there's no need to rush. I blow out a breath and explain it to him.

Why I ran away, how I got stuck here, why I'm staying here now. "If he dies or if the girls starve or die, it's my fault. Because I left, because I was selfish, because I was stupid. *So stupid!*" I feel myself getting worked up again, like the air in my lungs has turned to cement, so Thomas wraps his arms around me and puts his chin on top of my head.

"It's not your fault," he whispers, and I don't quite believe it, but the reassurance means something to me anyway. After a moment of quiet, he murmurs, "What if I could get you out?"

I pull back from my spot at his chest. "What?"

"What if I could get you out of here and away from Frank forever?" I search Thomas's eyes, but he isn't kidding.

"God, Thomas. You don't have to rescue everyone all the time! You can't *save* everyone. You can't save me!" I raise my voice at him.

"Can't I try?" he asks. His words echo mine from just this morning, when Virginia tried to convince me to go home and I told her I wanted to stay and save Hooverville. Oh, how much has changed in just a few hours.

"Thomas, tomorrow I'm turning myself in to Frank—"

"*NO!*"

"—and giving the reward money to the Abbotts. You can have some too, if you want, and you can get out of here and go see the world. Thomas, I know how you want to do that. It's wrong of me to stay. It's selfish."

"Weren't you the one telling me I deserve to be selfish once in a while?" Thomas shouts. I can't believe we're actually arguing about this.

"This is completely different than that! This is *me*! Not you!"

We're both so stubborn that it's like an unstoppable force meeting an immovable object, and I think he realizes that too because we both stop and stare at each other for a long, long time.

And then he grabs my face, and he kisses me.

When he pulls back, he says, "I'm sorry. I just wanted you to know what it's like to be totally loved. Just once." My lips are still tingling, and I'm too stunned to respond. "Don't go back to him. Promise me you won't."

Well now, this is really confusing, but I know what I want, and he's staring me in the face asking me to take it. "I promise," I whisper.

XII

I'm there in the morning when Arthur wakes up. He can't sit up straight, so I have to tilt his head up and help him sip some water from a straw. The girls play just outside his hut, loudly, and I shush them. I'll make a good mom someday, I'm learning. Arthur blinks slowly and turns his eyes over to me.

"Nobody told me," he says with difficulty because of his fat lip, "that Frank returned."

"I'm so sorry, Arthur. This is all my fault."

"You didn't beat me up. Frank did."

"Because I left," I try to explain. "This wouldn't have happened if I had stayed put—"

"Yes, it would have," Arthur mumbles. "It would have been you if it wasn't me." He's right, of course. If I stayed home and Frank came back in a foul mood, this might be me lying in a bed, with no use of my body. "He's a wicked man, Annaleise. Nobody deserves it." Again, he's right. I don't have to take Frank's beatings, and I don't have to take responsibility for who he hurts in my place. But it's so difficult not to.

I look at my hands and play with my fingers, dirt caked under my formerly pristine fingernails, with bruises and cuts on my hands from the last days. "So, what did you tell him?" I ask apprehensively.

"The truth." Arthur coughs a bit. "I told him I had nothing to do with your disappearance."

"Thank you," I whisper and look back at my lap. "And my mother?" He raises an eyebrow. "Is she safe?" I wish I could ask without being so transparent. I don't like my mother, but she's still my family. I don't want him turning his anger towards her either. Arthur smiles the best he can, which isn't much considering his busted-up face.

"She's just fine. So is Virginia. I've been sacked, though." I expected just as much from them. He's not a person in their eyes, just a little piece in their well-oiled machine. I'm sure they found a replacement before he even reached Hooverville. But Mia, Hattie, Gertie, and Molly come to my mind. I'm about to ask Arthur what in the world I'm supposed to do, but he falls asleep, so I leave him be. Most everyone around Hooverville has been asking questions about what happened. Who did that to Arthur? Are we safe anymore? And since we're trying to keep my identity a secret and not scare the girls, we're leaving them all in the dark. I don't know how Thomas came to find him, though. While Thomas and Peter are at work, I try to write the book I promised everyone I'd write. A book about Hooverville, to hopefully inspire some empathy in the hearts of the higher-ups. But everything I could possibly write just sounds selfish and dumb.

So, I try a unique method. I write what I see, instead of what I feel. Five women gossiping and washing their laundry. Two mangy dogs sniffing for scraps. Seven skinny children chasing each other around. One man playing a harmonica.

One man lying beaten by his former boss. One woman asking for donations so she can get to California. The summer sun makes Hooverville stifling hot. A few of the kids invented a game where they place a plastic tarp down on the grass and soaked it with water, and used the water to slide around on the tarp in. Their laughs fill the Hooverville with unbridled joy in the unbearable sun, and soon, I've tapped into the flow of words, and they come along easily after that. By midafternoon I've nearly filled the book up with details about Clara, and my argument with Thomas, and how it felt when he kissed me, and the games the kids play.

There's an entire chapter dedicated to the foods I've learned to eat. I haven't quite learned to enjoy a lot of them, but I do appreciate some good, canned beans. Some stories are funny, like when Peter threw a whole can of olives in the fire because he claimed, "Nobody even likes olives!" and a few seconds later, the can exploded and sent shrapnel and olives flying. Some stories are not, like when I was robbed or when I found Clara dead. Peter and Thomas return from work just as I'm finishing writing, so I tuck my diary into my bag and comb through my hair with my fingers, although it's been a couple days since it was last cleaned and it's been awfully hot today, so I know it doesn't look good.

I come out of my shack and jump backwards as Thomas appears with flowers. "I'm sorry!" he exclaims. "I didn't mean to scare you, I just wanted to give you these." He holds out a bouquet of handpicked flowers. I cover my mouth to stifle a laugh. So, it wasn't a dream he kissed me.

"Whose garden did you get these from? You'll probably get in trouble, you know."

"A little trouble never hurt anyone," he grins. "I just wanted to let you know that I was serious last night. I wasn't just trying to get you to stay. I meant everything I said." I look at my shoes. I wish he hadn't meant it. It would make it so much easier to let him leave and go see the world.

I'm about to respond when both of our attention is drawn by some shouting on the other side of Hooverville. We both turn our heads at the same time and spring into action. I drop the flowers to the ground. Though he moves first, I'm faster and I reach the screaming first. Three officers are grabbing at a woman called Leota, forcing her down on the ground and pulling her dark-colored arms behind her back whilst she shrieks for her husband. "No!" I cry and grab at an officer's shoulder to pry him off her, but a rogue elbow flies up and hits me in the temple, throwing me to the ground beside her.

My ears ring and the world spins around me. The next thing I know, Thomas forces himself between the police officers and Leota, whose tears soak into the grass beneath her. I push myself to my knees and take my place by Leota's side. "Are you alright?" I ask her, but she's trembling and weeping so badly that she can't make words.

"That's enough!" Thomas yells, startling even me a bit, and then he shoves an officer roughly. That officer pulls the gun from his belt and points it at Thomas.

"Don't!" I find it in me to shout, and before my mind even understands, I'm on my feet and moving in between them. The officer points the gun at me instead, but Thomas takes a calm step in front of me, blocking the weapon from my view.

Thomas doesn't turn to me, but he says, "I can handle this, Annie" in a flat, calm tone. My eyes move to the other officers with their hands on their guns, but I notice they all have papers in their hands. Flyers. Posters. And I begin to form a clear idea of what's happening here. I take a few steps back, hiding my face from the cops. I move behind Peter and Eva and keep a low profile. I need for Thomas to get them away from here, and I have to hope they didn't recognize me.

The cop's gun is shaking, either with fear or anger, and Thomas slowly puts his hands up in the air. "You have no jurisdiction here, officer," Thomas says calmly.

"She's a trespasser. You all are!"

"Why did you single her out?" Thomas asks. "She's old, she's fragile, she isn't hurting anybody. So why her?"

"Would you rather it's you, slick?" he spits. "I don't answer to you, Ville-ain." It sounds like a slur, but Thomas doesn't show any signs of hurt.

"Nobody's done any harm. We promise to keep it that way unless you make trouble here. I don't want trouble. Nobody wants trouble. We just want a place to live in." He's so soft-spoken, even in the face of literal death. He doesn't let a hint of fear slip through in his voice, and his argument never falters.

The officers are obviously startled by his interference, but the first officer eventually lowers his gun. "Fine, but one problem report and you're all out on your asses. And you'll be the first one I get, so be careful, slick." He gets up in Thomas's face, but Thomas doesn't flinch, even when the officer spits in his face. The three officers leave, sending angry glares at the five of us, and as soon as they're out of sight, Thomas's shoulder releases tension and drop.

He turns and sees all of us standing there, then looks at me and says, "What were you thinking?"

That's not quite what I was expecting, but okay. "You had a gun in your face and you're mad at me for coming to your side?"

"What if those guys recognized you? What if they tell your fiancé?" He lowers his voice so Eva and Peter don't hear. "That wasn't at the top of my mind when you had a gun in your face." I think he's going to be mad at me, but he just hugs me and lets out a breath of relief. He must have been more scared than he let on.

We check Leota for injuries. She's fine, just startled, but after that encounter with the cops, it feels like people look at me differently. Maybe it's just in my mind, but I think word is getting around. How many people did the cops ask about me? How many people said they've seen me?

Any one of these people could be ready to turn on me at a moment's notice. I take Thomas's arm and whisper into his ear, "Don't leave me alone with these people, please?" He frowns at me and then looks around at everyone else. He must sense it too, because he nods his head at me and holds my arm tighter. I feel at least a little bit safer with him by my side. We stay out at the fire after everybody else too, only leaving to check on Arthur and help get his daughters to bed. Then it's right back to the fire, where Eva and Peter dance with each other and Thomas and I don't dance, exactly, but sway in circles. Not for romance, but because it's the easiest way to keep an eye on direction in case someone is coming for me.

After everyone else has gone to bed, we finally give ourselves permission to sleep. We debate sleeping alone or sleeping together, but Thomas suggests waiting outside and sleeping on the ground to keep watch. I tilt my head up to him just before going to bed. "Sleep tight," I mumble. "And thank you for staying with me."

He smiles with his lips closed. It doesn't look genuine, but I don't stop to wonder why. I crawl into bed and watch Thomas's shadow lay on the ground by the door, just five feet from me. Even in the dark, I know that he doesn't go to sleep. He watches the stars up in the sky, and turns his eyes to me, but I pretend to be asleep before he catches me staring. And then, I really do fall asleep.

When I wake again, the sun isn't up and my hut is still shrouded in darkness, but I see that Thomas isn't where I left him. I push the blanket off me and go to my feet and stick my head out of my shack. Hooverville is silent and still, and Thomas isn't there. I walk around, looking for him, but he's gone. He's left me. It makes no sense. Thomas wouldn't do this unless he was going to Frank while my back is turned and he's going to pocket all the money and I won't get anything. Not to help the Abbotts. Not Thomas. Not freedom. I'm almost back to my hut when I see another person's shadow in the distance, walking towards me. With a flyer in his hand.

XIII

"Is this you?" the man asks in a raspy voice as he gets closer to me. There's nobody else around. Nobody would hear me if I screamed. My stomach flips, and my heart beats so loudly in my ears that if he says anything else, I don't hear it. I plant my feet firmly to the ground and straighten my shoulders.

"I think this is you, and I think I'm going to bring you in and get me a nice paycheck, *Miss Winston*," the man says, reaching for me with his long arms. He grabs me by the shirt with incredible force, nearly pulling my feet from the ground. His eyes search me like I'm a meal and he's been starving for years. I whimper and pry at his hands. He sets me down and grabs the back of my neck, half-steering, half-dragging me with him as he walks toward the edge of the park. It takes a moment for me to get my voice back before I shriek madly.

"Help!" I cry out. "HELP!" I kick at the man as we reach the last hut in Hooverville, and finally, we run into another person. Immediately my confusion and shock are met with anger and relief as Thomas appears before us.

"Let her go," Thomas commands, and the man tightens his grip on me. I struggle. "Or else."

"Or else? Kelley, you know this girl is worth twenty-five

hundred dollars!? Do you know what we could do with twenty-five hundred dollars? All the people we could feed for the cost of this girl, alone?" I know Thomas knows, and I don't like him being reminded of what the going rate is for my return.

Thomas's eyes narrow at the man. "I'm not going to warn you again. *Let. Her. Go.*" He says through his teeth, and rather than being happy that he's come to my rescue, I'm just angry that he wasn't there in the first place. When the man doesn't release me, Thomas shoves him to the ground roughly, and his grip on me slips. I push myself to my feet and stand at alert, ready to run from both of them. Thomas stands over him. "Touch her again, and you'll have way worse to deal with." Thomas turns to me and puts a hand on my shoulder, which I shrug off. "Come with me," he says.

I start to argue, but I don't want the man on the ground to get me again, so I follow, practicing everything I'll say to him as soon as I'm safe again.

Thomas pushes through the blanket he uses as a door to separate his hut from the rest of Hooverville, and I follow him in. He sighs in frustration and stands straighter to look at me.

"That guy didn't hurt you, did he?" he asks, eyeballing the scratches on my arms, though I'm sure I did worse damage to him by clawing. "I was afraid this would happen."

"Where the *hell* were you? You promised you'd stay so that *this* wouldn't happen!"

"Right," he says, turning around to rummage through his bag. When he twists back around, he has two thick strips of paper between his fingers. "I might be overstepping my boundaries here, Annie, but I can't stand by and watch this.

You aren't any safer here than you were with Frank. Especially not with him looking for you. You could be going through all this and still end up going back to Frank at the end of it, and *then* what?" He moves his hands around as he speaks, running them through his hair every so often.

"I know that," I jump in quietly, not getting his meaning.

"You have this idea in your head that this book thing is just going to work out." At my expression, he quickly back-tracks to clarify. "I have no doubt that it will, but that could still be years before you see any profit, and that's *if* Hoover lets a publishing house in the country publish it."

I hadn't thought about the prospect of nobody publishing it, and it makes me my shoulders tense and a lump rise in my throat as I feel like I just might throw up.

"So, let me make this proposition to you before you have time to shut me up." Thomas pushes the papers in his fingers toward me, and I see a drawing of a train on each of them, along with a date and a time, and the word "California" on it. "I know we agreed that you would stay here, but things are different now," he says with a crooked smile.

I look back up at Thomas, hoping it isn't what it looks like.

"I think we should leave." Thomas looks hopeful, as if he's certain of my answer, and for a moment it seems like a realistic goal, but then my fantasy comes to a screeching halt and I realize what he's really asking of me. He speaks again before I have time to counter.

"Hooverville isn't safe. Not that it ever was, but now it feels different. It's like I have more on the line. Or something." He takes a nervous breath, biting the inside of his lip as he looks at me with hopeful eyes.

"You want us to run away and *abandon* Hooverville?" I finally say. My tone conveys my answer for me, and Thomas's shoulders drop.

"Well, *yeah*," he stammers. "This Frank guy isn't going to stop until he finds you, and I think he's closer than ever. You aren't safe here, and this just proves it. I think we should go West like you wanted to. We could make it. We could be happier there." His voice lingers on the word *we* as if it's an unspoken promise waiting for him in California. If I knew the people here would be safe, if everyone had homes and food in their bellies every night, if Hooverville didn't exist—I would say yes to his proposition in a moment. But I know that at the end of the day, people will still be starving and dying, and Thomas and I are the best hope they have. How can he not see this?

"I would have been safe if you didn't leave me for some romantic gesture without thinking it through."

"I did think it through! That's all I did all night, lay there and realize that if we don't leave, you're going to go back to him, and he's going to kill you." He paces back and forth while he speaks, messing his hair with his hands, like I don't understand the importance of this.

"And *what about* everyone here? We just leave them here to die?" My question rings like an accusation in the air, and Thomas stiffens at the thought of it. "Do you know what would happen if we weren't here? More people would die. More people would be robbed. More people would starve." I say we, but if *Thomas* wasn't here people would die. I haven't fed anybody or offered anyone anything, but I know I have the power to make change, and I just have to see it through.

"Annie." He sighs as if I'm too stupid to understand the gravity of this.

"What did you think I would say to a request like that?" I ask.

"I thought you'd say yes. I thought you'd care enough about yourself to listen to me for once." His voice cuts like a knife as his frustration grows to match my own. "You said yourself, you can be selfish when your life is on the line. And ours are."

The Thomas I know cares more about other people than anything else in the world, and I've tried to emulate that pattern in myself. Selfless Thomas made me a better person, and now he wants me to abandon all theseeople? It's as if he's suddenly been replaced by someone from *my* world. And I don't like it.

"I made that statement at a different time, before I knew anything. You can't keep holding that statement against me. It's void. I was wrong!"

"But you weren't wrong! You were right!"

"Well tonight, my life *was* on the line. And you left me. So, what does that make you?"

He falls quiet for a moment and he says, "I'm just trying to protect you from Frank. I know you're not safe as long as you're here, so while I was laying there, I thought it was safe enough. I had to do something."

"I didn't *ask* you to do that, Thomas. I asked you to stay with me because I felt safe, and now I can't trust you to do even that. You knew that I wanted to stay here, and you made a choice for me anyway. One that YOU felt was best for me. What about what I think is best for me?"

"I just want you safe."

"And I want to know that the people here are safe. You used to, too."

Tears well up in my eyes, and my voice thickens and cracks. "I am so sick of people making choices for me because they think they know what's best. That's why I left that life, Thomas. Because why the hell would I want people to live my life for me, while I just blindly agree to it? How do you think I ended up in that engagement in the first place, Thomas? I am done with other people making choices for me! And right now, my choice is to stay and finish this goddamned book that *you* asked me to write, before a cop comes and kills them or they starve to death."

Thomas avoids eye contact with me. His jaw tenses with anger, and he takes a long, deep breath before looking back at me. "So, when are you going to make *a choice* to take care of yourself?"

"I don't know. But whenever it is, I don't need *your help* with it."

"And Hooverville doesn't need *you* to protect it." Thomas shrugs. We're at a crossroads again, and it never gets any easier to be here. So rather than fighting anymore, I leave. A couple of people are awake now after all the shouting, loitering around. I wave at them to go back to bed, and I have to hope nobody else tries to take me tonight, because I don't have any more strength to fight them.

I lay on my blanket and let fat tears roll down my cheeks and into my ears until I'm dehydrated and stare up at the sheet metal of a ceiling. I dissociate for a while, lost in thought about nothing at all, but hazily coming to the conclusion that I'm doing the right thing by staying.

He bought me train tickets to California. He bought me a way to see the ocean, to be free from Frank. If I were a smart woman, I'd say to hell with Hooverville and run off and marry Thomas by the Pacific Ocean. I could wear a white dress and he could wear a suit, and I would say "I do" wholeheartedly. But now, even if I wanted to leave, Thomas wouldn't. No. I can't think about Thomas like that anymore. I have a responsibility to Hooverville, and I won't stop until this book gets published and reveals the truth. I remind myself of my plan, as hazy as it is these days: write the book about Hooverville, publish it, give the money to Arthur, change legislation, and get rid of all Hoovervilles.

When I put it like that, it does seem a bit ambitious. Fear fills me and leaves my heart beating irregularly. But what if, like Thomas said, it doesn't work? What if I'm throwing away a whole future where I could be happy and bargaining on one that isn't even guaranteed? What if the rich snobs of my world don't listen and nothing changes? I'd be doomed. Everything would be doomed. A deep part in my soul considers dropping this project right now and apologizing to Thomas, running away and escaping Frank like he wanted. But another, stronger part, knows that if I don't take this opportunity to make my change, I'll never forgive myself, and who knows how long it will be before there's another chance like this?

I pick up the diary again and continue writing about what I see, despite the bruises on my fingers, the cracked calluses, the ink smeared all up and down the side of my palm and even on my forehead. I press my eyebrows together, putting the pen to the paper feverishly and writing so quickly that I soon realize I've stopped breathing and the muscles in my arm begin to cramp. I straighten my back with a loud crack and shake my arm out to loosen it.

"Writing good stuff there?" Eva asks as she takes a seat beside me. I hadn't noticed the sun come up, or life begin while I was working. "You're turning blue. Here." She hands me a cup of water and an open can of beans. "Take a break. You look like a crazy person."

I laugh weakly and hesitantly close the notebook, setting it at my feet. "Thanks." I take the food from her and relax the muscles in my back. Eva watches my face for a long time, seeing something in my expression I had hoped I could hide from everyone.

"Please talk to him," she says sadly. "Everybody knows he's the only thing makes you happy here."

"That's not true," I insist. "I'm perfectly happy."

"Are you, though?" She watches me closely, and when I don't answer, she says, "It doesn't make you any less of a woman to be happy in the presence of someone you love. This is an unhappy place, Annie. You've found something to be happy about. Embrace it. You and Thomas are both so stubborn and so fiercely loyal to the people you love. Love each other and let the other one love you in return." I don't know what to say in response, so Eva and I sit in silence and eat the beans.

XIV

The tensions in the town are high after the week we've had, but that doesn't stop a few of the older men from pulling out old instruments and playing music to brighten our spirits. I write that down, sitting far away from anybody else by the fire. All I've done the past few days is stress about the police officers and Frank and the wanted posters, and since that man tried to bring me to him, I've avoided most everyone around here. Except for a select few.

Thomas has been distant for a couple of days, leaving me even more alone than when I first arrived. Peter still talks to me sometimes. He tries not to be partial to either of us, but I wouldn't be upset if he took Thomas's side and ignored me completely. They were friends long before I ever came along. Eva is my closest friend here now, but something about her attitude makes me think she dislikes me.

I write so quickly about everything I've seen in the Hooverville that my hand slips and ink smears everywhere, smudging my entire page and leaving it completely illegible. That's the second time today. Enraged, I rip the whole page out of my diary and toss it into the fire, watching it burn like it soothes my soul. I can feel myself being irrationally angry, but I don't even care. A couple of shifty eyes glance at me, and I shoot daggers at them. They quickly look away.

A few groups dance to the music next to the fire, laughing and spinning. I clench my fist around my pen and grit my teeth together.

"Annaleise," Peter says as he approaches. "I could be wrong, but you look stressed."

"What gave it away?" I ask, my voice tense. He sits beside me and looks over my shoulder at my diary. I pull it away from him with big eyes.

"Worth a shot," he chuckles. He reaches his hand out and tries to grab the book from me, but I quickly pry it from his hands. I hug it to myself with a warning look, which he responds to with an eye roll. He holds out his hand again. I slowly hand my book over to him, cautious about what he wants. "And the pen," he says. I hand my pen over, and he sets both the book and the pen down on the ground, standing. "Come dance. You need to relax a little." He holds his hand out to me.

I'm suddenly hyper-aware of how tense my shoulders are, how tightly locked my arms are, and so I force myself to release the tension I carry and take Peter's hand.

The band plays a fast-paced folksy song. Peter puts one hand on my back and holds my other hand in his like a waltz, but instead of any actual dance that I've ever seen, we skip around the fire. He gallops like a horse and practically drags me with him, leaving me hopping to keep up. He changes the steps suddenly and without warning to be like a tango, and he spins me many times until I'm dizzy and giggling. Peter smiles big and continues spinning me until I nearly fall.

The song ends, and the band deliberates what to play next.

Peter helps stand me up, laughing himself. "There you are, Annaleise."

I stand up straight, catching my breath. I put a hand on his shoulder and laugh with Peter.

It feels good to be a madman occasionally. I've never known what that feels like until today. The band plays a slower song, and the couples around us start to sway. I drop my hand to avoid giving Peter the wrong impression, and I plan to go sit back down and finish writing in my new relaxed state.

"Thank you," I breathe to Peter. He looks over my shoulder at something in the distance, but his expression tells me it isn't something dangerous, so I turn around slowly. Thomas is slowly coming towards us, a cautious look on his face, but it softens into his trademark sideways grin when he sees me looking at him. I feel myself stiffen again. We haven't spoken since our fight a few days ago, but still, the sight of him makes me happy. *No. Don't be stupid, Annaleise.*

"Don't be pissed at him," Peter whispers in my ear. "He was just trying to help." I take a deep breath as Thomas comes face to face with us.

"May I have this dance?" Thomas asks, holding out his hand. Peter watches me, nodding as if he can control my head movements. I sigh and reach for Thomas's hand. Thomas seems to relax at my touch because his shoulders drop and a small smile forms on his face. Peter backs away from us, and Thomas puts both his hands on my waist. I jump slightly at the tickle, and he smirks at me. He holds his arms straight out in front of him, keeping me a safe distance from him, and he steps side to side awkwardly like he's trying to mimic a dance he maybe saw in a film once.

It's an obvious attempt at a dance from my world, which makes me smile, but I have to put an end to his misery.

"No, stop," I say, restraining the laugh that wants to bubble up. His face falls as I move his hands. "*Like this.*" I take a step closer so we're pressed together. My hands wrap around his neck, and his go around my waist. We sway and spin in circles, but not like the circles Peter and I spun in. More natural, like we spin with the earth's axis.

"Annie, I want to apologize to you for—" He pauses and considers what he's sorry for. "For everything, really. For going behind your back. For ignoring you these past few days. For making you dance with Peter." He throws in the last one as a joke, to ease both of our discomforts. "He's a horrible dancer."

"Well, he's no worse than you, I'm afraid," I say. Thomas chuckles, but not like usual. We're still distant. "I appreciate that you tried to help me, I do. But I can't leave in good conscious knowing all of this is happening. Not if there's something I can do about it."

"I understand," he says quietly.

"I have no doubt you could save everyone here if you tried, Thomas. But to change the minds of the upper classes? That's going to have to come from someone who is technically one of them."

"You're not one of them," Thomas says matter-of-factly. "You're one of us now." He motions around at everyone dancing, including Eva and Peter who skip around the fire arm-in-arm, laughing their heads off.

"Is Peter's dancing some sort of initiation ritual?" I tease.

"That's exactly what it is. Congratulations, you passed." Thomas chuckles and looks back at my face. "So, are we okay?"

"We're okay," I smile at him, and we sway. "I'm getting dizzy, though."

"Me too," Thomas says, but neither of us stops spinning.

I lay my head on his chest and find comfort in his arms, and I imagine a future without Hoovervilles, without Frank. I know it isn't realistic. I can't be free of both. But for tonight, I let that be my reality. There's no Frank, there's no Hooverville. There's just me and Thomas, and Eva and Peter, and acting like fools because nobody can tell us no.

XV

Eva and I tear down the last bit of the wall from Clara's shack and begin breaking down the boards. It was unanimously decided that her hut would be turned into a memorial of sorts since she wouldn't get a real grave. It was Thomas's idea to build a Hooverville Memorial for the first woman to live here, but Eva and I were the two most emotionally equipped to handle it. So, the plan is to break down the boards and turn one into a sort of headstone, so Eva can carve Clara's information into it as a standing reminder of her presence. Clara's writing with her name and her declaration of peace sits beside us, ready to take its place at the base of her headstone. Then everyone is going to walk around the Hooverville for a moment of silence and admire her sunchimes.

I can't take credit for any of it. Eva spent hours planning for this to be perfect. She doesn't act sad, but I know she is. She's just one of those people that prefers to stay busy, so she doesn't think about her sadness. My mother was the same way. For the first time since coming here, I miss my mother, and I never thought I'd ever say that. As hard as I try, I can't remember the bad stuff. Only the good parts of her. It makes it impossible to stay angry at her.

Starting when I woke up this morning, every time I breathe, a high-pitched wheezing sound comes from my lungs and a painful sensation fills my chest. I wouldn't breathe so hard or loudly if I wasn't so winded, but my arms and legs feel weak, like they could collapse under me at any moment.

"Are you okay, Annie?" Eva asks in her crisp accent, breaking down the boards. She stops what she's doing and looks up at me, a concerned look on her face.

"I'm fine. I guess the air is just dry this week or something," I lie with a hoarse voice.

Eva frowns and looks at the ground. I can tell she doesn't want to start trouble or be dramatic, so she carefully says, "You've been coughing for days, Annie."

I set down the board and think of my Pa when he first started getting ill, and how he claimed it was *just a cough* so as not to worry me. Before he was properly diagnosed, he stopped eating. He was so weak that he couldn't even lift a cup of coffee to his lips. He slept all day long and wanted to do nothing more than sleep. At the height of his illness, he hallucinated and shrieked madly at the doctors and nurses who tried to help him. He saw faces in the ceiling that weren't there and vomited anything he ate.

My only memory from the day he died is standing in the doorway while he choked on his own blood and fought at the doctors and nurses who tried to save him. He begged them to let him die; he pleaded with them and was an unrecognizable monster. Mother eventually pulled me away and locked me in a room with Virginia until his screams died down and my mother's got louder. Those screams of my parents have haunted me every day of my life.

"I'm fine," I say tonelessly and avert my eyes from her. I remember Clara, and the days I spent in such proximity to her prior to her death. I shake the thought away. She didn't get me ill because I'm not ill, I tell myself. I attempt to avoid coughing so nobody worries.

Eva and I finish up the headstone and sand it down with a scrap of sandpaper that hardly works anymore. Eva carves Clara's name and dedication into it. She crafts meticulously, leaning in close, biting her tongue to get every little detail right. It's an honor and even intimate to see an artist at work. I'm not sure I could ever care about anything so much as to make it beautiful, but Eva does it with ease. She carves intricate drawings of flowers in the bottom corners of the drawing and sands them down so they stand out against the dark wood. It takes no more than twenty minutes before she leans back and admires her work, then smiles at me.

In the center reads *Ms. Clara Sullivan, April 30th, 1852 - June 21st, 1932.* I reach out and touch Eva's careful work in disbelief. Then, directly below Clara's name, in a near perfect replica of her handwriting, reads, "*I am happy.*" Eva watches me for a reaction, biting her lip.

I wipe tears from my cheeks, my heart warm. "Eva, this is beautiful. Where did you learn to do this?" I ask her as I stand and admire it from afar.

"My dad." She smiles. "He was a woodworker. I picked up on it from watching him." Her voice trails off into a familiar one of nostalgia and loss, something I completely understand.

I lean into her and give her a one-armed hug. "I think our dads would both be proud of us," I say. She smiles sadly.

"My dad isn't dead," she explains cautiously, pulling her arm from around me.

"Oh, I'm sorry. The way you said that sounded like he had..." I stammer.

"I'm dead to them," she says. Her voice lulls, and her body shifts as if the memory is stabbing her over and over again. When I say nothing, she continues. "My family still has a home. I have two younger sisters and a mother and a dog..." She sounds as though she might cry. "But... they kicked me out. A year ago."

I frown deeply and take a step closer to her. What had she done that could make her family stop loving her? Surely a person as nice as Eva couldn't do anything wrong under the sun, and no decent parents would throw their daughter out if they ever really loved her. Here I am, running away from a family who loves me, and all she wants is one who does.

"Why?" I breathe. "If that's not a rude question."

Eva's silent for a long time, more vulnerable than I've ever seen her. She shrinks in size and wipes at a single tear down her cheek. "I don't want you to think differently of me," she chokes, her voice breaking. I begin to get scared of whatever it is she could tell me.

"Of course I wouldn't think differently of you." It isn't the complete truth. If she's murdered someone in cold blood and is living on the run, that would change my opinion of her. But I'm too intrigued now to let her go off without knowing what she did. It must have been awful, and I want to know every detail. I sit down on one of the logs and pat the seat next to me. Eva cries into her hands for a moment, then pulls herself together. It's the first time I've ever seen her look not pretty.

"I—" She hiccups and takes a deep breath before she says steadily, "I met somebody."

I understand immediately. "Your parents didn't approve of him?" I ask. Her face scrunches up, and she hides her face in her hands.

"No, it's not like that," she whispers. "They didn't approve of *her*."

It takes me a moment to comprehend what she's saying, and when I do, it shakes me to my core. I've heard of homosexuality, mostly in passing, or when Mother wants to insult somebody for being stupid, but to witness it is different and makes me guilty for any time I may have taken part in Mother's ridiculing. Eva looks at me for a reaction, so I'm careful to not change my expression to anything other than love and tenderness. I nudge for her to go on, and she spills everything.

She met a girl named Rose Calhoun in school several years ago, and while they both tried dating boys, it didn't work out for either of them. About a year and a half ago, Eva said she was afraid she might not like boys at all, but that she thought she was in love with Rose instead. Rose agreed with her and they started a hidden relationship. Her parents saw that she'd been happier and kept asking and asking her who the lucky boy was. Rose didn't want their parents to know and begged to introduce them to fake boyfriends, but Eva said she didn't want to live in secret. Eva told both of their parents over a rather messy lunch, and the next day Rose and her family moved to California without warning, and Eva's family kicked her out onto the street and told her to never return.

So, she walked until she collapsed in the street and was eventually found and brought to the Hooverville.

When she finishes, she lets out a breath and her tears stop falling. Finally, she looks at me.

"Do you hate me?" she asks meekly.

"Eva, of course I don't," I tell her. "I could never hate you." She sniffles and focuses on her breathing. "Does anyone else know?" I ask.

She shakes her head. "I couldn't deal with the reaction after what my parents did. It's too embarrassing. I think I'll just become a spinster or marry someone I don't even like just to make people happy so I can stop feeling like I'm a burden to society."

"Don't do that," I blurt out. "Don't. You don't want to marry somebody you hate."

She gives me a look, and then it's my turn to spill my secret. When I finish telling her about Frank and my mother, she laughs through her tears.

"So, it isn't easy for anybody, I guess," she cries.

"Not us," I laugh. "But I think there are bigger things to worry about than who falls in love with whom. At the end of the day, it doesn't matter how stupid we look, as long as we're happy and with who we love." I cough into my elbow when I finish speaking, and Eva smiles at me. We stay silent for a while, feeling less alone in our loneliness.

We eventually remember to stand and put Clara's headstone in the ground, and I set one of the flowers that Thomas brought to me at the base. We kiss our fingers and touch the headstone, then step back to give others the chance to say their goodbyes.

Thomas and Peter approach when a crowd forms. Peter has a bag in his hands and the knife he used on my first night tucked into his belt loop. He wears a massive smile across his face, while Thomas looks troubled. He stands by my side and wraps an arm around my shoulders.

"Are you alright?" I ask him quietly. Thomas purses his lips and motions to Peter.

"I'm *out of here!*" Peter says joyously. Eva and I frown in confusion. "I'm going to Washington!"

"Why would you ever go to Washington?" Eva grumps. "There's nothing there but corrupt politicians and monuments congratulating themselves for existing."

"No, that's exactly why I'm going!" Peter exclaims. We stare at him, not understanding.

Thomas speaks up for him. "Peter is going to join the Bonus Army. There's a rally in D.C. in a couple of weeks. Thousands of veterans and their families are going to ask for their bonuses."

The mood shifts between Eva, Thomas, and I as we face Peter. Peter's joy is clear on his face, but how could he leave us like this?

Eva speaks first. "You're kidding." Her voice is dry, almost angry.

"Of course not, Eva." Peter frowns. "There's nothing here for me in Hooverville. They're staying in a Hooverville in D.C. too! You know? Maybe I'll meet a nice girl. Maybe we can talk some sense into Hoover. Get him to figure himself out so none of us have to live in a Hooverville anymore!"

Neither Eva nor Thomas speaks, so I step forward and take

Peter into my arms, hugging him. "I support you," I mumble. Peter smiles and hugs me tighter.

"Thank you, Annaleise."

"Just promise us you'll be careful, and if there's trouble, you get yourself out. They won't hesitate to arrest you." I straighten his jacket and give him a kiss on the cheek. He looks at Eva and Thomas.

"I don't want to leave without your support, but it would kill me to stay," Peter explains. Eva and Thomas look at each other, then Eva steps toward him and hugs him. She whispers something in his ear that makes him laugh and call her a bitch. Eva steps away from him and wipes at a residual tear, careful to not let anyone else see.

Peter turns to Thomas. They stare in silence, and Thomas holds out his hand to shake.

"I'm going to miss you, brother," Thomas says, a nervous edge to his voice. Peter ignores his hand and goes straight for the hug, and they hug tighter than he hugged either Eva or me.

Thomas's back tenses, and I can feel his pain—in my back, in my arms, in my lungs. It's one of the worst pains I've ever felt, and it isn't even mine. I turn away from him in the hopes that if I don't look, it won't hurt so bad. Thomas and Peter open their arms to let Eva and me in.

We form a circle with our arms around each other and our heads touching, not a single dry eye in the circle. We laugh at how pathetic we must look, and I try to think of a way to never break our circle. I've never had a friendship like this one. I'd give anything to keep love like this forever.

"You're my best friends," Peter says. "I love you all."

It's met with a chorus of "I love you" from Thomas, Eva, and I, and Peter finally breaks out of the circle.

"I'm off!" he exclaims and saunters toward the exit. He doesn't stop to look back at us, and he doesn't say anything else as he leaves Hooverville. Eva and I put our heads on each other's shoulder, but my eyes shift to Thomas, who is barely holding it together.

"He'll be fine," I whisper, and the sick, weak feeling overcomes me again. Eva watches me closely, and I know by the look on her face that she suspects the same fear I have. I shoot her a look that communicates, *don't say anything*, and Eva looks away from us.

Hooverville is quiet without Peter to entertain everyone. There's hardly any music or dancing, though Thomas and I still try and dance together every night. Though he doesn't say it, I know it kills him the longer he stays here without Peter or Clara, and I feel guilty that I'm the only reason he's staying.

I wish he would take the tickets and go see the world, but it would be unbearable to be here without him.

Since Peter left a few days ago, Eva has been taking over his role around the Hooverville, coordinating the food donations from the grocery stores and hospitals, but she isn't quite as charming as Peter was, so the donations are lacking. Thomas tried his hand at asking for donations, but nobody even gave him a second look.

When the depression first started, a lot of people in my world actually did donate canned goods toward the cause, but that one-time donation didn't last long, and people like Frank and Betty complained about how they "*never stop asking! Can't they appreciate what they have?*"

I can no longer deny how sick I am, but at this point, I don't even think there's anything that can be done about it. I decide not to tell Thomas. It would be too painful for him.

My shoulders feel as though there's a wooden blank stuck between them. Every breath I take feels like my lungs fill with water. My eyelids are heavy all the time. My skin has turned green. For the first time, I understand how my father felt before he died. No matter how exhausted I am, it feels as though I'm a string puppet for the devil to play with, and if he sees me lowering my head, he yanks me back awake.

This week, two other people got sick, one of them a baby, and since there was nothing we could do and no hospital that would take them in, Eva and I sat and comforted them until they died. The band doesn't play music anymore. The bonfire has been burnt out for days, and I've managed to keep Thomas from seeing how sick I've become, too. When it first started, I told him I must have been allergic to something, and then it was that I'd breathed in smoke and couldn't stop coughing. Then I ran out of excuses and just hid from him entirely. I can't hold my own head up. I can't even hold a pencil anymore to write. My hands tremble badly and I'm not strong enough to keep it upright. I don't sleep because of fever nightmares and delirium. One night I lay awake and hallucinate Frank finding me, but I don't move. I just lay there.

I wrap my blanket around myself, but it doesn't stop my whole body from shivering, or my teeth from chattering. I've done my best to prevent Thomas from seeing me like this, but with how horrible I feel, I could die and not even care. I'd let Eva build me a beautiful headstone; I'd let everyone forget about the book. I don't even care anymore.

When Eva finds me, I must look mad. I'm weeping and sweating and partially delirious from lack of sleep. She brings a cool rag to try and lower my fever, but the minute it touches my skin, I hiss at her and pull myself away.

"Annie, please. You have to let me try and help you," Eva pleads, holding me still by the shoulder and forcing me down so that she can rub my face with the rag. I sob, coughing, and spinning my head.

"Just let me die, I don't care. Just let me die," I cry like a child.

"No, stupid," Eva declares, and I'm too weak to put up a fight. "Try and eat something."

"I don't want to eat!" I snarl like an angry cat. Eva leans back and looks at me with angry eyebrows.

"Do you want me to tell Thomas?" she asks firmly. I cover my face and cry into my hands. "That's what I thought. Just eat two bites of bread. An apple. Soup. Anything." I lay back and look at the roof of my hut, and nod weakly. Eva disappears for a while and returns with a crust of bread and kneels beside me. It takes like lead as I try to force myself to swallow it. Her eyes soften as I finish it and she says, "Thomas needs to know. He cares about you, and he will know what to do."

I think of myself at nine years old, hiding in the doorway of my father's deathbed. Watching him die. Watching him go mad with sickness. I couldn't do that to Thomas. Not after he's just lost Clara and Peter so close together. I blink slowly, too exhausted to speak, and just roll over onto my side.

I fall deep into a dreamless sleep but awaken with cold sweats and the feeling that I can't breathe as the world collapses around me. It's barely dawn outside, and the air is crisp and birds in the park chirp. I flutter open my eyes and see Thomas sitting above me, with his head propped up against the back of my wall and his hand holding my own. He sleeps with his mouth slightly open and a disturbed pinch to his eyebrows. I watch his face for a moment and feel the same intense pain I did when my father died. Only now, I'm the one hurting Thomas. I shut my eyes tight and let tears fall down my cheeks, and I pray to God to take me peacefully and quietly, so nobody gets hurt.

I mouth his name, but my voice is gone. I clear my throat to get my voice back and feel my mouth fill with the unmistakable taste of blood. My hands tremble as I realize this is the final stage before madness and death. I lean over and spit out the blood beside me, but my movement wakes Thomas, and he sees enough for his face to turn sheet white and his mouth to go dry.

"Annie," he whispers. "Annie, we have to take you to the hospital."

"No!" I say quickly, a bit of blood still in my mouth and on my bottom lip. "No hospitals." I'm too weak to put the edge I would like to into my voice, but I can't go to a hospital.

"Look, I'm sorry Annie, but we don't exactly have a choice here."

"I have the choice," I grunt. "Please, please, don't take me to the hospital. Just let me die here. Please." I'm crying again, and I must look pathetic.

Thomas reaches out and touches my cheek with the backs of his fingers. His touch hurts my skin, despite his gentleness. His face scrunches up, and I feel his pain again the same way I did when Peter left. "I can't let you die, Annie; you know that.

And if you won't do it for yourself, do it for the rest of people in Hooverville. You don't want to get them sick."

My face turns angry at his manipulation tactic. I recognize it immediately, but when I take a deep breath to argue with him, it's met with a cough and bloody sputum. I cough and choke on my own blood. It tastes like I've accidentally swallowed a big gulp of seawater when trying to go under. It feels my nose and makes my eyes water. I gag and vomit beside me, and slump over exhaustedly.

I've completely forgotten Thomas's presence when he wraps his arms around me and easily lifts me from my bed.

"Oh my God," he breathes when he feels how light I've become in the past two weeks or so. He puts a hand on my forehead and grabs my blankets, carrying me out of my hut.

Lights. Cold air. Birds. Clouds. Eva's here. She's sad. She's angry. They shout at each other, but it comes out as muffled distortions of real sound. Thomas's body is warm, so I tuck myself closer and try to go to sleep, but then he's moving quickly and the world bounces underneath his feet. I stare up at the sky and watch the trees float through my vision and make pictures in the clouds. I cough again into my elbow, a mix of mucus and blood erupting and resting on my shirt.

Suddenly, I realize where Thomas is bringing me, and I use all my energy to fight against him. It starts as a weak, "No," mumbled into his shirt, and then I manage to force my muscles to move. I reach up and try to push myself away from his chest. I kick my legs and thrash my head back and forth. I accidentally head butt him in the chin, and I hear his teeth click together against the force with which I hit him. He holds onto me tighter, like he's trying to tame a wild animal. I twist myself and shriek "NO!" as loudly as I can muster. I claw at his neck and weep into his shirt.

"No, Thomas, no. No, please!"

He stops running and uses all his force to hug me to him. "Stop!" he shouts, holding me tighter than he ever has before. "You aren't going to die! *I won't let you!*" I try to pull away from him once again, but he presses his face into my shoulder and holds me for what I suspect is the very last time. He looks at my face again. "Everything will be okay. *Trust me.*"

I want to yell at him again, but I don't have the energy. He begins running again, and I watch the city buildings fill my peripheral vision of the sky. My head lulls onto Thomas's shoulder and I try to stay awake as my vision is met with bright lights and yelling. They lay me down on a bed in the middle of the room, and faces look down on me, speaking words in that warbled tone. They shine lights in my eyes, and I let myself follow the blinding light down a long winding road straight into sleep.

XVI

〜⚜〜

I know I'm in a hospital before I open my eyes because of the softness of the bed. After weeks of sleeping on the ground, it's almost too comfortable. I see the bright lights between my eyelashes. I try to force myself back to sleep so I don't have to deal with what happens next, but my luck won't let me do that. I slowly open my eyes and take in my surroundings. I'm in a large room with about twenty beds and even more windows to let in the sunlight. Every single bed is empty and made. On my left side, there is a large vase of flowers, and at my knee, Thomas is resting his head on the bed, sleeping.

I try to bend my arm but wince with a sharp poking pain. I look down and see an IV pumping extra fluids, and likely medication, into me, making my veins feel funny. A nurse passing by me with extra bedsheets in her arms sees that I'm awake and gasps, nearly throwing the sheets up in the air. I guess I look as bad as I feel.

"You're awake!" she exclaims, waking Thomas with her loud voice. He sits his head up and looks at the nurse, then at me. He gasps, coming closer to me with a look in his eyes that I can't determine is happiness, sadness, or both. He lets out a sad laugh, his shoulders dropping like when he relaxes. The nurse checks my temperature with her forearm, then sticks a thermometer under my tongue rather forcefully. Thomas watches the exchange hopefully and lets out a happy breath when the nurse says, "You've gone down three degrees!"

"Do you want to sit up, Miss Winston?" asks a second nurse I hadn't noticed on my right side. The name makes my heart rate rise as my worst fear is realized. I stay silent, worried that if I open my mouth, I'll either start screaming or crying. I tighten my jaw like I've wired it shut and look at a spot on the floor. The nurse goes ahead and begins moving my bed into a sitting position.

"I'll go get you a pot of soup, Miss Winston," a nurse says once she notices I'm up. They both leave, leaving Thomas and me together, but it no longer brings me the sense of comfort that he used to.

"Annie," Thomas breathes. He leans forward and tries to take my hand, but I pry my hand from him and shoot him a look that doesn't convey half of the things I want to say to him.

His face falls, and he tries again to take my hand.

"Don't touch me!" I spit with more fury than I knew I had in me. I pull my hand away from him and hold it close to me, flexing it.

He sits back in shock at my reaction and opens his mouth wordlessly. He has the saddest look on his face, but I can't muster enough empathy to feel sorry for him. All I see when I look at him is a man who turned me in. He's no better than those men that attacked me to get the prize money. I hate him. If I had the strength left in me, I would tear him to pieces, but I'm forced to lie there like a vegetable, without the willpower to fight.

"Annie," he repeats, "I'm sorry, but I couldn't sit there and watch you die." As if he ever cared. I watch a shiny spot on the floor, inspecting the dirt particles. "Annie, will you please just look at me?" he pleads. I slowly turn my eyes to him, shooting fire at him. "You got worse. I didn't have a choice."

"You should have let me *die* instead of turning me in." My voice is flat, emotionless, and dry. He looks like he's fighting tears himself.

"You know why I couldn't do that, Annie," he whispers. Clara comes to mind, and I know he couldn't handle something like that again. "Get healthy. Get the best care." He places one ticket in my hand, and then kisses my knuckles, wary enough to know that I can and will punch him. "And then meet me in California."

The idea of it still makes my heart yearn, now more than ever. I should have gone with him when he asked. But he shouldn't have turned me in, and he knows that. He drops my hand, watching me hopefully for my answer. I try to imagine the future with him on the beach in California, but all I see now is a snake-like creature wearing Thomas's skin, and it makes my skin writhe and my chest ache. The ache makes its way into my shoulders and stomach, and hurts every nerve in my body, worse than any bruise Frank has ever given me.

"Do you know what I see when I look at you, Thomas?" He braces himself for whatever hurtful thing I'm about to say. "Nothing. I look at you, and whatever good things I previously thought of you are gone. I see someone who wants to act like a hero by any means necessary, but in reality, you're a coward. I look at you and see someone who wants to be some-body."

"Annie," Thomas whispers, and I know I'm cutting him deep.

"You can pretend like you know what's best for me, but you've known me for a month and a half. You don't get to make decisions for me just to make yourself feel better about having nobody else to save in your life." I'm not even sure which parts I mean and don't mean. I stutter over my words because of how angry I am. I don't have much time to think about what I say, or how many lines it crosses.

"Annie, I'm sorry," he pleads. "I know what I did was wrong, but I think you'll one day learn to forgive me once you get over the anger. I only saved your life. I only sold my belongings to get you a one-way ticket out of this town. I'm sorry if that's not what you wanted, but I can't say I think I was wrong. Do you know how much it would have hurt me if you'd died?"

"I don't care if you get hurt. How do you think I feel right now? You said you'd protect me. You're a liar, and I don't want to be in the same city as you, let alone the same room."

"Annie, would you please stop? You don't mean any of this. You're angry with me, I know."

"What gave it away?" I suddenly shout. "If I didn't feel like shit, I would rip you to pieces. That's how angry I am with you, Thomas." He sighs quietly and looks at the bed, and there's silence for a long time. Neither of us knows how to talk to the other in this state, and this is uncharted territory for us. Once I regain my composure, I run the next words over and over again in my head before I say them, debating whether to give him the last bullet. I do.

"This is different than buying me tickets without asking. This is unforgivable," I say flatly, watching him closely. He takes it in but doesn't react or beg from me anymore. He rubs his palms on his knees and avoids eye contact.

He swallows a lump in his throat and stands. "Very well." He takes one final look at me and says, "I really am sorry." Then he leaves.

As soon as he's out of the room, I regret saying it. I regret saying all of it. But I don't have the energy to deal with it. The morphine pulls me back into my sleep, and the world collapses around me.

My dreams are all about Thomas, with some about Frank. Thomas and I on a train to California, but the train crashes into a wall. Another one of me drowning and only Frank is around to help me, but he ties an anchor to me, and I sink to the bottom of the sea. The Hooverville burning down. Faceless men kidnapping me and then turning into Thomas. The fever must elevate the horror of my dreams, because every dream transitions into another horrific one, and I wake crying, reaching my fingers out to the empty bed.

The nurse returns and ups my morphine dosage once she sees my tears. "There, there." She brushes my hair from my face. "Your fiancé will be here soon. He'll help your pain go away."

"Fiancé?" I murmur. For a moment I hope my words to Thomas were only a dream. I hope that all of this has been just a bad dream and that my fiancé is the person I really want beside me right now.

"Mr. Alexander. He is your fiancé, isn't he?" She laughs softly and runs a damp rag over my forehead, making me shiver. "Your fever is still high. He was out of town on business, but he's getting on the first train he can and coming straight here." She leaves me alone. As the sun goes down, I watch out the windows at the city lights as they go from dark to light, but it isn't nearly as beautiful from here. I wonder where Thomas is and if he's watching them too.

I spend most of the night alone, and the nurses only come in when I start vomiting again to make sure I don't choke and die. After the third or fourth time, I become delirious and don't even really notice anymore. The nurses talk about me in front of me, but I can hardly keep my eyes open long enough to listen, and my head lulls back and forth. At one point I feel an icy hand on my cheek, but I don't open my eyes to see who it is, and my hearing becomes warped in my delirious state. Some part of me tells me it's my Pa coming to visit me, but I know that's not logical.

Frank makes an entrance the next morning, barging onto the hospital floor, shouting, "Where is she?!" My mother trails close behind him, looking like a mouse. I try to lull myself back into sleep, so I don't have to speak with him yet, but as soon as they see me, my mother throws her arms around me. I stiffen and don't move to hug her back. Frank stands behind her with an eager smile on his face, and I wonder where he thinks I've been for these last weeks.

My mother pulls back and looks at my face. "Oh, my girl!" She puts a hand on my forehead and feels my fever, then turns to the nurses. "Exactly where did you find her? How did she end up in this condition?" she shouts at the nurses. I hold up a single hand to tell her to quiet her voice, as it's giving me a headache.

"We don't know. The young man who brought her in wouldn't say where she's been," the head nurse tells them, turning up my morphine.

"A young man turned her in?" Frank repeats, shooting me a suspicious look. "Who *is* this young man?"

My head lulls back onto the pillow, then I lean over the side of my bed to the pot on the floor beneath me. I vomit again, though I'm not sure this is because of the illness. Frank covers his nose and mouth disgustedly with a handkerchief and pulls the nurse aside to speak with her privately. I lean back in bed and watch my mother with a flat stare on my face. I'm not sure if she sympathizes with me, but she doesn't immediately start scolding me for my matted hair or my un-maintained fingernails. She acts like a proper mother for a moment. It isn't enough to make me happy to go home, but it's enough that I don't want to claw at her.

"We're so happy to see you finally, Annaleise. We've been so worried about you." Mother runs a hand over my cheek, ex-amining the scratches on my face, and I twist away from her. "What happened to you?" I'm not sure if she's asking about the scratches or where I've been, but it doesn't matter because I don't respond.

"She seems to be in a bit of shock at the moment," the nurse suggests, to my relief. I'll have at least until the fever breaks to come up with a story. The nurse and Frank discuss the young man who brought me in, and I'm suddenly filled with a deep rage about Thomas again, specifically about the fact that he left me with Frank and my mother. He dropped

me here, and he left. For someone who cares a lot about protecting me, he sure doesn't care about my safety.

Over the next two days, I'm kept on a constant flow of
painkillers and sedatives until my fever breaks. Frank has vis-
itors in and out of the hospital to visit me, but most of them
I don't know. Betty and Johnny come by and drop off flowers.
They stay for several hours. Betty talks my ear off about everything under the sun and doesn't particularly care about me
not responding to anything she says. Johnny is the one who
convinces her to leave so I can rest, and I consider breaking
my silence to thank him, but they're gone before I can. My
room fills with more flowers than I can count, and Mother
brings in several of my old outfits to choose from when I finally leave the hospital.

By the end of the third day, my fever breaks, and I'm able
to keep down food without vomiting. They question why I
don't speak, but they don't push me. Mother declares that
we'll be hosting a welcome home party in my honor and
climbs behind me to comb through my hair and start practicing styles with it, occasionally muttering things like, "This
could be cute" or "No, that's not good enough."

The following day, I get another visitor. Thomas comes in
with my backpack of belongings from Hooverville and peeks
his head in, looking afraid. My heart lifts at the sight of him,
and any anger I previously had with him melts away instantly.
His eyes widen when he sees all the flowers. "Can I come
in?" he asks quietly. Frank looks up from his newspaper and
stands, each step firmly planted on the ground, and his shoulders sashaying as he walks.

"And who are *you*, exactly?" He looks Thomas up and down, squinting at his dirty clothes and self.

"Uhm." Thomas looks at me, then back at Frank. "Thomas. Thomas Kelley."

Frank lights up unexpectedly. "Thomas! You must be the lad that brought her in!" *Brought her in* like I'm a prisoner going to jail. Thomas swallows a lump in his throat and nods. I try to hide a smile. It would only give me away.

"Yeah, that was me. I just came to see how she is. But I can see that she's doing much better, so I'll just be on my way." He pauses for a moment, trying to figure out how to get my backpack to me without Frank noticing. I give him the tiniest shake of my head, and he purses his lips, turning to leave.

"Wait," Frank says. "As promised, you will get a reward for her safe return. Is there somewhere I should mail it to?"

"Oh, no, I can't accept that," Thomas insists.

"Nonsense. A promise is a promise." Frank pulls out his checkbook and a pen from his chest pocket and writes the grand total of dollars. I have never felt quite so literally like an item for purchase but seeing the cash exchange before my very eyes only proves it to me. Thomas glances at me with hesitation, and it takes only one look at me to refuse Frank's offer.

"I don't care about money," Thomas says, putting one hand up. Frank laughs in Thomas's face and turns to me in disbelief, as if saying *where did you find this guy?* He takes Thomas's hand, puts the check in his palm, and closes his hand around it.

"Perhaps you ought to start," Frank says like he's offering wise advice. He winks at him and clicks his tongue. "Money makes the world go round, my boy!"

"Well, it might, but you can't bring money to the grave with you, and that's where we're all headed anyway," Thomas shrugs. I try to stare at him into shutting up, but he doesn't.

"Fine then," Frank says frustratedly, then stares him down a moment too long. "Was there something you *wanted*, Mr. Kelley?"

Thomas falters and looks at me, then back straight ahead. "I just wanted to see how she was."

"Great, well, you can see she's fine. Now if you wouldn't mind, me and my fiancé would appreciate some privacy." Frank speaks so quickly that by the time it reaches Thomas's ears, he can only stammer a pathetic, "Yes," before he turns and leaves with my backpack of belongings.

I watch the space Thomas left behind and desperately want to follow him, or I want him to come back and steal me away. But he doesn't, and I'll doubt I'll ever see him again. My eyes roll toward Frank, who shouts at some undeserving nurse.

After knowing the kindness of Thomas, there is no way I could ever go back to Frank. I don't even care about the book anymore. Thomas is right. I deserve to be selfish.

XVII

❧

T he next days are a blur that seems long while
I'm in them, but suddenly it's the weekend and
the hospital is releasing me. Thomas left days ago and hasn't
been back to visit, but Frank says he'd like to have him for
dinner. I tried to convince him not to, but Frank said I was
being "incredibly rude" and "projecting a bad image of myself"
onto the lower class. Mother hasn't left my side even for a moment, which made silences awkward. Mother had nothing to
say to me and I had nothing to say to her, and since I couldn't
leave and she was too stubborn to, we sit in uncomfortable
silence for the better part of four days until Frank shows up
and at least forms a conversation with her.

Three doctors work to sit me up in my bed, and they help
me get re-dressed in clothes that feel too fancy for me anymore, while Mother pulls and twists my matted hair into
something decent enough for walking outside for the fifteen
seconds it'll take me to get from the hospital doors to the car.

I push myself to my feet too quickly and suddenly become
dizzy and weak, and the doctors have to catch me to keep me
from falling onto the floor. They lower me back to a sitting
position while my head clears, and they check my eyes. They
turn to Frank and instruct him, "Make sure she eats a good

meal to make up for her lack of protein. Keep an eye on her."
Frank nods and thanks the doctors politely, then wraps an
arm around me to help lift me again and walk with me leaning on him.

We take the steps down the four flights to the main level,
but Frank seems to forget how weak I am because he tries to
walk too quickly, and I nearly fall down the steps. After that,
he acts inconvenienced by the fact that he must walk slower
to keep pace with me and prevent me from falling on my skull
and dying. We eventually reach the bottom level and are out
the front door where dozens, if not scores, of photographers
crane to get a glimpse of me after the weeks I've been missing.
Every time a camera flashes, I only see Thomas's face in the
blank space left by my eyes. I hide my face from the flashes
and eventually, I'm ushered into a car.

An intense heat comes to the back of my nose and eyes
that I know to be tears trying to come out, but I won't let
them. Not here, not now. Frank smiles at the cameras and
gives a brief interview while Mother walks around the back
of the car and climbs in. Then Frank follows.

"Take us home, mate," Frank orders the driver, and the car
moves. I slump down in my seat and hide my face from the
photographers, but I feel my mother's eyes burning into the
back of my scalp. I turn my head and look at her.

"What?" I ask, more like an accusation than a question.

"I was just wondering where you learned such atrocious
manners, that's all."

I squint my eyes at her and slump down further in the seat.
"Are you going to do something about it?" I ask her. Her expression turns from some sour mix of disdain and disgust to

full-on fury. But she does nothing. She turns up her nose and faces forward once again. I smirk to myself and sit up straight again. "That's what I thought."

"You'd better be careful, Annaleise," Mother says.

"Enough, ladies," Frank says casually. "This is a happy time. I don't want to fight." From the corner of my eye, I see Mother scowling at me with every fiber of her being. The energy in the car turns dark, yet I'm too proud to let it affect me. I may not have had a say in when I could come home, but I have a say in how I act at home. I don't have to be her puppet. I don't have to act any certain way. It may end with Frank killing me, but at least then I'll be out of my misery. Again, Thomas's face comes to my mind and my joy at outsmarting my mother fades to longing. I miss him, as much as it pains me to admit. Still, if he arrived, I'm not sure anything would be the same. I can't be with him as the person I am in this life. There's no scenario anymore where I leave this life and live a whole new one with Thomas. I have to let him go.

We pull up to my family's mansion. The yard is overgrown, likely since the staff was so busy looking for me to take proper care of the household. The paint looks extraordinarily white in the blistering July sun and wiggles of heat radiate off the roof. I stand and squint up at the house and my bedroom window, where a glimmer of familiar rainbow light catches my eye. In my window is one of Miss Clara's suncatchers, the one with a monarch butterfly on it that Thomas picked out specifically for me. The one from my home in Hooverville. I keep myself from gasping, but I'm suddenly filled with a hope that I might see him again.

Then my hope moves to somewhere else. Virginia! She appears in the doorway, waving at me with her sweet smile, and I use every ounce of my energy to run to her and fall into her arms. She smells like home, and for a second, I don't regret leaving Hooverville.

I pull back from the hug, and she looks at me and feels my forehead. "How do you feel? You feel a little warm to me."

"I feel fine," I tell her breathlessly, fighting tears.

Frank and Mother approach from the car and walk directly past us to the dining room.

"Virginia," Frank says in a commanding tone. "Fix me a sandwich." My face falls and I look at him.

"I just got back. Can't I have a minute to have a conversation with her?" I speak up. Virginia gives me a look that says *don't*, but I ignore her. Frank himself seems taken aback by my new personality, and he straightens his back to make sure I know he's in charge.

"I'm sorry?" Frank scoffs with a disturbing laugh. "Annaleise, she's the help. She gets paid to help us so you can do things you want to do, and nothing you don't. She is not here to be your friend or your companion."

"Well, as far as I'm concerned, you aren't her boss. She works for my family, and we aren't married yet." Mother and Frank stare at me with wide eyes, and without words I can tell what their thoughts are. They're wondering where the hell I've been where I've suddenly come back a whole new person. Before Frank can argue with me, I take Virginia's hand and drag her up the stairs to my bedroom.

"What the hell are you thinking, standing up to him like that?" Virginia asks as soon as the door shuts behind her.

I approach the window and look at the suncatcher up close. "How did you get this?" I ask, a nervous lull in my voice.

Virginia squints her eyes at me and says, "That boy came by the house and dropped it off." She tilts her chin down like it gives her an advantage in reading my expression. "Along with this." She opens my closet door and pulls out a bag of all my belongings from the Hooverville, including some paintings I made at Clara's, my book, and one of his shirts. I pull the shirt out and hold it up to my nose, smelling his familiar scent. It makes me relax and tense at the same time, and I don't know if I want to smile or cry. I pull out the book slowly and flip through the pages. All my words. All my hard work has gone to waste.

A hot ache burns a hole in my heart until I can't bear it any longer, and I start crying. "Why did he have to bring me home?" I throw the book with a thud and bury my head in my knees. "Why did he ruin it?"

Virginia doesn't answer, but I hear her walk across the room and pick up the book. "Anne," she whispers.

"I don't want it."

"Look up," she says firmly, and when I do, I see she's holding a piece of parchment folded three times with my name written across it. "This fell out of the book." I take it in my hands and slowly open it. The first line makes me cry again, and I hug the shirt to me.

"My dearest Annie,

I can't apologize enough for taking you to the hospital. I know it wasn't what you wanted, but I would do it again if it meant you were healthy. I wish I could give you the life you deserve away from this place, away from Frank. I wish more than anything I could take all your worries and carry them on my shoulders so you'll never have to feel that burden. If like you said, you never want to see me again, you can just ignore this letter and I will disappear and never try to see you again. But, if you want to see me again, stay strong. I know you can handle anything they throw at you until I can be with you and we can handle it together. Stay safe, my dear. I promise I will figure out a way to right my wrong and get you out of there. Eva and I are brainstorming every possible idea. We're still working on one that isn't illegal. I miss you, Annie, and I'll see you soon. Somehow.

Love, T.K."

I close the letter and breathe in deeply, then hand it off to Virginia. She scans it quickly and then folds it back up and puts it in the book.

"Well, ain't that some shit?" she says, drawing a laugh out of me.

"I don't want to think about Thomas right now." I set the book aside. "Or Hooverville or anything else that might have happened while I was there. I just want to..."

"Pretend like it never happened?" Virginia interjects.

"*Sleep,*" I finish. I stand and crawl into my bed. "Thomas still thinks we stand a chance. I don't see any possible way, so to entertain the idea is just torturing myself, and him, more than I have to. With any luck, Frank will kill me within the year, and I won't have to deal with any of this anymore."

Virginia frowns and closes the curtains, but I quickly stop her. "Don't," I tell her urgently. "I want to see the lights." Virginia opens the curtain again slowly, and the rainbow spots dance on my floor, and then up my wall as the sun goes down.

I don't sleep. The lights form pictures that dance across my eyes and remind me of everything I've lost. Above all, I think of Thomas. I prop myself up on my elbow and look at Virginia, who sits in a chair next to the door to stand guard.

"Would you do something for me?" I ask her, mind racing with this new idea, even though it's risky.

"Depends."

"Would you get a letter to Thomas for me? So I can tell him I'm sorry and that I forgive him and so I can..."

Virginia's face stops me mid-sentence. "What?" She presses her lips together and raises both her eyebrows like what she really wants to say is going to come bursting out of her at any moment. "Spit it out."

"I think it would be better for you to have no contact," Virginia breathes. I frown in confusion and throw my blankets off me.

"*What?* No, no, I—"

"You're engaged to Frank. And you admitted it yourself that there's no way for you to be with him, so the longer you hold onto this idea of him, the worse it will be. You *have* to let him go."

This hurts worse coming from Virginia than it would coming from my mother or even Thomas. I fight tears and my heart beats in my ears while I swallow a lump in my throat. I finally work up enough courage to say, "I can't."

"It may seem impossible now, Anne, but it will get easier and I promise I'll be right by your side to help."

"Thomas and I are better when we're together." I can sense her frustration with me by the way her eyebrow quirks, and she looks away from me. "I need to say goodbye."

"You do whatever you want, Annaleise." Virginia sighs.

Her eyes look like she's given up on me, and it hurts my chest. I plead with her, but she takes my wastebasket and leaves the room with it. I blow out a breath.

Seconds later, I'm down the hall and making my way toward Frank's office. I peek my head in the glass door and he immediately hangs up the phone at the sight of me.

"Darling, I'm so happy you're up. You look healthy. You look beautiful," Frank says, then he runs two fingers along my cheek. "I have exciting news."

"What?" I ask him.

"You'll have to wait until dinner to find out, my love." He leans in and tries to kiss me, but I turn my head, so he kisses my cheek instead. "Right. Smart. Germs."

"Speaking of dinner," I say and take a seat at his desk. "I've been thinking about what you said, and I think you were right. We should invite Mr. Kelley to dinner," I say cautiously, so as not to draw any extra attention to myself.

"Really? What made you decide that?" He leans back in his seat, resting his feet on top of his desk. If I were to do that, Mother would scream at me for an hour and then not talk to me for days.

I pause for a beat. "I owe him my life, really," I say. "The least we could do is give him a meal and a conversation."

Frank looks torn, but then he smiles to himself. "Consider it done, my love. I'll have Virginia send out an invitation immediately." He gives my cheek another kiss and walks past me out of his office. I let my shoulders relax.

I dress in my best dinner clothes, a lovely pink gown that was specifically made for me, and I make myself look as pretty as I can despite the dark eyes and the pale skin. Even with my exhaustion, I feel more alive than I have since I left Hooverville, and it's all credited to seeing Thomas again. I fluff my hair and peek out the window. Our new driver and Virginia left about forty minutes ago. For a second, I fear something happened, but then I see the flickering of the car lights through the trees surrounding the house, and I relax. I take one last look at myself in the mirror and go down the stairs to meet Frank and Mother.

"Frank," I call. "He's here." Frank emerges from his office and takes a second look at me and my outfit, scrunching his nose.

"Now why can't you *always* look this pretty for me, darling?" He grins and wraps an arm around my waist. My face falls and I face the door. A butler opens the front door to reveal Thomas, my glorious Thomas, standing there holding a single bottle of wine that I know he couldn't have purchased for himself. Arthur must have chipped in to help him make a good impression. I make a mental note to give Arthur a big *thank you* later.

Frank takes the bottle from Thomas, examines it for a moment, pretending to be impressed, then hands it off to Virginia. "Welcome, Mr. Kelley. Please, come in," Frank says extra-kindly.

He steps out of the way for Thomas to enter. Thomas meets my eye and communicates a thousand words without speaking. We hold an entire conversation using just our eyes and minuscule muscle twitches in our eyelids or brows. I have to keep myself from leaping and hugging him, but with Frank's arm around me like a leash, I'm reminded that I can't. Not now, at least. I give him one more playful look before stepping into the role of "Mrs. Frank Alexander," arm in arm with Frank while we give Thomas an extensive tour of my home.

As we make our way through the mansion, I look back at Thomas and notice he appears physically ill. Not nearly as bad as I must have last week, but he appears uncomfortable. So, in my best rich girl voice, I tell Frank, "I think we're boring our guest. Shall we go to dinner?" I urge. Frank opens his mouth to say something, but Virginia butts in.

"Right this way, Mr. Kelley," she says, and leads us to the dining area. I smirk inconspicuously and catch Mother scowling at me.

We sit at the big table for dinner, typically only reserved for parties and other celebrations, but this dining room has intricate paintings on the ceiling and a massive gold chandelier, so I suspect this is another one of Frank's intimidation tactics. Frank sits at the head of the table on the far side of the room, while I'm seated at the other end. Thomas is directly between us with twenty feet of empty table on each side of him. He sits across from my mother, who stares him down like she's personally offended by his mere existence. Thomas may not fit into my world, but I would give anything to fit into his.

I sit up straight in my seat as two staff members I've never met before appear with two plates, one in each of their hands, before they set it in front of each of us. I thank them politely and glance at Thomas, who seems confused.

Despite the expensiveness of the meal, there isn't much food. Three pieces of asparagus, a small bit of lamb, and three cubes of potato. He curls his lip and glances at me. I urge him to eat his food, and he does, rather quickly. So, when Mother is still just biting into her lamb, he's finished the whole plate.

"Charming," Mother mutters, biting daintily into her meat. Thomas turns red and looks at his lap.

"Ah, don't judge the man," Frank says, the food rolling around in his open mouth as he speaks and points at Thomas with his fork. "He's hungry! Aren't you, Mr. Kelley? That's nothing to be ashamed of." I squint my eyes at Frank confusedly, expecting the other shoe to drop. And it does.

"That's my good deed, for the year, Mary," Frank adds with a chuckle. I set my fork down and lean closer to the table.

"What's your good deed for the year, darling?" I ask with a raised eyebrow. Frank doesn't seem to want to answer. He picks the bits of lamb from his teeth with his tongue.

"You know." He shrugs and looks at Thomas. "Feeding the poor."

"Oh," Thomas says immediately, setting his napkin on the table. "No, I don't want charity. I don't want this to be like that."

"You would turn down an extravagant meal with your new friends just because we feel sorry for you?" Frank coos. I harden my face and glare at him.

"That's enough, Frank," I say lowly.

"Yes." Thomas nods. "I would, actually."

"What kind of Villeain are you?" Frank asks aggressively. That's the same word the cop called Thomas a few weeks ago. It *has* to be some type of slur.

"FRANK!" I shout at him. "That is enough!"

"Quiet, Anna," Frank spits at me. "I'm just teasing our new friend."

Thomas gives me a look that says, "it's okay," and turns back to Frank. "I'm the kind of Villeain who would rather be treated as an equal than an enemy. Believe it or not, I think lots of us would feel the same way. I don't think money makes the man." He gives Frank a mischievous, winning look, and I have to hide a smile by biting into my asparagus. Frank is speechless and tense, and a second later, he clears his throat.

"Anyway," Frank changes the subject, and Thomas smiles triumphantly. "As for my big news..." Mother and I look up from our plates mid-bite. "To celebrate our Annaleise's return," he pauses dramatically and smiles at me, "we have been invited to a gala at the home of President Hoover himself in Washington!"

Mother jumps to her feet, letting out some sort of squeal. I choke on my asparagus and cough it up violently until it lands with a clink on my plate.

"*What?*" I say rather loudly once I catch my breath. Frank looks disgusted but is too excited to do anything about it.

"Oh, Frank, that's wonderful!" Mother claps her hands together and begins pacing around, muttering to herself about everything she must have the servants do before we depart.

"Mother, calm yourself." I pull myself together and turn my chin down at Frank. "You're serious?"

"When you vanished, I was on business with him, and he was very concerned for you. He *personally* called just this afternoon to welcome you home and invite you."

"I-I..." I look at Thomas, frantic to find a way out of this. "I can't go. I'm not well enough to travel."

"Annaleise," Mother shouts. "You would dare to turn down

the *leader of your country* when he is throwing a party just for you?"

"You would think he could find a better use of that spending, rather than throwing a gala for a person he has never met, just to pretend as though he has some sense of control over what's happening in the world! How can I attend a party when the person who saved me comes from a Hooverville? Wouldn't a better thank you be putting money toward helping that problem?" The words spill out of my mouth before I can stop them. I release thoughts I didn't even know I had, and immediately after I say it, I shrink away from what is sure to be an explosion of wrath on Frank's part.

But he stays silent. The whole room is silent except for a tiny *tink... tink... tink...* as he taps his fork against his plate. Thomas stares at his plate like he's trying to vanish into the table itself but cannot. Mother's breathing becomes heavy the longer time passes.

Finally, Frank speaks. "If you're so concerned about the wellbeing of this man, perhaps he should come with us and state his case to President Hoover himself. In any case, it would be rude to have a party thrown for you and then not show up. So, we *will* be attending the party. Is that clear?"

The words "*Yes, sir,*" come out, and I swallow down some puke. Nobody says another word for the rest of dinner.

Virginia shows Thomas to a room he can stay in for the night, at my pleading with Frank, insisting that it's the least we can do. But I fear Frank won't be so accepting of many more favors for Thomas after this. If he catches onto anything more than a vague acquaintanceship between the two of us, he'll kill us both and get away with it. He'll say my sickness took me, and nobody would even notice if Thomas went missing. No. I have to play my cards incredibly safe if I want to protect Thomas.

Virginia fetches Thomas a pair of pajamas that don't fit him quite right because they were tailored to fit another man. When he emerges from the bathroom in them, I tilt my head some.

He holds up his arms and stands with his legs slightly apart uncomfortably.

"Do you have any larger sleep clothes?"

I laugh softly. "Those were my dad's. He was not the tallest man." I approach him and try to stretch them out any way that I can, but they won't budge. "Your best bet would be to just..." I blush slightly and hesitate. "Sleep in your underclothes." Thomas smirks at me and raises his eyebrows flirtatiously. I playfully hit him in the chest. "Stop." I laugh softly, and then suddenly my arms spring out and hug him.

"I'm *so* sorry, Thomas," I breathe. He wraps his arms around me, as best as he can with the tight pajamas, and presses his face into my neck. "I'm sorry for everything I said. I wasn't thinking."

"I'm sorry too, Annie," he whispers. Hearing the nickname again calms me down. "I shouldn't have brought you back. I just didn't know what else to do. You got worse, and—"

"Shh," I whisper. "It's in the past. As for the future..." We both know nothing can truly happen, but the fantasy is enough to lie to ourselves for a little while longer. "We'll figure something out." I pull back slowly and admire his face, both making up for lost time and saving some for later. "I have to go before Frank comes looking for me." I take a step away from him, but then return and say, "Thank you for coming back."

"I couldn't stay away." Thomas smiles. I lean up and kiss him on the cheek before I scurry out of his room and find my way back to my own.

I almost make it back home-free before I turn the corner and come face to face with—

"Mother!" I exclaim, jumping back slightly in shock and raising my arms like I'm ready to fight. I relax and drop my shoulders. "You frightened me."

"Anxious, Annaleise?" Mother looks at me up and down like I'm a bug, pressing her lips together into a tight line that reveals how judgmental her thoughts are. "I didn't see you after dinner."

"I went to Mr. Kelley's room to thank him for saving me, and to make sure he's settling in well." I walk past her, but she stops me by grabbing my arm forcefully and pulling me face to face with her. Up close, I see through her facade. Her wig is sliding off the back of her head, her skin is flaking, and it appears cracked despite her powder. Her brows are drawn on in a painfully dark line and no amount of makeup can hide just how *tired* she is. It couldn't have been easy raising me.

"I'd be more careful if I were you. You're already walking on dangerous ground."

XVIII

⁓⁓⁓

I can't tell if she says it like a threat or a warning, so I tug myself out of her grip and smooth out my dress.

"I'll keep that in mind. Goodnight, Mother." I walk past her directly to my room and lean back on my bedroom door, replaying every moment with Thomas, and then thinking of Washington, D.C. *Hoover wants me to visit his house?* It's a bit of irony, all things considered, but I have a feeling that this party might be my best shot of ending up with Thomas. We could easily escape the party without being noticed. Frank would be too busy with the politicians to notice me leave, and by the time I got away, we could already be on a train to California.

But then again, Frank found me last time. He would find me again, and then we'd still be in danger. As long as Frank is alive, I belong to him. It's fun to fantasize about, but Virginia's right. The longer I dream about it, the worse it will be when we eventually split.

But being without him is unbearable. How am I supposed to do this? I strip my dress off me and get in the tub with water that's way too hot, as if I can boil the day off me. The heat makes me ill, but it feels good and gives me something else to think about other than Frank. I get out when the water becomes too cold and dry myself off with a large towel. I plait my hair down my back and tie it up so it'll be lovely tomorrow, and go to bed.

My dreams are filled with Thomas. One in particular where Thomas and I lay happily in a bed with blankets and sheets strung up to become a little tent, with Clara's suncatchers filling our little fort with light. Thomas and I have a conversation, none of which I can remember, and then Thomas showers me in kisses. On my forehead, on my cheeks, on my ears and my neck. It isn't sensual at all. My dream self laughs through it until the door opens and my Mother peers in, catching us. She appears angry for a second, but then she just says, "I guess this is what they do when they're engaged."

And I wake up with a yearning in my heart for that. That feeling. That moment. To marry Thomas and have him all to myself, to be accepted. I feel an ache in my heart, but just as quickly I get the feeling that I'm not alone. I sit up, looking around blindly in the dark of my room, and squint my eyes. Sure enough, a figure darker than the rest of the room is leaning against the wall, watching me.

"Frank?" I whisper confusedly, as my eyes adjust to the new light. "What are you doing here?" He approaches the bed quickly and with such a strange demeanor about him that for a moment I think this is just a nightmare. I pull the blankets up to my chest to hide my night-dressed body from him and try to scoot away as he comes nearer and stands above me. Fear fills me, but not the fight kind. The kind that makes me freeze in place and want to cry.

Frank grabs me hard by the hair and tilts my head back, so I'm forced to look at him. He leans in close and whispers, "If you try anything in Washington, anything at all..." He reaches his other hand up and puts it around my throat but doesn't tighten it. It just rests there, with the possibility and the knowledge that he could choke me lingering in the air. "I'll fucking kill you," he finishes in a sinister whisper. I've known he could, but this threat feels much more real than it has before. When he releases me, I find I'm trembling. He brushes a finger along my cheek and leans down to kiss me. I recoil back, and Frank stands.

"Behave," he says firmly, and his word lingers in the air like a gun ready to blast at any moment. He leaves my room and shuts the door behind him, but I still feel him in the room with me. I don't sleep for the rest of the night. I sit straight up, staring at the doorway. In fact, when Virginia opens the door to get me for the morning, she asks if I'm okay, and immediately I break down into tears and sob in her arms.

Maybe there's no way out. Maybe Thomas and I have to pull a Romeo and Juliet and kill ourselves to be together. Then there's no Frank, no Hooverville, nothing standing in our way. I'm embarrassed to admit that I consider killing myself a way out, but I see no other alternative. I tell Virginia what happened, and even she doesn't know what to say. Instead, she stands me up and gets me dressed in one of my best travel dresses and packs a bag for my time in D.C.

She does my hair and powders under my eyes so I don't appear so puffy, then escorts me downstairs to the car. Frank acts as though nothing happened last night, holding a cheerful conversation with Thomas.

We get in the car and begin our long road trip. As we pull out of the driveway, I wave back at Virginia. Frank holds my hand in the car, while Thomas holds my gaze. I give a minuscule shake of my head and then rest it back against my seat. I still feel his eyes on me, but I choose not to acknowledge him. It's about an hour to the airfield owned by Mr. Roosevelt and his wife Eleanor. When we arrive, we're ushered into a private plane of his.

We must shout over the volume of the engine, so we save all conversations for when we're on the plane.

"Annaleise," Mrs. Roosevelt says, holding her arms open for me. "It's wonderful to see you again. I believe the last time I saw you, you were... what, not eleven yet? You've grown up beautifully."

I hug our old family friend and then shake hands with Mr. Roosevelt. Roosevelt turns to Frank and Thomas and shakes each of their hands, saying something I can't quite hear. Frank holds out his hand to Mrs. Roosevelt, but she just looks at it and quirks her eyebrow, unimpressed. I stifle a laugh, but something also concerns me. Have I given her reason to suspect he isn't trustworthy? No, I couldn't possibly! How could she know?

Thomas, on the other hand, is greeted enthusiastically by the Governor and his wife. They ask him all sorts of questions about his childhood and where he's from, and Thomas doesn't sugarcoat the answers.

"I'm from a Hooverville," he says. The Roosevelts watch him in intrigued shock, and it takes a second before either of them can fully process it.

"By 'a Hooverville,' you mean..." Franklin says, trailing off, but Thomas sits quietly, challenging him to finish his sentence. "A homeless encampment, correct?"

"Correct, Mr. Governor," Thomas says, smiling to himself.

"This isn't appropriate flight conversation," Frank tries to interject, but he's quickly silenced by Eleanor's right hand going up.

"Tell us more about that." Roosevelt leans forward in curiosity.

For a minute, I think Thomas will lie about the state of the Hoovervilles and claim that everything is great, but Thomas tells the complete truth without hesitation. He tells about the disease and how many people die, about the robberies that occur and the sexual assaults on their women. He tells them about the starvation and the freezing to death on long winter nights, and how when someone dies, the cops throw the body in the back of a truck and bury it in an unmarked grave on the other side of town. Even Frank looks, for a minute, slightly horrified by the conditions, but he quickly hides his expression.

"Well, aren't you a bluenose?" Frank says, expecting to get a big laugh. When he doesn't, I see the anger grow on his face, and I know he'll somehow find a way to blame me for this later.

Franklin asks some questions about where their food comes from, and how many children live in the Hooverville, and when Thomas answers them, the Roosevelts are left stunned and silent, only the sound of the plane engine filling the air. I distract myself and look out the window at the clouds as we fly past them, and the skyline of the city. I try to look disinterested for Frank's sake, but I listen in closely to their conversation.

"Well, Mr. Kelley—" Mr. Roosevelt says.

"Thomas, please, call me Thomas."

"Well, Thomas," he corrects himself with a smile. "I'm sure you know I'm running for President this year, and if I win, I'm going to do everything in my power to ensure you all get back on your feet."

Thomas and I both scrunch up our noses at his pathetic promise, which sounds like nothing more than a campaign slogan. If I were Thomas, I'd just smile and nod and accept his promise as complete bullshit and not give it a second thought. But, of course, I'm not Thomas, and Thomas isn't like anybody else.

Thomas clears his throat to hide a laugh, "Please don't take offense to this, Mr. Governor.

I'm sure you'll make a great president and I'm sure you're going to do a lot of great things for other people. But don't bother making promises to us if you can't keep them. It's a waste of your precious hours and ours, too."

Frank's eyes get huge and his mouth falls slightly open, and he stammers out an apology, but the Roosevelts just smile sincerely at Thomas. "Thank you for your honesty," Eleanor says kindly.

Franklin Roosevelt squints his eyes at Thomas and smiles to himself. "Come to my office when we return home. I think we have *a lot* to talk about." And that's the end of the conversation. The look on Frank's face is a hilarious mixture of anger and shock. I've never seen another person render him speechless before.

The plane lands after only a few hours, and we're welcomed with camera flashes and reporters shouting questions in our faces. We smile and wave, but don't stop to answer questions or pose for photographs. I glance behind me at Thomas to make sure he's okay, and while he looks overwhelmed, he seems to handle it okay. We slide into the car and I cross one knee over the other, earning a scowl from Frank and a laugh from Eleanor.

Thomas carries on a happy conversation, but his voice drops off as we round the corner to the White House. His mouth drops open, and he stares out the window. I find myself watching Thomas instead of the view because his reaction is so cute. Frank rolls his eyes. Across the road are thousands of people carrying signs. At first, I believe it's for me, but then I recognize that it's a Hooverville, and the people are protesting. *The Bonus Army.*

I smile and tap Thomas on the arm to see if he recognizes it too, and we both excitedly think of Peter. It's unlikely we'll have a chance to visit him on this trip, but what are the odds that the three of us could all end up in Washington together?

We pull up in the circular driveway and Thomas opens the door, but I shake my head as the driver gets out and opens it for him. Thomas turns slightly red as we both get out and stand before—

"President Hoover!" Frank exclaims as he slides out from the car. He rushes up to him and shakes his hand enthusiastically, thanking him for inviting us. Thomas and I shoot each other a look and return our gaze to the man for whom our home is named after. He looks much more human than I would have expected. He doesn't have snake eyes or a lizard tongue, he doesn't have claws or devil horns. He's just... *normal.*

Hoover sees me from over Frank's shoulder and says something along the lines of, "Is that our guest of honor?" He approaches me like a hunter would a deer and holds out his hand for me. "So glad to finally meet you, Miss Winston."

"Annaleise, please," I say politely but flatly. His handshake is loose and pathetic like he's nervous to even be touching me.

He turns to Thomas and holds out his hand. Thomas straightens his back, holds his head up high, and shakes the president's hand. "And you must be our Mr. Kelley. Well, it's a fine thing you did, rescuing this woman. You're one of America's finest! Come in, I'll give you the tour."

Thomas gives me a look and raises his eyebrow. I hide a laugh as we head up the stairs into the home.

The President slips away halfway through the tour, citing some "important business" and sharing a laugh with Frank because "this job never ends!" while Thomas and I don't find it quite as funny, but luckily the others don't notice our unenthused glance at each other.

At dinner, Thomas and I make faces at each other as the politicians and manly men discuss money and the economy and such. The goal is to make the other one laugh without getting caught, but after I let out a giggle, Mrs. Roosevelt looks over at us. She gives me a knowing look but continues eating her peas.

"So, Mr. Kelley!" Hoover booms across the table at one point. Thomas looks up from his plate with gigantic eyes and eyebrows raised halfway up his forehead. He swallows the bite in his mouth, and everyone from further up the table gets a kick out of how clueless he is. "Tell me, where are you from?"

Roosevelt chimes in before Thomas can. "Thomas here comes from a Hooverville! Isn't that nice, Herb?" Everyone senses the tension like it's an unwelcome visitor making its way into the room. It makes me sick to my stomach, and Thomas can't even do anything to stop it.

"I don't like that name," Hoover says, aggressively cutting his meat with a fork. "I think it's so vulgar. It's as if they're blaming me for their misfortune."

"Well, you aren't exactly making it better," Roosevelt says.

"It should not be my job to get people out of a hole they dug themselves."

"Yes!" Roosevelt exclaims. "That is exactly your job!"

"Can we get dessert?" I ask, looking around for a servant.

"Your job is to protect the people of this country, and I personally think the fact that you aren't is a good enough reason for them to throw it back at you like that," Roosevelt continues.

"Franklin," Eleanor chimes in.

"Dessert?"

"You are a disgrace to this presidency!"

"Franklin!"

I can't say I don't disagree with him, but it makes for an awkward few minutes after the argument eventually comes to an end. Hoover orders that we all go to bed. Without dessert.

One of Hoover's many assistants, Ruby, is assigned to be my personal attendant for the day. She helps me flee questions asked by reporters who happen to catch me en route from the hotel to the White House. When we reach the White House, she brings me to a bedroom away from anyone else and helps me into a ball gown that was specially picked out for me by one of the press secretaries—and my mother, of course. It's a light gold-colored gown with golden thread embellishments like little roses along the breast line and the hem.

"They said gold is your best color," Ruby says as she takes it off the standing mannequin and holds it up to my chest. "It's very lightweight, so if you get too ill, the dress won't weigh you down."

I get undressed and put my arms above my head so Ruby can slide the gown right over my arms and down my body. She takes a few seconds to tie me into the corset and button up the back, then she straightens the hem and turns me around to see myself in the mirror. After so long of wearing plain clothes, it feels foreign. The underskirt scratches my legs, and the fabric is itchy. Ruby's eyes soften like she's never seen such lovely fabric in her life, and she shakes her head in awe.

"You look amazing, Miss Winston." She takes my hand and leads me over to a vanity chair and begins pulling out various makeup products from a thick bag. "It isn't often that I get to do girlish things for the people I assist. Usually, it's just getting these men their coffee. This is fun."

She holds me by the shoulder and leans in close to my face, squinting as she plucks and thins out my eyebrow hairs. She draws on eyebrows for me, paints a thin line of eyeliner, and smokes out my eyelid. She layers on mascara until every time I bat my eyes, my lashes hit my cheeks, then she adds on a dark red lipstick. She turns me around to face the mirror, and I'm completely unrecognizable from who I know now.

"You look lovely!" Ruby says as she twists my hair back into an updo. She pins my hair in place and slides heeled shoes on my feet. "And you're ready."

Ruby acts as an escort as we head to a separate room to take exclusive photographs for the magazine. In the small gathering hall is a photographer setting up his camera, along with Hoover, Frank, and another man wearing a suit. I take a couple of seconds to even recognize him, but when I do, I feel my cheeks get hot and my heart beats faster in my ears. As Thomas turns around, he freezes slightly as he has the same reaction to seeing me dressed nicely as I did to him. His jaw hangs slightly open, but he corrects himself and gives me the smallest hint of a smile.

He looks good in a suit. Not out of place, only slightly foreign, but still like he was built for it. Though I prefer it when it's all-natural, they've combed his curly hair back and slicked out with some gel or some other product. I bite my lip while I look him up and down. Thomas catches me and quirks an eyebrow. He mouths, "You look good" and smiles softly. I blush deeply and I'm so caught up in my moment with Thomas that I jump when Ruby clears her throat.

"That's the guy that rescued you, right?" she whispers casually, leaning in so only I can hear her. "He's cute. Do you know if he's seein' anybody?"

I feel myself get angry that she would even ask me that but have to remind myself that I'm engaged to Frank, and nobody knows about me and Thomas. I don't even know about me and him. I know how I feel about him, and I'm almost certain how he feels about me. I know neither of us wants to spend another moment apart, but how could we be together if Frank would kill us for it? How are we supposed to make this work?

Ruby nudges me. "Did you hear me?"

I watch Thomas as he speaks to the photographer about how the camera works. He looks dorky and charming, different but so right at the same time.

"Sorry," I tell her. "I think he's taken." She clicks her tongue.

"Rats. That's a bummer. I guess I'll have to keep looking. We can't all get lucky with fiancés like Mr. Alexander, can we?" She giggles slightly.

"No," I hiss. "No, we can't." I finally take my eyes off Thomas and glance at my engagement ring on my finger, which feels like a noose.

The photographer finally lines us all up in a row, with my back to Frank's chest, and Thomas standing across from us. Frank puts his hand on my waist, and it makes me feel ill. The photographer takes the photograph, and then we're free to go eat lunch before the party.

Frank and I leave together, but he runs off to join his colleagues walking down the hallway. I sigh, alone again as I turn down a dark hallway to go back to my room. My arms swing in a way Mother would hate and I slump my shoulders.

"Boo," Thomas whispers as he sneaks up behind me and pokes me in the ribcage.

I squeal and laugh, hitting him in the chest. "Don't *do* that."

"Sorry, I couldn't help it. You look really pretty," he whispers in my ear so nobody who might be around can hear, and he pushes a strand of hair behind my ear. I shudder under his fingers as they just slightly brush against my cheek. I bite the inside of my mouth and blush.

"You look good too," I whisper. "This look suits you." I wait for him to get the joke, but he doesn't. He just looks down at the suit with a new appreciation.

"Thanks. I've never owned a suit. I've also never had my photograph taken."

"Well, you're a natural at it." I pause. "It seems all the girls here have a thing for you. Ruby asked if you were single."

"What did you tell her?"

"What should I have told her?" I raise an eyebrow. "You have your pick of all the girls in the country now if you wanted."

He frowns deeply and takes my hands in his own and squeezes my fingers. "If all the girls in the whole world were lined up for me to choose, I'd still pick you, Annie." My heart melts. I hate it when he says cute stuff like that because it will eventually make saying goodbye all the more difficult. "If I could, I'd marry you right now." The idea of marriage that I had previously rejected only feels right if it's with him.

There's only one person I want by my side for the rest of my life, and that's Thomas Kelley. I let it sink in, then I throw my arms around his neck and bury my face in his shoulder. "Is that a proposal?" I ask him jokingly. He smiles and wraps his arms tighter around me.

"One day," he whispers, "I'll be your husband, and you'll be my wife."

We live in our fantasy for a few moments, embracing each other with not a care in the world. But it can't last, and eventually doubt creeps into our little world.

"What about Frank?" I whisper. "You know he'd never let me go."

"I don't know. Don't think about him though. Keep him

out of our world." He smiles that sweet smile at me and any concern I have fades away. I've never known a person with that kind of power over me. I should be afraid of it, but I'm not.

I stand up on my toes and kiss Thomas lovingly, pulling closer to one another. When we separate, I open my eyes and look up at my future husband and admire every inch of his face. He's everything I never knew I wanted. For a moment, my soul is at peace.

And then that peace fades.

Heavy footfalls fill the silence between us, and out of the corner of my eye, I see a shadow appear around the corner. But by the time I turn my head, it's already gone. Thomas opens his eyes and catches onto my nerves without me saying a word. He squeezes my hand.

"What is it?" he asks gently.

I turn my face back to him and whisper, "I think we're in trouble."

Thomas drops my hand and goes down the hall to see who it is. He stands for a few moments, and when he turns around, he's sheet white. Confused, I rush forward and turn the corner, only to see Frank's stocky figure walking away from us down the hall with his fists clenched. I fill with fear, and I cannot focus on the words Thomas says. I shake my head uncontrollably.

"Hey, *hey*," Thomas whispers, taking my hand and turning my body to him. "It'll be okay."

"No," I choke out. "No, no, it won't."

Thomas wraps his arms around me and whispers "I won't let him hurt you, okay?" I reach as far as I can just to get air into my lungs, but it evades my grip and leaves me breathless. I grab Thomas's arm and search his eyes to steady myself, and then I hug him again, trembling.

"Everything will be okay," Thomas whispers in my ear, and my heart wants me to believe it.

After we separate, Ruby finds us and tells me it's time for the party to start, and to go back to the foyer. She swiftly leads us there, and Thomas and I take one last look at each other before entering separately so as to draw even less suspicion. Maybe Frank didn't see us together; maybe I'm wrong about all this. Maybe there's nothing to worry about.

I enter the foyer first and take my place at Frank's side, but judging by the look on his face, it's obvious he saw Thomas practically propose to me. The whites of his eyes appear black, and his facial muscles twitch. Yet, his expression remains passive.

As Thomas enters a moment later, every man in the room stands and turns to him, standing straight with accusing fury in their eyes. Before I can ask what's happening, two of the men charge at Thomas and force his arms behind his back.

"Whoa, whoa, what's happening here?" Thomas asks, just as casual as ever as he struggles against the men.

"Mr. Kelley," Hoover says as he stands. "It has been brought to my attention that you stole from Mr. Alexander and Miss. Winston."

"What?" Thomas and I exclaim at the same time, a mirrored look of confusion on both of our faces.

"Oh, shut up, won't you, *Annie?*" Frank scolds me, using that nickname just to assure me that my relationship with

Thomas is why this is happening. My blood runs cold. Thomas catches it and I see the remorse spread across his face.

"This man here stole a sizeable amount of cash from me," Frank announces to the room of politicians. "And why shouldn't he? He is homeless and useless in society. In fact, he lives in one of those so-called camps that makes a mockery of your very name, Mr. Hoover."

The men shift uncomfortably and murmur amongst themselves. "You see what happens when you try to give these creatures anything they did not earn themselves? They just take, and they take, and they take until you're bled dry."

"Frank!" I urge. He holds up one hand to silence me. One man, a bespectacled man in a wheelchair, speaks up from the crowd.

"Where's the proof that he stole anything?" Franklin Roosevelt asks, much to my relief. Frank laughs in the governor's face.

"Don't believe me?" Frank shouts at the crowd and turns to Thomas. "Search him," he tells the two men who are holding him down. Thomas shouts profanities at them while I grab Frank's arm.

"Frank, you know he stole nothing. It's me you're angry with. Punish me, not him," I insist. Frank grabs me by the wrist and pries my hand off his arm.

"I plan to," he breathes. "Until then, though…" He turns me to face the men as they pull a thick wad of cash from Thomas's pocket, while he shakes his head wildly with huge eyes.

"I swear to you, I did *not!*"

Hoover stands slowly, and all eyes go to him. "You make a mockery of my name, you come into my home, and now this?" he tells Thomas. Thomas pleads for mercy. "Cuff him. Frank, you can have your way with him. Then send him back to where he came from."

"Very well, Mr. President." Frank smiles and starts heading toward Thomas as he's shoved to his knees. Thomas shakes his head swiftly, and the men step back as Frank raises his fist.

And then my feet are moving and I throw myself between Thomas and Frank, and his fist stops just before it hits me.

"Annaleise. Out of the way," Frank says through his teeth.

"No," I breathe. "I'll *not* let you hurt him when he did nothing."

The men watch in shock as Mr. Alexander's Obedient-Little-Wife suddenly disobeys him and throws herself in front of a perfect stranger. A few of them snicker at the power Frank has lost in his own relationship. Frank looks around, knowing I have him backed into a corner. If he hits me, he's a monster. If he gives up, he's a coward. His eyes fill with fury again, and in one swift movement, Frank throws me to the ground and kicks at Thomas' stomach. Thomas doubles over and groans in pain. I shriek horrifically, and one man pats me on the shoulder.

"There, there. I know it's frightening."

Thomas's suit jacket stains with blood and Frank finally stops the assault, which even the politicians think is brutal for stealing a small sum of cash. What would they think if they knew his actual crime? Frank leans into his face and whispers something, and Thomas pushes himself to his feet, his nose obviously broken, but his dignity not crushed.

Hoover turns up his nose and says, "I believe there's another homeless encampment across the way. You run along."

The two men who'd grabbed him begin half-carrying, half-dragging him out the door and away from the building. As soon as Thomas is gone, everyone lets out a sigh of relief. Ruby looks stunned and embarrassed that she ever fancied him. Frank turns around to the group and nonchalantly asks, "Shall we go party?"

XIX

〰️

A s everyone else leaves the room to head downstairs to the main ballroom area, Frank lags.

"You complete asshole," I spit at him with all the fury I can muster, but he doesn't flinch. To fight with Frank is like fighting a wall while the room gets smaller.

"You're the one being a whore, Annaleise." Frank pulls his gloves back on. "Now, here's how tonight is going to go. You're going to smile and stay by my side. You're going to dance with me, you're going to act grateful, and above all, you're going to behave yourself. If you say anything that makes people think twice about us, I will kill you *and* your lover boy. If you try anything, you'll both be dead by the end of the day. Is that clear? Don't make me prove myself, Anna. I'll kill him first and make you watch. You're *mine*. Don't forget that. I'll see you downstairs."

Frank walks past me, leaving me alone and afraid. I search my mind for any escape, any loophole that I can get through with Thomas. I'm smart enough to know Frank's not bluffing. I look out the window and see the two men dragging Thomas through the protesters and across the road toward the Hooverville encampment. That's probably the safest place for him right now—in a Hooverville, away from me, and away from Frank.

I leave the foyer quietly and descend the stairs, and I hear one of Hoover's men announce, "Here she is! The spectacular Annaleise Winston, in the celebration of her return!" Whatever crowd there is cheers as I come around the corner of the stairs and curl my lips into an uncomfortable smile. My eyes fall on Frank, who stands at the bottom of the steps with his hand outstretched. My eyes flash to the door, but guards protect it. The windows lie too high on the ceiling for me to escape through. I'm trapped. I reach the bottom step and take Frank's hand.

Frank smiles proudly at me for doing as he said, but my mind still tries to work a way through this. Frank leads me through the party to greet every person, and at each guest, I must repeat, "Thank you so much for your support until I could come home." Lots of people ask where I was, but Frank concocts the story that I had fallen while out and about and got amnesia for a short while and forgot how to return home. At that, everyone begins treating me as though I'm stupid. They talk loudly with their mouths wide open like I'm deaf.

"I don't believe you're familiar with the term amnesiac, are you?" I ask after I've had enough of it. Frank tightens his grip on me as a warning. After we've spoken to every single guest and thanked them for coming, we're allowed to join the other couples on the dance floor. We take our spot in the center and spin circles in a waltz. He doesn't step on my toes like Thomas did.

"You're doing remarkably well," Frank says. "Now you just have to keep this up forever, and we should be fine." He says it like he means for it to be a joke instead of a threat. "Smile, act like you love me." There it is. The tone, the disdain for my love with Thomas. He wouldn't ever let it show. But I figure out that my relationship with Thomas is an embarrassment to Frank's manhood. His fiancée loves someone else more. I can be a smartass and I can be unladylike and it's not the end of the world. But to choose someone other than Frank, that's the biggest mistake I could have made.

"I don't know what you have up your sleeve, but you'll never escape me, Annaleise. I'm with you forever."

He spins me and I start to get dizzy and nauseous. He leans forward and kisses me, tasting of smoke and tobacco and liquor. I scrunch up my face and pull away, returning to the dance.

"I don't have anything up my sleeve," I say, and he searches my face for any hint of a lie.

"I don't believe you. You always have something up your sleeve. You're a troublesome girl. If you had any brains at all, you'd submit to me and we wouldn't have this problem. He has nothing. I can give you the whole wide world, Anna." His voice softens, and he gazes upon me adoringly. "I'm only mean because you don't listen otherwise. We could be happy together. Just give it a chance. You aren't even trying."

His words echo in my skull as the room spins around us. The protesters outside chant even louder, disorienting me. I catch sight of security guards pushing their way through the party, and Henry Banner looking confused and making his way towards the exit. Confusion fills me, and I plant my feet to stop Frank from spinning us.

"Wha—?" Frank asks, suddenly fearful that I'm going to do something.

"Something's wrong," I whisper as the guards rush out the front door, guns in their hands. A guard whisks the President out of the room and out of sight. "We have to go," I say, backing away from the center of the room.

"Get back here you little—" Frank never finishes his sentence as the glass window above us shatters and a brick lands between us. I jump backwards and cover my head just before the next window shatters, raining glass on top of me and everyone else around me. A third object shatters the window, and a moment later it releases a thick smoke from one end.

The party erupts into chaos. Women scream, people trip over themselves. Mostly, they pace around in circles, disoriented, while protesters climb through the window into the room and continue their protests inside, shouting, "WE DEMAND OUR BONUSES!"

I find Frank lying on the ground in the thick smoke and I think he's dead, but a moment later his hand reaches up and he cries out, "Annaleise!" His voice disorients me. He sounds desperate. I finally see his face. The top of his head is bleeding from where he must have been hit with a brick. I take a step back. Now is my chance to run and get away. But he pleads with me to help him, and I must. I am a better person than he is, and I won't let him die. Not here.

He's not good enough for that.

I curse under my breath and help Frank to his feet, and together we stumble through the smoke toward the staircase. I sit him down and examine his injury. I tear a strip off the long curtains that line the hall and place it on Frank's head and urge him to hold it there to stop the bleeding. Catching my breath, I look back over my shoulder at the ballroom. The attack is over as quickly as it started. Nobody is too severely injured, mostly just shaken up, and the guards arrest the veterans who infiltrated the party.

"You're going to pay for that," one guard says to a gentleman. I quickly scan the room for Hoover or Banner to see what their next move is, but when I don't find them, I look back at Frank. He places his hand on top of mine and smiles up at me. Without words, I can read his thoughts. He believes he's won me. I saved his life, so he thinks he's won me over somehow. I have to find Hoover. Now. I stumble backwards, then run past him up the staircase we came down in.

"Annaleise!" Frank shouts after me, but I leave him behind.

I run down the hall as quickly as I can toward my quarters, but as I pass Hoover in one of his offices, I slow to a stop and back up into the doorway. Hoover shouts on the phone with someone, his face bright red and beads of sweat forming at his hairline.

"I need military forces here. Send them out. I want them gone." He sets the phone down and sits down at his desk. Outside, I hear the chanting of the veterans as they swarm the building and suddenly, I understand. President Hoover sorts papers into stacks, digging through drawers, throwing papers, as if he's looking for something. Only then does he realize I'm still standing here.

"*Out*, Miss Winston," he says breathlessly, like I'm an inconvenience to him.

"Call off the troops," I say forcefully, coming close to his desk.

"They aren't going to hurt anybody, I assure you. They're just going to get them off the government property and send them back to where they came from."

"*That* sounds like a lie." My voice sounds almost like a growl.

"You care an awful lot about a bunch of homeless looters. Go back to your party and act like you're grateful for all we have given you."

Why does everyone keep telling me to be grateful for the bare minimum?

I scowl at him. "There are innocent people in there! People who have nowhere else to go but here. You would really send the militia to attack homeless veterans and their families? What's the matter with you?!"

"Get out, you stupid girl!" Hoover shouts at me, echoing off the walls.

"Please, call off the order! There are *children* down there!"

"They shouldn't be trespassing! They, like yourself, should be grateful for everything they're given and not demand more like that pathetic friend of yours."

Out of ideas, I rush toward the window, where the guards and officers downstairs are shooing the protesters away with teargas. They move as a singular crowd back toward the Hooverville across the way, and I turn to Hoover.

"They're leaving. *Make* it *stop!*"

Hoover approaches the window as the crowd dissipates, but guards follow them with batons and teargas fueled by rage. "It's too late," Hoover mutters, horrified by his own mistake. I realize what this means. I steady myself on the wall and without another moment's thought, I turn and run out of Hoover's office.

XX

"Annaleise!" Frank shouts after me. "Where are you going?"

I ignore Frank as I flee past him down the spiral staircase of the mansion, through the banquet hall where my guests pace around confusedly, and out the door. I jump down the steps, skipping three or four steps at a time, and look around to orient myself in the city. My breath is heavy, and while I hear the chaos and the shouting, I'm not sure which sound to follow. On the other side of the trees, I see smoke rising that I recognize from back home. *Hooverville*, my lips mouth, and my feet break into a sprint again. I force my way through passersby.

"Move! Get out of my way!" I scream at them.

I curse under my breath as the street ahead of me is blocked by tanks and armored military vehicles, swarms of soldiers marching beside them. I come to a halt so quickly that my heeled shoes skid on the gravel beneath me and send me to the ground.

A few of the soldiers look down at me, and I can see the remorse in their eyes. It just takes one to refuse this job. Just one to save all my friends. But they don't. They just continue marching. Expressionless. If I want to save my friends,

I'll have to do it myself. I push myself back up to my feet and cut through the wooded area that leads directly into the Hooverville. My dress catches on branches and the twigs and thorns cut at my legs, but I don't slow down.

"Thomas!" I scream as loud as I can. "They're coming!" But I know they don't hear it.

I reach the edge of the woods and run without stopping across the road. Several people stare at me, appalled by my behavior. A trolley nearly hits me, but I don't stop. I jump to the next sidewalk and into the park.

"Everybody out!" I scream once I reach the shanties. I wave my arms madly, earning stares and confusion among the veterans. "Move! Go!" They must believe that I'm one of Hoover's people come for them, because despite my exhaustive efforts, they don't sense the urgency. Two men stride up to me and shove me down, shouting. The force with which I hit the ground knocks the wind out of me.

"Try and force us out!" one of them challenges.

"No, listen to me!" I scream, but it comes too late. Across the road, the tanks and vehicles and soldiers arrive and march onto the lawn. They form a line in front of us and block the entrance.

Nobody moves in the Hooverville. Nobody runs for their life. Instead, the veterans smile and cheer for joy, while I shake my head in confusion. They believe the Army is here to protect them, but as I open my mouth to speak, I recognize General MacArthur from his photo in the paper with his pipe in his mouth. The General shouts something incoherent, spit flying out of his mouth, and the Army draws their batons and charges the Hooverville.

It takes a second for the realization to set in, but when it does, screams erupt from within the crowd and dozens of them push their way through to find another way out. I can't push myself to my feet fast enough to stop the screaming stampede from trampling over me. They step on my hands and my head; they trip over my legs and back. I curl up in a fetal position and protect my head until I'm certain I'm safe, and I pick my head up.

Ahead of me, the two men who pushed me to the ground run headfirst into two soldiers and tackle them. They wrestle and roll around on the ground, and I can't tell who's winning. We look like we have a chance until two gunshots ring out and the men slump over. They're obviously dead.

My body recoils at the loud bang, but after I recover, I can't take my eyes off their bodies. The people around us suddenly realize the severity and run in different directions like mice in an experiment. I realize I'm not breathing when the ringing in my ears subsides, and some stranger in the crowd running past me helps me to my feet.

"Get up! Go!" the stranger yells. He's gone just as quickly as he came, but I realize immediately that I likely owe my life to him. I run as fast as I can into the crowd and look above the heads for Thomas's blond hair. Hoover would have sent him here, wouldn't he?

Amidst all the chaos, the people are very slowly penned in, surrounded by the police on every side. There's nowhere to run. Nowhere to hide. We're at their mercy now. Children fall on the ground and scream as they're stepped on. Some of the protesters fight against the soldiers at the front of the crowd. Others continue shouting and holding up their signs.

I continue to shout Thomas's name, but I go unheard in the crowd. Near me, tents and flags go up in flames, and the protesters scream as their belongings are destroyed. The heat of the July sun and the flames make me ill.

No. It's not the heat. Another woman near me has vomited as well.

Something is wrong.

That's when I notice the thick yellow smoke filling the camp. Where it's coming from, I can't see, but with us distracted by the fire and the smoke, the police slowly inch away from the crowd with proud little smiles on their faces.

"Cover your mouths!" someone shouts over the screaming, but it's not enough.

The coughing begins almost immediately. A thousand people choking on nothing. They heave and gag and a few of them vomit. I cover my mouth and nose with my elbow, but it doesn't stop the gas from reaching me. My eyes water and my lungs feel like a rubber band is squeezing at them until there's no air left. My nose burns. My head starts to ache. The world starts to spin around me, and I stumble backward and lean across a wooden crate. I force my eyes to open to take in the scene around me. *Do not fall asleep*, I tell myself.

The protesters disperse and vomit or collapse elsewhere in the park, gagging and dry heaving. To my right, a horrible screaming sound that shakes me to my core brings me back to reality. A young woman no older than me, holding a limp infant, shaking her, screaming at her.

In my confusion, I don't understand. The General's face remains blank, like this is just another day at the office.

A younger, scrawny looking soldier appears at his side and

says, "Hoover's ordered the end of the raid. Shall we leave now sir?"

The General looks over the shanties and shakes his head. "No," he says, like this is a game. Like it's *fun* for him. "Burn it. Burn it all." He turns formally and marches away with his hands behind his back.

"But sir!" The scrawny second soldier calls back uncertainly.

"This is war, Eisenhower!"

The second soldier, Eisenhower, turns to his men and says, "You heard orders." And they enter the Hooverville again.

The Army soldiers go into every tent, including the burning ones, and pull out every personal item they can. Photographs, notebooks, jewelry. They toss it all into one spot in the center of town and return to find more belongings. They pour thick gasoline on the fire and take a step back as it grows taller than the shacks. The heat hits me like a wave and almost sends me back to the ground. The soldiers high five each other and then whoop around the fire. I can't take my eyes off it. It's a bright red color, unlike the bonfire back home. This is a raging inferno.

More soldiers appear at the other side of the town with long metal weapons that look like hoses. I think for a moment they'll use the water and put out the fire on the belongings, but instead, they aim the hoses at the tents. The hoses shoot not water but fire directly at the tents. I gasp and jump backward as they throw fire at shack after shack and tent after tent, letting the flames eat at the homes until they collapse one after the other with a creak and a crash.

If there are any stragglers left after the gas attack, the soldiers corner them. I hide behind the burning pile of items, pulling myself out of my stupor and holding my breath for my life. My eyes catch sight of an old dingy jacket that's thrown in the pile. I know it. But how do I know it?

I search my memories for where it's from, but a scream pulls my attention away from it.

My eyes lock on a woman guarding three young children as the officer approaches with a baton in his hand. Tears stream down her cheeks and she hugs her children close to her as the officer raises the baton above his head. I close my eyes and look away, preparing for the horrible cracking sound of a skull breaking. But none comes.

Instead, I hear a grunt and a thud on the ground. I open my eyes again to see a young man—no, a boy—with a knife in his belt loop tackle the officer. He appears to be winning, though it could hardly be considered a fair fight. The officer struggles, but he can't even get up from where the boy is pinning him to the ground, screaming at him. And that's when I recognize him. Two other officers sprint over and pry him off by his arms and hold him at attention. He fights and kicks at them, but they don't release him.

My feet start to move towards him, just as the first officer cracks his baton down on Peter's skull.

"PETER!" A horrible scraggly sound escapes me as Peter gasps and crumples to the ground. He makes a sound unlike anything I've ever heard before, and his hands fly to the top of his head as if he could somehow stop the inevitable. I try to take a step, but instead, my legs go numb and I find myself on the ground again. The officers stand over him and swing their batons down on Peter's body until he goes limp, then they're distracted by someone else. Peter searches for breath like a fish out of water. I know I need to move. I know I could help him. But I'm frozen and my feet have cemented themselves in place.

I cannot leave him alone. I won't do it. Peter would never leave anyone alone in their dying moments. He would be there to crack a joke or make you smile. I have to be there for Peter.

I push myself to my feet, trembling as I cross the field and drop myself beside Peter's face. He's staring at the sky, dazed, with silver tears slipping out the corner of his eyes.

His eyes drift to me, and for a moment he seems confused by my presence, like he doesn't believe I'm really here. Then he smiles.

"Annie..." he whispers. His voice is scratchy, and I can sense how scared he must be. I have to hold myself together and not cry. I won't let myself.

"Hi, Peter," I whisper, cradling his cheek. His eyes drift to the other side, like he's looking for something else. Or somebody else.

Thomas.

His lip shakes and he wraps his hand around mine, gripping it with every ounce of strength he must have left.

"Annie?"

"I'm here," I whisper. A dull ache forms in my chest and it takes every ounce of courage I have to keep the tears at bay.

"I want my mom," he cries. I see for the first time his age. He's still a child. A boy.

"I know," I whisper and brush back his hair. My fingers touch the bloodied part of his skull where the police cracked his skull open, and Peter's grip on my hands slips. His eyes gloss over and look at some spot in the distance, and with his final breath, he whispers something I don't quite hear, but I'm almost certain it's Thomas's name.

My hands tremble as I realize he's really gone, and I lay Peter back down. I kiss him on the forehead and cry a pathetic, *"I'm sorry"* from somewhere in my chest. Peter deserved better. Thomas deserved better. I deserve better.

I remove Peter's knife from his belt and lock eyes on the officer who killed Peter, who looks neither happy nor upset, but walks with a certain prideful swagger about him. I wrap my fist around the knife, push myself to my feet, and take huge steps toward the officer with the knife raised over my head. Just as I'm about to sink the knife into his back, my eyes catch sight of a man sprinting towards me at full speed and it brings me to a halt.

He's still wearing the dress shirt and slacks from the party. His hair is still slicked back, but he's covered in dirt and blood. Whose blood is that? He's screaming at me, but I can't hear what he's saying.

"Thomas?!" I scream over the fire, squinting in the sunlight and the thick smoke. I drop my hands

He yells, "Run!"

But before I can, a round metal object appears on the ground in front of me and the soldiers. It ticks for a second, then Thomas and I are thrown backward with a blast of air, and my vision goes dark.

XXI

My eyes open and I'm staring at the sky. Gray clouds inked with veiny black smoke. Pieces of floating ash. Dust. My senses come to one at a time. First, my smell returns with the scent of burning rubber and chemicals in the air. I hear the dying down of the fire, and I taste metallic blood in my mouth. My entire body is numb, and I fear I must be dead. Maybe it would be better if I was dead; then I wouldn't have to worry about anything anymore. My ears ring a high-pitched tone that drowns out any sound around me.

One thing becomes increasingly clear to me. *Thomas is dead*. He must be. The *only* reason he would leave me behind is if he were dead.

Thomas is dead. Peter is dead. I lost them both. I failed. No doubt Hoover will order similar raids on every Hooverville in the country. Eva and everyone else from back home will die. Every word written in my book will be forgotten.

Right now, I cannot find it within me to care about any of this. Maybe it's better off forgotten.

My Thomas. Sweet Thomas, who makes sure everyone else has eaten before he even starts. Who gets too nervous to tell a girl that he likes her. Who's never had a pet dog. Who talks in his sleep. Who moves his lips when he reads a book. He's gone. And he'll never *know*.

Ash from the sky falls onto my shoulders and hands and face like impure snowflakes, and somewhere, I hear the faint roar of fires still burning out as the ringing in my ears subsides. I listen hopefully for a sound from any soul, any at all that signifies I'm not alone, but there's nothing.

No pain I've ever known has prepared me for this pain. It's deep and consumes me, but at the same time, it's empty and cold. Hopelessness fills me, and I lay back on the ground, ready to let God take me now. I've put up a good fight, but I didn't fight enough. I completely lose both of my worlds. The home I grew up with and the home I've grown to love. I have no place in the world.

While in my numb stupor, Frank appears in my mind. The only reason he would leave me is if he too was dead. I turn my head slowly, and my eyes find Peter's knife glistening in the light a few feet away from me. I stretch my fingers and pull the blade back toward myself.

Eva engraved it with *Property of Peter,* and the handle is red with Peter's blood. Peter is dead. Thomas is dead.

But I am still alive. Despite Frank, despite my illness, despite every attempt that's been put out for my life—I'm still alive, and I still have a chance that others don't. I may not have been able to save the Bonus Army, but I can still protect the rest of the Hoovervilles in the country from the military force that wants to rid them.

The world swirls around me as I force myself to prop up on my elbow. A sting of intense pain rips through my side, and I reach down to find deep welted burns covering my body. I tuck the knife into a belt loop of my dress and slowly sit up. I wince with every movement, and when I'm finally seated, I can see just how severe my injuries are. I'm covered in cuts, burns, small blisters. I think I must have a concussion, and my whole backside is scraped and bruised from where I hit the ground after the grenade went off.

I take a moment to look around. The Hooverville is empty now save for some body-shaped lumps, most of which don't appear to be dead, just stunned like me. There are piles of charred items, what's left of the tents and the shacks, and nothing more.

Twenty thousand protesters, and this is what happens. No one is safe in a war. Not even in your own front yard.

I stand, trembling with pain until I don't even notice it anymore, and I stumble forward.

My heels crunch on burnt wood pieces used on the homes. Broken glass. A child's stuffed rabbit. I come close to one of the body-shaped lumps, but it's been so severely burnt that it's unrecognizable other than a horrified expression on its blackened, otherwise featureless, face. I try not to think too hard about who this person was, if I knew them, so I push myself forward, the pit of my stomach lurching.

Behind me, I hear a glass break, indicating someone else is here. I spin on my heels, blind hope filling me. A mangy black cat scavenges for food, paying no mind to me. All hope leaves my body as I realize that the only souls here are me and the stupid black cat.

Peter flashes in my mind. Then, horrifyingly, Frank does too. A chill goes up my spine as I suddenly feel as if eyes are watching me. I look around in fear and stiffen my shoulders in defense, my fingers wrapping around the knife still at my waist.

In the distance, beyond the smoke, I can see the Capitol Building shining white as if nothing monstrous has happened to thousands of people right on their own front lawn. It feels as though is taunts me for all we've been through. I begin to walk in that direction.

Outside of the park, there are a few stragglers who don't look nearly as beaten up as I do, but none of them resemble Thomas. I keep my emotions in check as I stumble four blocks to the Capitol Building, where a small group of protesters still shout at the guards who protect Hoover from the rest of us. The people who weren't as injured as I gawk at my ripped and burnt and torn clothes that expose my bloodied and blistered ribcage.

As I approach angrily, a guard puts his hand up.

"Back away, ma'am," he says forcefully, readying his gun. I don't know what I thought I would do, so I just stand my ground.

"I have to speak to Hoover, sir." The guard looks me up and down at my outfit covered in dust and ash and scoffs in my face.

"I won't ask you again. Get off of government property." He points his weapon at me. I take a step back, ready to back down when two of the other protesters step forward and put their hands on my shoulder.

"If you shoot her, you'll have us to deal with." The twenty-five or so Hooverville-ites stand straighter behind me in my defense and square their shoulders. The guards squint their eyes at everyone and turn their guns to them instead.

"Please," I say, stepping forward. I feel too weak to play the part right now, but I have no choice. "My name is Annaleise Winston, I'm engaged to Frank Alexander. Hoover threw a party for me today. Now if you'll please, I have to speak to the President." I turn up my nose in the hopes that using my name will work one last time to get me what I want. The people behind me seem uncertain, as if I'm a traitor, and they begin to withdraw their support.

The guards whisper between each other, and one heads inside while the other lowers his weapon. The guard returns a moment later and says, "Okay, go in."

I step past them with my head held high and glance back at the protesters. I lower my head at them and nod softly, giving them a signal that it will be okay.

The door shuts between us, and I'm plunged into near darkness. As I take steps, the dirt and ash on my body leaves black marks on the marble white floor. I look up at the high vaulted ceiling with a chandelier and am filled with unbridled anger. At Hoover, at High Society, at myself. How could I have ever lived like this knowing people were dying miles away?

I go up the steps to Hoover's office, where he and three other pale-skinned old men sit arguing: Henry Banner, who must have escaped the party early, William Hearst, and Franklin Delano Roosevelt. They all shout over one another, not noticing me in the doorway.

"You *have* to publish something," Banner shouts at Hearst. "Hundreds of people were attacked by their own military today. Veterans! You might as well have murdered puppies."

"That's precisely why we can't publish anything!" Hoover

slams his fist on the table. "Do you know how it would ruin me if people knew?"

"Then you shouldn't have made the order," Banner says through his teeth, leaning in close to the President. They say that the enemy of my enemy is my friend, and I despise Mr. Banner less knowing he hates Hoover just as much as me.

"If you publish this story, you'll be charged with treason, and that goes for everyone," Hoover seethes.

"Herb—" Roosevelt butts in, but he's quickly silenced.

"I'll *not* have people thinking I—" Hoover starts, but Hearst clears his throat at the sight of me standing in the doorway covered in ash. The men all look up, and all except for Roosevelt stand, left speechless. Perhaps they can't tell who I am. "Miss Winston," Hoover drawls, looking me up and down. "What's happened to you?"

"What do you think happened to me, *Mr. President?*" I suddenly shout, stepping into his office. "You set the military on innocent people." I shout at him, fuming. The men just stare at me. *"How could you?"* I spit. "You're a *monster."*

"Anne, you're clearly just emotional."

"I was *blown* up!"

"Are you alright?" Hoover asks.

"Don't ask stupid questions, Hoover," Banner jumps in, and suddenly I see a similarity between the two of us. Roosevelt removes his suit jacket and hands it to Banner to cover my torn dress. I thank him wordlessly with a nod of my head, then look back at Hoover, who raises an eyebrow as if this is a minor inconvenience to him.

"I'm sorry that you got caught in the line of fire, Annaleise. I really am," he says. "But this is a war."

"It wasn't a war. You made it a war the minute you made the order."

"And what exactly do you expect me to do about it now? Your fiancé is okay. Why don't you go back home and let me deal with this? It doesn't concern you."

I squint my eyes at him, so angry that I don't even know what words to use.

"You attacked thousands of veterans. You killed them," I say in a low tone. "You're going to regret this, Hoover. If it kills me, you will regret this."

The look Hoover gives me isn't necessarily one of fear, but more resignation to his fate. He knows I mean it, and I believe part of him knows he deserves it. I storm out of his office wearing Roosevelt's suit jacket over top of my torn gown.

"Wait!" Banner shouts behind me, and I hear footsteps chasing after me. I run down the stairs to avoid a conversation with him, but I'm not fast enough, and his hand grabs me by the shoulder. "Annaleise, I'm—I'm sorry."

"I have somewhere to be, Banner," I say indifferently.

"No, really, I'm sorry. If there's anything I can do to help…"

I look out the window at the burnt Hooverville and then over Banner's shoulder into Hoover's office.

"Fine. You really want to help me? There is one thing," I whisper, leading him away. And I explain everything. I explain where I disappeared to, and the book. How it can help turn around the ideas people hold about the Hoovervilles. He looks cautious and leads me to a quieter corner where Hoover won't hear us.

"That's risky. You heard Hoover; I could be charged with treason."

"And I could too," I whisper. "But if I don't do this, who will stop Hoover from attacking whomever he wants and keeping the support of the people like you and me? I have to show them the truth."

He thinks for what feels like an eternity and then clicks his tongue. "Okay, I'll do it."

"Mr. Banner, *thank you,*" I breathe out and then hug him around the neck. He pats my back awkwardly, thankfully nowhere near my burn, and pulls back with his lips pressed together. "I have to get to work now. I'll see you in New York."

XXII

I exit the Capitol Building and pass the same veterans and protesters I saw earlier, only now they've concluded that I'm just another aristocrat who doesn't give a damn about them, and they become angry and relentless again. They shove at me as I pass through, aggravating my burn, but I soon push through the crowd and into the street.

I'm suddenly hyper aware of how alone I am. I want a hug; I don't care who from. I'd even accept a hug from Mother right now. I drag myself to the Hooverville, where a few extra people wander around, searching the rubbish pile for salvageable items. There are only a few dead bodies, and I know there were more people in this camp than are here now. I stop and look around at the remnants and approach one of the other people. It's the stranger who helped me to my feet after the attack first started.

"Where did everyone go?" I ask him.

"A bunch of people were arrested," he explains. "The injured ones are all over there." He points to the crowd on the far side of town that I already scanned for Thomas's face. I don't want to let myself hope that he's still alive in case I'm wrong, but what if he is and I let him rot in a jail cell?

The stranger gives me a pathetic smile. "There's a good chance that whoever you're looking for is still alive. The death toll as of now is six. It may still rise as the injuries take people, but right now it's six. Six out of twenty thousand isn't bad."

But two of those six were my family. The people I love most in the world. It's easy to say it's not bad when they're strangers. I thank the stranger quietly and allow myself just enough hope to get me to the jail. It's several blocks away, and my feet are already so exhausted after all the running to-day—in heels!—that I almost don't make it. But I do.

The jail is overcrowded with at least twenty people to a single cell, with only standing room. The air is stiff and smells of blood and vomit. Some people cry out in pain from their burns, others vomit from the gas. It's mostly men in jail, but there are some women and even a few kids.

They look at me in my bloody and burnt ball gown as I pass through, confused about whether I'm a friend or foe. I scan each of the faces for Thomas, but the longer it takes and the more faces I look at that aren't him, the more hopeless I become.

"I'm looking for Thomas Kelley," I say loud enough that each of the cells can hear. The prisoners look around, calling out his name, and finally, a blond head pops up from the crowd and limps toward the front of the cell.

"Annie?" he breathes. "You're alive."

A relief like nothing I've ever known floods my body, and I can't contain my emotions. I begin to weep openly and fall to my knees in front of the cell. I reach through the bars and grab his shirt, clinging to him, and vowing to *never* let him go.

"Thomas, I thought you'd... I thought you had..."

"Shhh, shh, it's okay. We're fine." He reaches through the bars and wipes my tears away.

"I thought you'd died. After that grenade went off and you weren't responding..." he trails off. "They arrested me immediately after it went off. I thought I left you behind. I'm so happy you're here."

I smile weakly, trembling with all my emotions. "What happened to your leg?" I ask him. His leg is poorly bandaged with blood soaking through.

"It's not that bad," he says immediately. "I'll be fine." I can tell by the tone of his voice that he's not sure of it himself. "They got the bullet out when I got here. I'm fine."

"Bullet?"

"I'm okay, I promise," he assures me. "Don't worry about me. You need to go to a doctor and get bandages on those burns."

"No, I'm not going anywhere until I find a way to get you out of here," I say firmly. I look around for a guard. I'll pay for his bail. I'll do anything. He smiles weakly at me and stares at my face like it'll be his last time ever seeing it.

"Okay," he says with his natural charisma and optimism, but it's unconvincing this time.

"Thomas, trust me."

"I trust you." His smile fades slightly despite doing his best to keep it on. "Have you seen Peter anywhere?" he whispers, and suddenly I'm filled with fresh pain. He doesn't know. The image of Peter's last moment flashes in my mind, and it must flash across my eyes too, because Thomas's whole demeanor shifts.

"Annie?" he breathes, hope still in his voice. "Where's Peter?"

I swallow a lump in my throat and can only shake my head. Thomas's breathing hitches and he leans back as if it's physically hit him across the chest. "He was protecting a family, Thomas. A mother and her children from some cops. They got him instead," I whisper. Thomas presses his tongue to the roof of his mouth and tears form in his eyes, but he doesn't let them fall. "I tried to help him, but it was too late. There was nothing I could do."

He takes a moment and then nods, one tear falling on each cheek. I know he can't cry in front of all these other men in jail, but I wish he would let himself. "I'm glad you were there," he mumbles.

I reach across my belt loop and pull out Peter's knife. "Do you want this?" I whisper so the guards can't hear me. "It's his."

A sad smile spreads across his face, and he puts his hand over top of mine and slides it back to me. "You keep it. He'd want you to have it." I hesitate and tuck it back in my belt loop. When I turn back around, Thomas is still holding my hand, turning it over in his. My fingers have Peter's blood dried on them, but there's no way he could know that.

"Miss, you have to leave now," says a guard appearing beside me. I squeeze Thomas's hand and kiss his fingers through the bars. We bring ourselves to our feet. I put my hand to his cheek and start to say the words that have been plaguing me all afternoon, but he stops me first.

"I know. Don't waste it. Go," he whispers. I don't understand what he means about *wasting my I love you*, but I don't ask him about it before I leave. I walk the miles back to the White House, feet aching and bloodied with blisters.

When I arrive, guards guide me back to my stateroom wordlessly, either for their safety or mine. They shut the door behind me with a click, and I squint my eyes at it before turning back to the room. The air is stale; the room is cold.

Everything is perfect, as if this room is a showroom in a museum. I peel off Roosevelt's suit jacket from my body and examine my burns on my arms and my back. They're blistered or scabbed over already, while the rest of my skin is red and raised with welts.

I look in the mirror at my once-immaculate ballgown. It's black in places where it was burned off, with other parts torn, but the whole front of it is covered in blood. My blood. Peter's blood. My hair has been burnt off in places. I do not look like someone who belongs in a mansion or a ballgown. I look away from the mirror, for if I look at it too long, I see myself transform into a monster.

I run myself a cold bath and move to unzip my dress, but the mere movement of my arms sends hot, electric pain down my arms and chest. I try again but break open one of my blisters on accident. I gasp for breath and grip my hand to relieve the pressure. The pain subsides and I take an angry breath. Angry at who? I don't know. Nobody. Everybody. Herbert Hoover.

I claw at my dress to get it off my body, but I'm given no such relief. I scream in frustration and climb into the tub with my dress on anyway. The dress floats to the top of the water, wrapping me in a bubble, and I sigh in relief as the cool water soothes my burns. I duck my head under the water and consider staying under forever. But when I open my eyes and see the water has turned rust colored, I come back above the surface.

The blood in my dress has started to seep out into the water. I gasp and jump out of the tub. I can't breathe. The dress seems to tighten around me. Every time I close my eyes, I see Peter crumple to the ground and bleed out from his head. I grab onto the counter, dripping wet, and dry heave into the sink.

My fingers wrap around Peter's knife, and I tighten my fist around it. I hold the knife up to my chest and begin slicing the dress off me directly down the center. I slide it off my shoulders and throw it to the ground, tossing the knife away with me with a clink against the floor.

I gasp for breath, and soon I feel normal again. I drain the rust-water and wash the dirt out of my hair by holding my head under the faucet and letting the water run over my neck and head. Then I let the tears come and flush out my soul. I drown out the sound of my tears with the sound of the water hitting the tub. Each time I close my eyes, I see Peter's face. His voice comes into my head, telling me a joke. I smile at the memory of him dancing around the fire like a madman, but then I cry again.

I dry myself off with a large towel and clothe myself in some pajamas I find in a drawer, then I help myself to the liquor graciously offered to me by our hosts until it dulls the pain. I lay on the ottoman, drained and motionless, staring into space, or a spot on the carpet that occupies exactly none of my thoughts. The dehydration wants me to sleep, but I don't.

How could Hoover send an entire Army to attack Veterans? Veterans and their families and homeless people. How could he? I think of the children who died as a reaction to the gas, or the woman who lost her baby, and feel a pang in my chest. Yet, I can only think of one thing. How could he? How could he have betrayed all those people who once fought for him? I think of the scrawny aid that came to the General's side and second-guessed his orders but agreed, anyway. I wonder how many people he could have saved if he ignored orders.

Is it too much to ask to live in a world where people simply love people? Where abuse doesn't happen, and nobody is better than anybody else? A world where you can pass a shantytown and you don't avert your eyes, but instead you offer them a meal and a conversation. A world where the police don't attack their own citizens with wartime weapons and call it justice. Where boys don't fight in a war they never signed up for. How can this be the world we have formed for ourselves? All these years of existence, and this is the best we can do?

I sit straight up as the doorknob clicks and turns open, and his broad figure steps into the doorway. I straighten my spine and harden my face, preparing for another battle.

"Frank," I greet. Frank steps past me and closes the curtains to the window without a word, but I can tell by his stature that he's angry with me. His cut from the brick today has scabbed over and he's chosen not to wear a bandage, probably to show how tough he is. His back is tense, his forearms flexed, and he grits his teeth so hard that I can see his jaw twitch. He turns to me with tight eyebrows and a dull expression on his face. And he just stares. I stare back, challenging him. This has turned into a game between the two of us as to who frightens who the most. And after today, I think I might have the upper hand.

"I don't even know where to begin with you, Annaleise," he says, turning his nose up at me.

"So, don't, and we can skip this altogether." I try at a joke, but he doesn't smile.

"You made a fool out of me today. In every possible way." His voice is monotonous, which scares me more than if he would raise it.

"Sorry, but I think being blown up was retribution enough," I say.

He raises his hand to slap me, then restrains himself, which unnerves me. "I'm furious with you," he finally says calmly. "Furious. Do you understand that?" I don't answer. "Do you realize what it looks like for me to have a fiancé go missing for weeks, and then when she reappears, she's suddenly a-a..." He stammers, looking for the word. "Traitor," he finally decides. Not the word I expected, but because I know it isn't the truth, it doesn't hurt me.

"What do you think that looks like for me, Annaleise?" He takes a menacing step closer to me. I swallow a lump in my throat and keep my head high, ignoring his question. "*Answer me!*" he screams and balls my hair into a fist. He slams my head back against the footboard of the bed and then drags me from the ottoman to the wall and pins me there. My brain feels like it bounces around in my head, and I blink hard to focus on the world again. Frank is staring me down like a madman, with eyes that seem to turn yellow and steam practically coming out of his nose. He puffs himself out to make himself look bigger, and huffs to breathe.

"How does it make me look, Annaleise?" he repeats. He wraps both of his hands around my throat and tightens his grip. Even in his worst times back home, he's never gone this far. He presses his thumbs into the sides of my throat and his face twitches with anger. He leans in close and whispers, "It makes me look like I have no control over you."

My eyes water. I gasp for breath but feel as though I'm being submerged in water. I claw at his hands to get him off me, to no avail. He presses harder, and my vision goes dark at the corners and I gasp for breath, a raspy noise coming from my mouth. Just before my body goes fully limp, I muster all my energy to my legs and I force my knee forward.

He drops me and moves his hands to his crotch area. "You little bitch!" he grunts.

I drop to the ground and cough, heaving and catching my breath, crawling toward the bathroom. Toward Peter's knife. It's hidden under the strips of my ballgown, but I can just see the blade. I reach my hand out for it when I feel Frank's grip around my ankle, and he pulls me back toward him.

"No!" I screech. I dig my fingernails into the floorboard as he drags me by the ankle. I flip myself over to face him as he steps over me.

His fist comes down over me, but I block it with my forearms, and he hits me in the stomach instead. He straddles me and I know there's no way for me to escape him this time. Not now. I can still see Peter's knife from the corner of my eye, but I can't get to it. Frank's crazed look in his eye makes me realize that Frank will kill me here and now and get away with it.

He slams me into the floor over and over again, but somehow, I reach my arm out into the fireplace, pull out a log, and smash it over his head.

With Frank dizzy and distracted, I run to the bathroom and grab Peter's knife. I jump to my feet and grip the handle in my fist and point the tip at Frank as a warning not to come any closer. Frank shakes himself back into reality, and I see a flicker in his eyes, but then he smiles, disorienting me once again.

"What are you going to do with that, Annie?" He sneers and steps closer to me with his arms up. "Are you going to kill me? That would make you look like a hero, for sure. Crazy girl runs away from her fiancé, returns, and murders him in cold blood? Think of the picture that would paint for your precious Hooverville."

I stand straighter and try not to let his words get to me, but he makes sense. I narrow my eyes at him as he circles me. My brain works overtime to think my way out of this.

"You'd be doing everyone you fought for today a disservice. Everyone will believe they're a bunch of savages with the power to turn perfectly innocent people evil too. Imagine what they'd do to your little friends. They would *never* let Mr. Kelley out of jail."

From behind me, he grabs my hand and points the knife at my throat. The knife shakes as our strengths fight against each other, and I lean my head away, but then understand what I must do. He leans into my ear and whispers, "I don't have to kill you. But I can. So, I suggest you drop the knife and be a good wife."

It seems there's no way out of it now. No ending where I

live my life free from Frank. I look at Frank in the mirror. He knows he's won the battle, and he looks entirely too pleased. He presses the icy blade against my throat. I struggle against him for a moment longer, then smile twistedly at our reflection in the mirror, and my smile shakes Frank enough to disorient him.

"I've never been a good wife," I say with my raspy voice, struggling against his grip. "And *you don't own me*," I declare, and then use all my force to push his hand back, twist myself out of his arms, and plunge the knife into Frank's chest. With his hand still wrapped around mine, and the knife in his heart, Frank staggers and takes a step back. He looks at me with an unexpectedly vulnerable face, like he's shocked he could have lost our game.

I catch my breath as Frank stumbles for a moment, then collapses on the bathroom floor, dead. I reach up and touch my swollen throat, then ceremoniously remove his engagement ring and set it on the counter. I watch Frank's body for a moment, waiting for him to move. It's too good to be true. But as a puddle of dark red blood forms beneath him, I drop my shoulders and breathe for the first time in years.

"Goodbye, Frank," I whisper as I turn and leave the bathroom. I shut the door behind me as I leave and pack up my things in my bag before I leave my stateroom.

XXIII

When they find Frank's body, I confess to killing him, and it's my lack of remorse that makes them put me in handcuffs and cart me off to the madhouse. I'm kept separate from the other patients—the ones who scream at invisible faces or slam their heads into glass windows— since no one can agree on whether or not I should go to jail. The one thing they can agree on is that I'm not mentally stable enough to be on my own in public. That's just code for they know I'm angry and they fear what I'll do to others who have upset me, which right now is a lot of the officials who keep me here.

They treat my wounds with antibiotics and some fancy creams that remind me of Mother's bathroom back home, but sting on my open sores. The doctors here are the worst sort of people. I've seen them shove and berate the other girls here, so I stay on my best behavior to prevent being treated the same. The nurses aren't as bad. One of them, Lucy, told me she thinks I was very brave, and that she hopes she could be as brave as me someday. I don't feel brave. I feel reckless and stupid.

Someone brought my things from my stateroom, like the suncatcher and my diary. The doctor says that writing in it is a productive way to cope, but I don't do it for him. I do it for Thomas. And for Peter. I write about the Bonus Army and about Frank's murder. I may or may not want to remember it when I'm old and frail, but just in case I do want to remember it, I don't want to leave out a single detail.

I don't have any windows in my cell, so I don't even know what day it is, but based on how many times they've fed me, it must be Sunday.

"Miss Winston," a kind guard named James says. "You have a visitor."

I stand and watch as my mother comes into the cell, dressed down in a way I haven't seen in years. I'm not sure who I expected, but I'm disappointed with who it is. She wears no makeup, and her hands tremble with tremors. Her hair is a matted mess atop her head, still making her look older than her mere forty years. She's truly hideous. She looks me up and down, confusion on her face. She must have expected me to have become some monstrous creature, but when she sees only her daughter, she's horribly confused.

We stare at each other in silence. Her silence stems from her fear of me, and mine comes from my anger with her. I realize she isn't going to say anything, so I sit and face the wall.

"You can leave," I tell her. I feel her eyes on me and hear her heavy breathing.

"I don't want to leave," she finally says, and puts a hand on my shoulder, inadvertently aggravating my burns. I jump away from her so quickly that James moves from his post beside the door in case he needs to get between me and her. They honestly think I'm the monster here. Where was this protection for me when Frank tried to murder me?

"It's okay," my mother tells the guard. "She wouldn't hurt me; I'm her mother."

"Oh, are you?" I spit angrily. I glance at the guard, who stands ready in case he must pull me away. I slump back to the floor. "If you're here to lecture me, I don't want to hear it."

"I came here to ask you why you did it," Mother says, biting her tongue in anticipation.

I turn my head towards her, squinting my eyes. "Don't tell me you didn't know," I scoff. "You're just as vapid as I thought," I mumble under my breath. She outstretches her neck and shakes her head. "Frank tried to kill me, Mother! Daily!"

Mother swallows a lump in her throat and blinks. "I thought he was just trying to make you a better wife. You couldn't be taught."

My mouth hangs low, and I feel anger rising in me again, but there's no fire left in me. "I worried every single day about if I was going to live to the next morning, and you knew? You didn't care to do anything?"

"Annaleise, it's not that I didn't care. It's that I thought it would *stop* after a certain point." She folds her hands nervously in her hands and plays with a handkerchief, so she doesn't have to meet my eyes.

"I was never going to be a good wife, and instead of accepting it, you sold me to someone who would try to beat me into someone I'm not? Will you *look at me*?" My hand flashes out and steals her handkerchief from her. James stands straighter at the door, and I see his finger tighten on the trigger on his gun. Mother jumps back and turns to me, her buggy eyes even bigger than they usually are if that's possible.

Finally, we see what we've become. I'm something to be feared—or something capable of inducing fear—and she realizes there's nothing she can do to control me anymore. She relaxes her shoulders.

"It's not quite as dramatic as you make it out to be. There was no selling. I never sold you."

"You completely misunderstand."

"Then help me understand!"

"I ran away from home to get away from YOU, Mother! I left because I couldn't stand to be near someone who could do that to me and feel no remorse," I shout. James is pretending not to listen. Mother stiffens. "I killed Frank in self-defense, but you're the one that I *truly* hate."

"Maybe if you hadn't been so difficult," Mother says, then stops herself before she says too much. My eyes burn into her skull, and she squirms uncomfortably under my gaze.

"Fine," I finally say dryly. "Here's how this is going to work. You move out of the mansion and find somewhere else to live, and you don't speak to me *ever* again."

"Anna—"

"You missed your chance to be a loving mother. Don't start now."

She looks at the floor, then pushes herself to her feet. "I hope you can learn to forgive me, Annaleise. I do love you."

I stare back at the wall and listen as she leaves. The door shuts behind her, echoing in my large cell and probably making the same sound in my empty heart.

Doctors come in to check on my neck every hour. The bruises Frank left are my only evidence that it was self-defense, so they check on it frequently to make sure I'm healing fine. They feared my voice may permanently change, or that I may not even get it back, but I could speak again after a couple of days, although I chose not to. There are scabs where his fingernails dug into my skin, which will eventually turn into little white scars to remind me of him every time I look in a mirror.

I still hear Frank, even though he's dead. His voice in my head telling me I'm not good enough. I feel his presence appear at times as though he's just entered the room, but there's no one there. Instead of being relieved with his death, I feel him always now. When the door opens and its guards or detectives or doctors, I retreat into a corner of the room and turn myself into a ball until I'm certain he hasn't come back for another fight.

I overhear the doctors at one point when they think I'm sleeping, and they say that my anxiety and fear are at the same level of soldiers with battle fatigue, which baffles them.

Even after I've finished it, I can't stop rereading the diary. It makes me crazy, yelling at my past self for what a fool I was. Yelling at the author for not being smarter in her choices. Eventually, I ask Lucy to take it away from me and give it to Henry Banner.

While I lay in bed at night, I feel the need to cry, but I can't make the tears come. I don't belong in Hooverville. I don't belong at home. I don't belong anywhere. Maybe I should just stay here for the rest of my life, so I never have to deal with anything bad again. No more wars. No more lying politicians. No more heartbreak. Just pure safety. I could stop feeling for everyone else so much and just not care about who lives and who dies. It wouldn't matter.

But I don't get to live out my fantasy for long, because just as I'm getting used to a routine at the hospital, I have another visitor. I stand from my bed and watch the door open, and Governor Roosevelt wheel himself inside.

"Hello, Annaleise," he says kindly, with a sweet flicker in his eyes. He doesn't look at me like the others have. He doesn't fear me, not even a little bit.

"Governor," I say hoarsely.

He sighs and looks at the ground. "Annaleise, I'm sorry about all of this."

I'm not sure which part he's sorry for. My engagement to Frank? The Hoovervilles? Putting me in a high-security madhouse? I frown at him.

"For, first of all, the homeless crisis. I know it's my duty to help it. Mr. Banner showed me your writings. You're talented. And I want to make a promise to you I will do everything in my power to fix it."

It sounds like a politician's lie, and I'm not immediately inclined to believe it.

"And second, I'm sorry they put you in this cell for so long. It's obvious to anyone watching that you did what you had to do." He observes my neck and grimaces. "Annaleise, I've pardoned your crime."

I steady my feet and swallow a lump in my throat with difficulty. "You've what?"

"You're free. I've come to take you back home to New York." Roosevelt smiles at me, and his eyes twinkle and scrunch up at the edges like my father's used to. I take a deep breath. I'm happy. I should be happy. Why am I not happy?

Roosevelt picks up on my uncertainty and frowns. "What's the matter?"

I think of home, but will it even be home anymore? Without Peter and Thomas, without my parents, without even Frank. Everything's changed. "If you pardon me," I start, "can you pardon the veterans who were arrested?"

He hesitates. "I've been trying, I promise. But that's not my jurisdiction. That falls on Hoover."

My shoulders slump, and I nod, staring at the floor. "There's just one person who I was hoping I would get to see again."

He nods understandingly and stands. "I will fight to make sure that happens, Annaleise. After everything, I want you to be happy. Truly happy." He opens the door for me and stands out of the way to let me leave. I leave without taking another look at my cell.

They give me my things and find some clothes for me, since the clothes I came here with were taken for evidence. They bring me downstairs and Roosevelt warns me that "It's a little crazy out there, Annaleise." But "a little crazy" doesn't begin to describe the madhouse waiting for me outside the jail. Once my eyes adjust to the sunlight for the first time in a week, I'm met with screams and cheers. Some people scream at Roosevelt to lock me back up because I'm a menace. Others throw their support my way. Up front in the crowd are photographers and reporters trying to get exclusive photos or interviews, but I'm forced past them by Roosevelt and the prison guards.

They put me in a car with blackened windows in the back-seat, and I wait while Roosevelt wheels around the car to get in on the other side. We drive off, and I lay my head against the window. I fall asleep.

When I wake, we're still in the car, but it's dark outside now and I recognize the New York skyline. The lights are on, but the city is silent.

Roosevelt gives me a list of people to call if I need anything at all, and he informs me he's going to keep two officers in my home at all times until the scandal dies down. For my protection.

We pass Central Park, and I see the pit and the bonfire in the Hooverville, with figures dancing around. I suppose they still have no idea about Peter or Thomas, and I don't want to be the one to tell them. Not tonight. I look away from the Hooverville as some stranger, not Arthur, drives toward my house. My mansion.

They watch me go in and wait for me to shut the door behind me before they drive off. The house is cold and empty, and everything is exactly the way it was the morning we left for D.C., except my mother's things are gone. Her coats, her shoes. All of her photographs, including the ones of my Pa.

My bravery falters and I take a shaky breath into my lungs. I hang my coat up in the front closet and then move into the living room. Every move I make or step I take echoes in the house and fills me with dread and loneliness. Virginia is nowhere to be found, and Arthur must still be in the Hooverville, so my home is empty.

On the table in the living room is a single envelope with Annaleise written in beautiful cursive letters. I debate whether to take it, so when my hand reaches out for it, I brace myself.

I pull it open and pull out a letter written in my mother's handwriting.

It reads:

My Annaleise,

They told me you'd be pardoned for your crime, so I decided to listen to you and leave.

I've moved into a smaller home on the eastern side of the state, and I won't return until you request to see me again. I leave the offer to you. The moment you choose to see me again, I will be there, and should you not, I want you to know that I love you deeply, and I'm sorry for any harm I've caused you. Looking back, I can't justify my actions other than blind hope that your future could be brighter, one created without lies and deceit, like my life was.

I believe your father would be proud of all you've accomplished, even if I cannot yet accept it. Mr. Banner told me you wrote a book, and I look forward to reading it. I promise to be your biggest supporter from a distance.

I love you, and I hope you'll one day forgive me.

Love,

Your Mother

I fight tears as I read her letter, and I fold it back up and place it in the envelope again. I might one day consider forgiving her, but for now, I can't.

I lay on the couch and try to sleep, but none comes. Instead, tears start. Thick, heavy tears that run down my cheeks and soak my hair underneath me. I don't have the energy to sob or throw things, so I just let the tears come. Every time I feel I'm close to stopping, I think of something else that hurts me again. Frank. Peter. Mother. Virginia. Arthur. Thomas.

It's at least two days without another soul. When I hear

the door open downstairs and Virginia call my name, I stumble downstairs and right into her arms, eventually falling to the ground with tears.

We go to the Hooverville together and bring Eva and Arthur and his daughters home with us, and soon my house is filled with joy and love like it never has been. But although they all seem happy, I still feel empty. The day I tell them about Peter is the worst, but I have to try to be strong for them, since I've had more time to grieve.

Banner comes by a few weeks later with a hard copy of *Hooverville*. Printed, bound, painted. I run my fingers over the beautiful cover and do something I never thought I'd do: I hug Henry Banner and thank him. He pays me seventy-five dollars for the book and tells me that more is coming.

Soon the book hits the shelves. I don't even know it until I'm in the park one afternoon in early October and I see a woman reading the book, engrossed. I run to the nearest bookshop and sure enough; the sellers put up copy after copy of *Hooverville*, each one promising juicy details about the disappearance of one Annaleise Winston and about the Bonus Army attack. It's enough to send copies flying off the shelves.

Banner comes over for lunch with us twice a week, and we get to know each other better. He tells me stories about my father when they were young, about me when I was young, and then all about how he overcame his alcoholism. He tells me in passing, "your writing inspired me to fight for good again." And I haven't stopped thinking about it since.

One afternoon while eating grilled cheese sandwiches, I

run an idea by Banner, Virginia, and Arthur, that I've been stewing on for months.

"I want to turn the mansion into a soup kitchen and let people use the bedrooms." They pause for a minute, but then smiles spread across their faces, and I let out a breath of relief to have their support.

"I think that's an amazing idea," Arthur says, and then the lunch turns into them excitedly discussing how it'll work, what we can do. Banner suggests we do a special re-release of *Hooverville* with an epilogue about the soup kitchen so 'people can really see what a hero I am.' Virginia suggests helping people get back on their feet with some clothes for interviews, or resources for jobs.

It takes some planning and work, but Eva and I turn each of the twenty bedrooms into a luxury bedroom set with first aid supplies, fresh clothes and blankets of all sizes, female products, and as many books as a person could read. Word gets around about our project and people like Betty and Johnny Lyndon start donating things from their own home to the cause.

We open our free bed-and-breakfast to the people of the Central Park Hooverville first, and single-handedly make the soup from Miss Clara's recipe and feed the people and their children. I give Arthur and the girls' my mother's old bedroom, which is more than large enough for all of them.

With the noise and laughter in the home, my loneliness subsides, but an ache stays with me always.

"What are you thinking about?" Eva asks me one night when she catches me in the backyard looking at the city lights. I jump slightly and turn around to face her. She grins and I hardly have to answer. I've hardly thought of anything else in months. "Wherever he is, I'm sure he's thinking about you too."

I have to hope so. The day I told Eva what happened to Peter was the worst. But somehow it made me feel less alone, having someone else miss him as much as I did. It started as hours of crying, followed by laughing about the dumb things he would do, followed by more crying and hugging to get through our grief.

I feel for the first time that I've done something right, but something doesn't sit with me. I head back to my bedroom one afternoon and find Thomas's train tickets to California, and I stare at them. I consider it for a moment. I told Thomas I wouldn't leave until I was certain everyone would be safe. I look around at what I've created, the soup kitchen and bed-and-breakfast. Eva has already told me she'd be happy to run it if I ever left, and I know they'd be in good hands, so what's keeping me here?

I go for a walk in the now near-empty Hooverville and make mental notes of where things happened. This is where I met Thomas. This is where Clara died. This is where Peter played the knife game, and this is where he danced every single night. How could this have happened?

I do a lap around the park and come back around to the Hooverville sign. I never want to forget a single moment that happened here. No matter how awful. No matter how painful. I wouldn't have done any of it differently, but every time I pass the park, or see Eva, or catch someone reading *Hooverville*, a pain like electricity hits me in the heart and makes it impossible to breathe. I can't stay any longer.

A sound from behind me stirs me, and I jump into a fighting stance before I remember nobody wants to turn me in anymore, but when I see him, I stop breathing. He's thinner, with long hair and a stubbly beard, but he has the same smile. Same eyes. It's Thomas. My Thomas.

"They said you might be here—" Thomas hardly gets his sentence all the way out before I jump on him and wrap my arms around his neck. He stumbles back a little but catches me and wraps his arms around me. We bury our faces in each other's shoulders and hold each other until things feel like they're finally okay.

XXIV

⟨⟨⟨❦⟩⟩⟩

E va, Thomas, and I stand at a distance and watch the last person leave Hooverville for my home, and as we stare at the empty shacks, none of us can say a thing. It feels like sacred ground now. Nothing's technically changed, other than the people leaving. The shacks still have stripped and chipped off paint falling like snowflakes onto the ground beside them. The bonfire is now a lump of ash sitting between a pile of blackened bricks. The only difference is that the belongings are missing. The *life* is gone. The little touch that made the *Hooverville* a *home*. No pictures are hanging by a pin on boards. There are no newspaper ads turned into board games for the kids. No chess table, but a cardboard box. It's just as dilapidated and run down as I remember it being when I first arrived, but I'm not sure this is the same Hooverville I left behind when I went to D.C. It's just a hunk of garbage now.

I press my tongue to my teeth. Eva stretches her shoulders. "Why don't we just let the authorities deal with it?" she asks, clearly uncomfortable with the idea of tearing it down ourselves. I consider agreeing with her, but Thomas shakes his head.

"No, I don't want anybody else doing this but us," Thomas declares, and glances at me. "It's our home."

I take his hand and nod at him, giving him my whole support. We pick up the axes from the ground below us, and one by one chop down the huts into piles of paint-stripped wood.

Eva weeps while she does it, Thomas acts as though he has a mission to accomplish with this, and I release my anger into my fingertips and the handle of the axe while tearing them down strip by strip. Angry that they ever existed in the first place. Angry at the people who killed Peter. Angry at myself for killing Frank. No, no, I'm not angry about that. I don't even know why I'm so angry. It festers inside of me and the more I try to release it, the more it stirs within me until I'm swinging the axe madly and Thomas has to come up behind me to stop me.

The last time somebody held me like this, I killed him. But Thomas just wraps his arms around mine and hugs me to him until I drop the axe and collapse crying in a rubble pile that used to be the Hooverville. It's catharsis that I don't think any of us knew we needed, a collective grief. Thomas shhh's in my ear and rocks me until I stop crying and waves off Eva when she comes near.

"They told me," Thomas whispers. "About Frank."

I don't know what my plan was for when he asked. I had hoped he would just accept that Frank was out of the picture and never ask questions.

"I killed him," I whisper. "I murdered him. I'm a bad person." A wave of pain goes through me, not because of Frank, but because Thomas fearing me the way I feared Frank is unbearable. If there's even a moment of hesitation, I might as well kill myself here and now before I become more of the monster I fought so hard to defeat.

"Hey. Look at me." Thomas grabs my cheeks and looks me in the eyes. "You're not a bad person. Okay?"

"I killed somebody," I whisper. "I don't want you thinking of me differently."

"No!" he insists immediately. "Annie, nothing could ever make me think of you differently. I've seen you in every way, or at least in a lot of ways, and I love every single version of you." He searches my eyes for a reaction, but I can't bring myself out of my sadness to even feel joy for his statement.

"I messed a lot of stuff up," I whisper, my voice breaking again. He brushes my hair from my face in his gentlest way. I used to flinch when he did that, but I don't this time. He's my shelter from every storm.

"The world's messed up on its own. Don't give yourself so much credit." He grins painfully. I let out my first laugh in ages, and it feels foreign compared to the months of crying I've done.

Eva returns with a headstone just like Clara's made from some of the wood from shacks, and she's carved Peter's name into it. She stands over us anxiously and gently holds it out.

Thomas's jaw drops, and then he breaks too. Not as unbearable as when he first found out, but to see him in pain hurts me too. I feel it in my chest and up my spine and into the nerves in my cheeks. His face twists up and turns red. He hides it in his hand, but his shoulders shake as he sobs. I try to soothe him, but I'm not as good as he is at that.

The headstone reads: "For our Peter, our friend, our brother, our hero."

"Do you like it?" Eva asks anxiously. Thomas reaches out and touches it, nodding with a kind smile.

"I think he would hate it," he jokes. "He'd want something sarcastic." We all laugh, but it comes out as a strange, warbled, laugh-cry sound. We put the headstone in the ground right beside Clara's and silently mourn them. This is the closest we'll get to funeral services for them, but I don't think Peter would have complained.

Eva, Thomas, and I eventually crack open a bottle of some type of alcohol that tastes burnt and drink it until we're too drunk to be sad. We pass along stories of Clara and Peter and our time in the Hooverville. Then it gets sad again and no one quite knows what to say.

The walk back to the house is awkward. We let Eva walk ahead of us, and Thomas and I walk with our arms around each other. When Eva is out of sight, I stop walking. We've cut through the park, the trees shielding us from the city lights, and only the moonlight shining on us. Our breath turns to fog around us, and Thomas tugs on my hand to pull me close to him. We sway in light circles again and Thomas hums, chuckling slightly.

"You need to trim your beard," I whisper and reach up to touch it lightly. It's only a symbol of how long we were apart. I hate it.

"You like the scruffy look," he smirks.

He takes a step closer to me, looking from my eyes to my lips. He presses his forehead to mine, our noses tickle each other's, and we shut our eyes as if it's a way to make this time slow down.

"Annaleise, can I kiss you?" he whispers so quietly that

only I can hear, and so close I can feel his breath on my cheek. I nod, and he leans down the last couple of inches and lowers his lips to mine. We both desperately need this, and so we hold onto each other, too afraid to let go. He is warm and gentle and tender and holds me like he's afraid to break me. Thomas smiles a bit against my mouth and kisses me again, and I let him. Even in the cold winter weather, I've never felt warmer inside.

He pulls back too soon and rests his forehead against mine. "Annie, can I ask you something?" He whispers into the air. I nod. "Do you regret coming to Hooverville?"

I open my eyes, pull my forehead back, and look at him. I have to think long and hard, which I think makes him nervous. "I regret parts of it. I don't regret you, though."

When we get to the house, most everyone has gone to bed, so Thomas and I sit in the library. I give him a copy of Hooverville to read, but he mostly skims it.

"You don't like it?" I ask, deflated.

"It's just hard to read," he says, fighting a bubble in his throat, and I realize it was rude of me to force it on him. He adjusts himself in his chair and takes my hand. "I haven't fully processed everything that happened. I mean, I have; I had plenty of time to dwell on it and think about it, but it's not real yet. None of this is real."

I completely get what he means. Even while I'm living this new life, I still wake up in the same bed as always and expect to find I'm still engaged to Frank, that this has all been some amazing, terrible dream. But every day, the sun rises, and I wake to find it's all real. The good and the bad. It's sometimes tough, but I try my hardest to live each day, so if I wake up tomorrow, I'll remember today as a marvelous dream.

"I missed you and Peter so much, and things weren't clear in there, and I got pretty bad in the head. I would have hurt myself if not for this one shining beacon of hope, something to fight for." He plays with a loose string from his sweater and wraps it around his finger so tightly it swells up and turns red.

I can't imagine Thomas needing anything to give him hope. He's always seemed so strong. What did they do to him in that jail to make him want to hurt himself? Suddenly I'm kicking myself for not fighting harder to get him out. I don't know that I would have survived if Thomas had killed himself after all of this. One more loss could kill me, I swear it.

I move closer to Thomas, holding onto him so he can't slip away from me.

"What was it?" I ask nervously.

"You." Thomas says. "You keep telling me I'm selfless, but..." he sighs. "I'm not. Everything I've ever done has been in pursuit of my own personal gain, because I don't want to be alone. I'm... terrified of being alone."

"Thomas, you're not alone," I whisper.

"But I *was*. I did everything right, and I still ended up alone in the jail. And at first, I didn't think I would survive it. I even tried to get ahold of a rope to do it with. But knowing that I would get out and see you again made it all worth it. I didn't know if Frank was alive or dead, or if you were alive or dead at that point, but *you were my hope*. You got me through long enough to heal on my own. I eventually figured out that even if you weren't there when I got out, I could survive on my own. I'd made it that far on my own and I would be okay."

I don't know what to say. So instead, I lean forward and kiss him.

Thomas deserves better than the constant reminders of his loss. I deserve to go somewhere I can walk down the street without being recognized for what I've done. The good, the bad, everything in between. I deserve to go somewhere that I am more than the character Banner turned me into in the book. Somewhere that I'm not a hero, but just me.

I think of the train tickets and pull back from the kiss. "Do you want to run away?" I ask Thomas. At first he looks confused, and he searches my eyes for the explanation. "I want to go to California. We can start anew. Have a farm or something. Get away from this city, just you and me."

He bites his lip for a minute and looks around him. He has comfort in this house, for sure. All the books any of us could ever want. Soft beds and a spacious garden of fresh vegetables, which have mostly died out in the last few weeks. He looks like he's going to say no, and I can hardly blame him. He has security for the first time in who knows how long, and it's a big thing I'm asking of him.

"Will you marry me?" Thomas asks, and a smile creeps up on me. It was only a few months ago that Frank asked me the very same question, but it feels so much better when you're in love.

I jump at him and throw my arms around Thomas's neck and kiss him again, and when we release each other, we both say, "I take that as a yes?" and erupt into fits of laughter.

"Sorry that I don't have a ring," Thomas says timidly.

"I don't need a ring. I just need you."

XXV

We don't tell anyone about California or the engagement just yet, but when Virginia catches me dancing in the kitchen at breakfast, I think she senses something, because she gives me a little smile, and makes pastries for Thomas and me in the afternoon, which everyone in the house likes.

I pull on my Pa's old coat again and go for a walk. Protesters argue in favor of Franklin Roosevelt for President as I pass by. The Bonus Army attack sealed Hoover's fate, and he'll be kicked from office by the end of the season, although I don't think he ever really stood a chance against the working class.

The line at the employment office and at the food shelter still wraps around the block, and stores are still bricked up with "CLOSED" signs, but the crisp fall air promises the end of an era. Like the fallen leaves in Central Park, rebirth is promised.

I find my way to Mr. Banner's office and sit in the waiting room with his secretary. She scurries into his office and a moment later he emerges, looking fatter than usual, with a cigar between his teeth.

"Annaleise! What a pleasant surprise!" he says, opening his

arms for a hug that I do not return. "What can I do for you today?"

My book has afforded most of the luxuries in this building alone. I'm sure he can afford to give me more, as it will be the last time I'll ever ask for money from him.

"I wanted to tell you that I'm leaving," I say. "Thomas and I are going to California to get married."

He blinks, stunned, then says, "Congratulations, Annaleise."

"I've come for my last paycheck to help us get started out there." I plant my feet to the ground, prepared to fight if he says no. "After this, I want my percentage of the book earnings to go toward the shelter."

He taps his foot and looks around. "Very well." I had expected more of a fight. "Come inside."

Twenty minutes later I leave with a check, made out to *Annaleise Kelley*. Seeing it in writing, and not just in my imagination, stops me in my tracks, and this time I really do hug Henry Banner and say goodbye.

As I pack my bag for California, I really realize how few material belongings I have, or even want with me. I find the blue gown I wore to Betty's party the night Frank proposed and all my things from Hooverville. I only pack a few things. Some pairs of pants, some shoes, my check, and Clara's gifts like the suncatcher.

I don't even have a picture of my family. Not of my father or of Peter or Clara. What if I forget all of this while I'm in California? I know the goal is to forget the bad things, but what if I forget the good things too? I don't want to forget.

I sit down on my bed and envision our house in California.

A little cottage near the beach, dogs roaming around, maybe children too. A garden to grow vegetables in, a sea to get swept away in, and everything seems so perfect.

***

The next morning is the same as always. Chatter, chaos, laughter filling these walls like there never was before. We pretend like nothing is happening until late afternoon, when Thomas and I enter the dining room with our bags in our arms. Nobody knows we're leaving until the chatter dies down, and one by one, they start to realize.

"You're leaving?" Eva asks, standing quietly and approaching us.

"Yeah, we're leaving," I say.

"We're going to California!" Thomas announces excitedly.

She's frozen for a moment as others push past her to say their goodbyes. Family after family thanks me for all I've done for them, though I don't feel like I've done anything worthy of praise or thanks. Do I deserve to run off and miss all of this? Is it cowardice to leave? Have I earned any of this? I hug each of the Abbott girls for a long time and tell them I love them, and I give *The Reign of the Abbott Sisters* to Gertie to keep and read. I kiss Arthur on the cheek and promise to write to him, and then it's Virginia's turn.

We hug each other tightly and rock back and forth. "Thank you," I say into her ear. "For everything you've done. Forever. I love you."

"I love you more, little girl," Virginia says and kisses my hair.

Virginia and Arthur each turn to Thomas and grit their teeth. "You," Arthur says and gets close to Thomas. "If you hurt that little girl—I don't care in what way—if you hurt that little girl, you're going to be in a whole world of trouble. We'll hurt you."

I have to laugh a little bit. Thomas's eyes go big and he shakes his head wildly. "Never, I'd never hurt her."

"Don't try and control her either," Virginia says. "She's not gonna be your normal housewife. This girl got dreams, and you're going to support her come rain or shine."

"Give him some space, guys. I trust this one," I tease. Thomas laughs a bit nervously, but I think I catch Arthur mouthing words to him. I take Thomas's hand. "We're getting married," I announce, and squeeze Thomas's hand to steady myself. For the first time, I can say it with complete pride and rejoice in the reaction of my friends and family.

They cheer and hug us once again, and I find Eva's face in the crowd. And that's when I remember. Eva and her love, Rose, somewhere in California. The one thing she's tried to accomplish all this time. And it's happening for Thomas and me and not for her.

Her face breaks my heart. Tears come to her eyes and she looks like she's trying to find a way out of this room, out of this crowd. She looks the same way I did the morning Frank proposed, and just like I did, she bolts out of the room.

I drop my bag to the floor, release Thomas's hand, and push through the crowd, crying her name. "Eva! Eva!"

I follow her into her bedroom and immediately start the apologies. "Eva, I am so, so sorry. I completely forgot about you and Rose."

"No, no, it's fine. It's just that my best friends are leaving me to do the thing I've been trying to do for a year and a half.

But it's fine. I'll just stay here and take care of the mess *you* made."

It stings, but I deserved that.

"I promise it wasn't like that. I just forgot. I'm sure we can get another ticket."

"No, no, you can't." Eva says, sighing, and I'm confused for a moment. "Who's going to take care of this place? Virginia doesn't want to, and Arthur has his own life. You can't just drop this and leave and expect us to carry it for you."

She told me months ago that if I ever wanted to leave, she would take care of the safe house for me, but she probably didn't think I'd ever really leave. I don't know what to say. She's right though.

"Maybe Banner can watch it and you can still come with us."

"Mr. Banner is a pig and will pocket all the money for himself."

I start to dispute, but she's right again. "I'm so sorry." Thomas enters with his eyebrows stitched together.

"What's the matter, Eva? Aren't you happy for us?" he asks, taking my hand again, but it feels wrong to flaunt our love in front of her.

"Of course I'm happy for you guys," Eva half-shouts. "It's just..."

"We're going to miss you too," he says gently. I sigh. Bless his clueless little heart.

"You're an idiot," Eva says. "There's *somebody*." She waits for Thomas to understand, but he doesn't. "There's somebody in California that I want to see again."

Lightbulb.

"You're in love with somebody?" Thomas's face lights up. "Why didn't you say anything?"

"Because I don't need to make a big deal out of it like you two, apparently." She closes her eyes a moment and breathes to help her anger. "We couldn't be together here, and I hoped we'd somehow be together in California. And now you two are going, and I'm happy for you, I really am. But everyone I love will be there, and I'll still be here. I'm always going to be here."

As Eva shuffles her feet, I know exactly what's going on in Thomas's head. I gently shake my head, but the words are already coming out of his mouth before I can stop him.

"Take my ticket," Thomas says, taking a deep breath. I grab his hand and hold on tight to him. "You deserve to be with the person you love."

"No, I'm not going to take your—"

"I'm serious," Thomas says. No amount of convincing otherwise will get him to change his mind. Eva takes a moment to embrace the news, then her face lights up and she leaps to hug Thomas, crying "thank you, thank you, thank you." She bounces with excitement, and it's too late to take it back.

"Thomas, I'm not going without you," I tell him.

"Yes, you are." He takes both of my hands in his and kisses them. "You can have a new start just like you wanted."

The thought of it now feels like a puzzle with missing pieces. "What about you?"

"I'll be okay," he reassures me. "I know that now. I'll be okay."

Will I, though? He would be better off without all the trouble I've caused him, and even though he should rightfully resent me, he doesn't. He adores me with every fiber of his being, or at least I thought he did before a few seconds ago. If he really loved me, he wouldn't give me up so easily.

Eva packs a bag and thanks us at least ten more times before we go back downstairs to a confused crowd. Nobody seems truly certain when they learn Eva is leaving instead of Thomas, but they accept it anyway and give her the same eager goodbye they gave Thomas and me a moment ago. Albeit this time, they give me and him pitiful sideways glances like they know my heart is breaking in my chest.

I take a moment to say goodbye to the house I grew up in for the last time. Hand in hand with Thomas, I run my fingers along the gold trim, which has gathered dust since Mother dismissed the staff, and breathe in the scent for the last time. I pick up my bag, give a sad smile to Virginia and Arthur and the girls, and Eva waves excitedly at them as she joins Thomas and me. "Bye," I whisper, bearing a hand-squeeze from Thomas as he looks at me closely to make sure I'm okay. This house never really felt like home, and so when I walk out the front door and shut it behind me, I feel nothing. No pang, no ache, no regret. I step out into the sunlight and into my new future with ease.

We walk to the train station in silence, listening only to the rocks crunching under our shoes. I don't think either of us would know what to say if we tried. We pass the bookshop and my feet slow to a halt as *Hooverville* stares back at me in the stand, and Thomas's and my reflection in the mirror, holding hands. Thomas tugs on my hand lightly and nods his head, asking me to leave.

The train is already in the station when we approach it.

Eva rushes forward and gives her bag to the conductor and shakes his hand, while Thomas and I stop and turn to face each other.

I open my mouth to say something, then stop, because I don't even know what to say. I haven't prepared for this, so I look at him, hoping he knows what to say. He simply pulls me into his arms and hugs me tightly, brushing my hair with his fingers the way he always does.

"Be safe out there, Annie," he tells me, trying to keep the mood light. I laugh softly.

"You too." I pull back and straighten his jacket so I have something to keep myself busy. "Just promise me you won't go finding some other girl too quickly." I grin, even though the idea of Thomas with another girl hurts me.

"No chance of that," he says seriously, then puts a grin on his face and turns to Eva, who is running back to him with open arms. "You didn't think you'd get away without saying goodbye, did you?" He chuckles and they throw their arms around each other.

"Thomas, I can't thank you enough for this," Eva says sincerely.

"You deserve love more than anyone else in the world, Eva. I wish you luck." He smiles at her, and they embrace again. When they pull back, Eva looks at me.

"I'll let you two say goodbye now," she whispers. "I'll see you on the train, Annaleise!" She skips off and jumps onto the colored section of the train. I touch Thomas's arm to bridge the gap between us. Thomas looks down on my face, and I just know he's trying to memorize this moment just as much as I am.

"Thank you, Annie. For... everything," he says. I press my eyebrows together confusedly. "You may not see it, but your crazy actions saved a lot of people from living in a homeless city forever. Me included. So, thank you."

His thanks makes me uncomfortable but puts some things into perspective. I hug him again. "I know you'll do better things than I do, Thomas." The train whistle blows, cutting our time together short. I scrunch up my face and bury myself in his shirt. I fear that if I have to look at his face, I'll lose all my resolve and decide to stay.

Thomas hugs me close, puts his mouth beside my ear, and whispers, *"I love you, Annie."* My heart rate slows, and I think I stop breathing. I pull back and look at his face. He chuckles at my face and points his chin at the train. "Go." He lets go of my hand, gives me my bag, and backs away from me. I force myself to pry my eyes off him and turn to get on the train.

It's as if my feet have cement blocks tied to them because walking away is impossible. I climb onto the train and take another look back at Thomas, who mouths, "Goodbye."

My heart shatters in my chest as I realize it's really goodbye. I rush onto the car without responding and take my seat beside Eva. While she stands and waves out the window at everyone saying goodbye, I can't look up from the seat in front of me. My chest aches and my heartbreak finds its way into my veins and down my arms. My blood pounds in my ears so loudly that I can't hear anything happening around me. I force myself to look out the window at Thomas, still standing there with his red, puffy eyes, and I think of how just two nights ago he proposed, and I was the happiest I've ever been in my life. How could so much change so quickly?

I think of the cottage by the sea, with the garden and the dogs and the kids, and it's lost its luster. And it feels just as damning as New York. The train starts to move, and I press my face against the window as Thomas moves from my right to my left and he gives the tiniest of waves.

"It'll be okay, Annaleise. We're starting a new adventure!" Eva says, trying to be helpful. But no adventure feels right without Thomas in it. He's been there for all the best adventures of my life. I don't want any adventure if he's not there.

I take deep breaths, then I'm on my feet, moving through the aisle back toward the door, dizzy as the train gains speed under me. The conductor tells me, "Sorry miss, I can't let you off, now."

But I practically throw him out of the way with a force I didn't know I had and pry open the train door. The ground beneath me is moving faster and faster until it's just a blur, and I don't even think for a second before I throw my bag out the train door and jump.

The split second I'm in the air seems like much longer, but then time speeds up to catch itself as I hit the ground at rapid speed and tumble, but I hardly notice if there's any injuries. I stand up and look toward the crowd of people, then begin running back to them. I yell Thomas's name, though I don't know why. He knows I'm coming back to him.

Thomas pushes his way from the crowd, shouting, "Annie, what the hell!" But we don't slow down as we crash into each other with open arms, embracing so tightly that Thomas loses his footing and falls on the ground beneath us. I lean down and kiss him, both of us crying.

"You're so stupid! What were you thinking, Annie?" he

cries, pushing my hair from my face and showering me with kisses between his words. He pulls back and stares into my eyes, holding me tightly to make sure I'm really here. "What were you thinking? You could have killed yourself!"

"I couldn't leave you, Thomas. Not again. Never again," I cry. A boyish smile crosses his weepy face, and he kisses me again, holding me tight and not letting me slip even an inch away. "Let's go *home*," I whisper when I pull back. We smile at each other with understanding, and we stand and wave at Eva, who's excited face peers back at us from the window of the train, cheering. We both got our happy ending.

We watch the train and the sun each disappear over the horizon, and we walk back toward my mansion but agree not to go inside.

Instead, we go back to the place we met. Even though there's no Hooverville anymore, we lay on the grass and wait for the city to light up the sky around us. I intertwine my fingers with his and lay my head on his shoulder.

I don't know what the future holds. I don't know if things will ever be the way they were before, but that's okay. The beauty of it is that with Thomas by my side, there's nothing we can't tackle. I don't need to know everything, because I know that even if we lose everything but the clothes on our back and the shoes on our feet, we have each other and that will *always* be enough.

***

THE END

Acknowledgments

Surely, it can't be easy to fit two-and-a-half years of supporters onto a single page, but I'm going to do my best, so please, bear with me.

My first thank you must go to those who donated money, shared, or lent support in other ways while I was crowdfunding to publish Hooverville, without whom this book *would not* have made it past the second draft. Thank you to my high school U.S. History teacher, Mr. Thomas, who first put the word Hooverville in my head, and to Sara Cedar Miller of the Central Park Conservancy.

Of course, I must thank my *amazing* cover designer and artist LiGraphics for the *beautiful* work she did, and my editor Kat Nics for enthusiasm, kindness, and smiley faces while she made this story sparkle. Thank you to my dearest friends Cody Castillo, Kayla Arellano, Presley Vaughn, and Nicole Moriarty for their collaboration and support along the way, and to my writing friends around the world (there isn't enough ink to name them all, but they know who they are.)

To Cody, Mackenna, Sharon, Mimi, Karley, and Lisa for general support, snacks, listening to rants, or whatever else.

Thank you to Mum, for helping when the words wouldn't come (and encouraging many re-watches of Pride and Prejudice for creative reasons), to Dad, for always answering questions that if I had Googled would have put me on some kind of watch-list. To both of them, for their unwavering support. I promise to one day write a book where both the parents are alive and decent people...

The last thing I'm going to say here is that there was a time when a group of male writers read an excerpt of this book and decided *Hooverville* would never succeed unless a man wrote it. There was a time I was told that if I tried to write books, I would end up working at a drive-thru, so I had better not try. I'm thankful every single day that I was taught at a young age not to listen to criticism like that, and I wrote Annaleise with a singular message in mind for the young girls who may look up to her: *do not listen.*

The Hooverville Theme
(I'll Write Our Story)

Lyrics by Presley and Kayla Joy
Available on all streaming platforms, or at
presleysworld.com

The battle is over, I've lost his game
And I alone am left to blame
I tried so hard to win this fight
But vic'try means nothing, when it's some-
thing he'll buy

How far can I go with you if I have to stay?
How many days will I suffer in pain?
I don't want his diamonds, I don't want his
pearls
I want a love I don't have to ask for.

So I'll write a story
I can't read out loud

Take your last name in secret
When he can't hear a sound
Lovers in the moonlight, strangers in the day.
And when we say goodbye,
I promise to write the ending you'd like

I tried not to love you when you stole my
heart
Now my love's an inferno and you are the
spark.
His ring's on my finger, but you're on my mind
I'll dream for the day when I'll hold you tight

And the beggars, they beg, for someone to care
How can this world be filled with such de-
spair?
You're my escape, but I cannot go
But you were the only home I've ever known.

So let's write a story
We can't read it aloud.
Take your last name in secret, when he can't
hear a sound
Lovers in the moonlight, strangers in the day.
And when we say goodbye,
I promise to write

the ending you'd like

It's getting harder to live in our dream
When this nightmare world is all I can see
So many people are hurting and yet
I have you
And yet I'll lose you.

So I'll write a story
I can't read out loud
I'll say your name when he's not around
Lovers in the moonlight, strangers in the day.
When we say goodbye,
I promise to write
the ending I'd like
the ending you'd like
the ending we'd like

Author's Note

However based in reality it may be, *Hooverville* is, at the end of the day, a work of fiction. Historical figures in this book may be presented as either good or bad, but we must remember that *nobody* is 100% good or bad. We all have the capacity to be both, and the highly featured characters Franklin Delano Roosevelt and Herbert Hoover both had good *and* bad in them and were only painted the way they were for the sake of the story and for the sake of historical accuracy at the time of the story's setting.

I don't condone *any* form of racism, homophobia, sexism, or xenophobia, nor does Annaleise Winston, but I want readers to be transported to a day in 1932 with all the modern knowledge and ideals, and recognize how far we have come and just how far we still have to go.

All my love,

Kayla

About Kayla Joy

    Kayla Joy is an author and artist living in the Pacific Northwest with her many animals. At 20, she has already self-published two books: *Morbid Tales from Behind the Mirror* (available on Amazon now) and her first novel, *Hooverville*. She has lived in 8 states, visited 37, and New York is not one of them. You can follow her writing journey at kaylajoybooks.com.